IAN RANKIN

Watchman

A CRIME CLUB BOOK
DOUBLEDAY
New York   London   Toronto   Sydney   Auckland

A CRIME CLUB BOOK
PUBLISHED BY DOUBLEDAY
a division of Bantam Doubleday Dell Publishing Group, Inc.
666 Fifth Avenue, New York, New York 10103

DOUBLEDAY and the portrayal of a man
with a gun are trademarks of Doubleday,
a division of Bantam Doubleday Dell
Publishing Group, Inc.

Library of Congress Cataloging-in-Publication Data
Rankin, Ian.
Watchman / Ian Rankin.—1st ed. in the U.S.A.
p.   cm.
"A Crime Club book."
I. Title.
PR6068.A57W38   1991
823'.914—dc20   90-19585
CIP

ISBN 0-385-41809-4

For Alistair

Acknowledgements

When I started researching this book, one person whose brain I'd just been picking begged me "For God's sake make it realistic." He was fed up with stories which exaggerated the "glamour" of the spy and the ingenuity of his tools of trade. However, the following six months' worth of conversation and reading left me more than a little confused. It seemed to me that the problem in writing a novel about the security service was that reality was sometimes so much more unbelievable than fiction. I showed part of the first draft of the book to my acquaintance, and he telephoned the same night. "How the devil did you know that?" he demanded, citing one particular passage (extant). "I made it up," I replied, quite truthfully. "Oh no, you didn't . . ." he began, and then fell silent, having said too much already. . . .

Some of *Watchman* was written while enjoying the hospitality of Hawthornden Castle International Retreat for Writers, and my grateful thanks go to the staff there.

I should also add that, really, MI5's surveillance section is known as the Watcher Service. But I find the terms "watchman" and "watchmen" more resonant, as fans of Alan Moore will doubtless agree.

I.R.

Contents

Prologue

It was said that his ancestors had come from Donegal, and for that reason if no other he had decided to spend a holiday in Ireland. The lush countryside, so quiet after London, and the little villages around the coast delighted him, and the people were polite and, he supposed, as friendly as they would ever be to an Englishman. Ah, but he was quick to point out to them that his roots were in Donegal; that in spirit if not in body he was, as they were, a blood-hot Celt.

Having spent long enough in the west, he travelled east, driving through Fermanagh and Monaghan until he reached the coast, just south of Dundalk. The days were balmy and clear, and he breathed it all in, resisting the occasional temptation to telephone back to London with news of his trip. He could wait for all that.

A few of the men along the coast were fishermen, but not many, not now that the economy was dragging itself, along with the country's social problems, into the twentieth century. The north was a ferment of naive idealism and brutish anger, the whole concoction spiked by foreign meddling of the most malign nature.

In particular there was one young man, his hair wild and with a beard to match, whom he met in Drogheda, and who had spoken to him of the fishing industry and the village pubs and of politics. Politics seemed to pervade life in Ireland as though the very air carried whispered reminders of bloodshed and injustice. He had listened with an unjaundiced ear, explaining in his turn that he was on holiday, but that really he was recovering from a broken heart. The young man nodded, seeming to understand, his eyes keen like a gull's.

In one of the pubs they sat for night after night, though he could feel, through his happiness, the end of the holiday approaching. They drove into the countryside one day, so that the young man, Will, could spend some time away from the gutting of fish and the rank posturing of the boats. They ate and drank, and, with Will's directions, approached a quayside as dusk was falling. He pointed over to a small boat. The air was rich with the smells of fish and the endless screeching of the herring gulls. The boat, Will told his companion, was his own.

"Shall we take her out?"

As they did, out past the green-stained walls of the quay, out past the bristling rocks and the wrack, into the choppy Irish Sea, the older man trailed his hand in the bitter-cold water, feeling the salt cling to his wrist. Will explained why the wind was slightly warm, and spoke of the hunt for some legendary giant fish, a shadowy monster which had never been caught. People still caught sight of it, he said, on moonlit nights with a tot of rum inside them, but if it were still alive then it would be hundreds of years old, since the first such tales had been told centuries before. The sky gaped above them, the soft spray like an anointing. Perhaps, thought the Englishman, he was the outdoor type after all. He would return to London, throw up his job (which was, in any case, about to scupper him), and drift, seeing the world through rechristened eyes.

The engine stopped, and the lapping of the water became the only sound around him. It seemed a pure and a miraculous peace. He looked back in the direction of the shore, but it was out of sight.

"We're a long way out," he said, one hand still paddling the water, though it was growing numb with cold.

"No," said the younger man, "it's only you that's a long way out. You're way too far out of your territory."

And when he turned, the gun was already aimed, and his mouth had opened in the merest fraction of a cry when it went off, sending him flying backward out of the boat, so that his body rested in the water, his legs hanging over the edge, caught on a rusty nail.

The younger man's hand shook only slightly as he placed the gun on the floor of the boat. From a bag concealed beneath one seat he brought out a load of stones, which he hoped would be sufficient for his purpose. He tried to pull the corpse back into the boat, but it had become sodden and as heavy as the dead weight it was. The sweat dripped from him as he heaved at his catch, growing tired quickly as though after a full day on the boats.

Then he caught sight of the face and he retched, bringing up a little of the dead man's gifts of food and wine. But the job had to be done, and so he gathered up new strength. He had done it, after all, he had killed his first man. They would be pleased with him.

PART ONE
The Arab's Smile

CHAPTER 1

Miles Flint wore glasses: they were his only distinguishing feature. Billy Monmouth could not help smiling as he watched Miles leave the club and head off towards his car, which would be parked some discreet distance away. Miles and Billy had joined the firm around the same time, and it had seemed inevitable that, over the years, they would become friends, though friends, in the strictest sense of the word, were never made in their world.

Miles was feeling a little heavy from the drinks. Billy had insisted on buying—"the prerogative of the bachelor's pay cheque, old boy"—and Miles had not refused. He fumbled now at the buttons of his coat, feeling a slight and unseasonal chill in the London air, and thought of the evening ahead. He had one more visit to pay, a few telephone calls to make, but apart from that Sheila and he would have their first full evening together for a whole week.

He did not relish the prospect.

As suspected, his car had collected a parking ticket. He ripped it from the windscreen, walked around the car once as though he were a potential and only half-informed buyer, and bent down as if checking for a bald tyre or broken silencer. Then, satisfied, he unlocked the passenger door. The Jaguar's interior, pale hide complementing the cream exterior, looked fine. He slid across into the driving seat and slipped the key into the ignition, turning it quickly. The engine coughed once, then roared into life. He sat back, letting it idle, staring into space.

That was that then. He was not about to be blown up today. He knew that the younger men in the firm, and even the likes of Billy Monmouth, smiled at him behind his back, whispering words like "paranoia" and "nerves," going about their own business casually and without fear, as though there were invisible barriers between them and some preordained death. But then Miles was a cautious man, and he knew that in this game there was no such thing as being too careful.

He sat for a few more minutes, reflecting upon the years spent inspecting his car, checking rooms and telephones and even the undersides of restaurant tables. People thought him clumsy because he would always drop a knife or a fork before the meal began, bowing his head beneath the tablecloth to pick it up. All he was doing was obeying another of the unwritten rules: checking for bugs.

The car was sounding good, though it was a luxury, much detested by
Sheila. She drove about in a battered Volkswagen Beetle, which had once
been orange but was now a motley patchwork of colours. Sheila did not
think it worthwhile paying a garage to do repairs, when all one needed
were a handbook and some tools. Miles forgave her everything, for he too
had a quiet liking for her car, not so much for its performance as for its
name.

Miles Flint's hobby was beetles, not the cars but the insects. He loved to
read about their multifarious lifestyles, their ingenuity, their incalculable
species, and he charted their habitats on a wall map in his study, a study
filled with books and magazine articles, and a few glass cases containing
specimens which he had caught himself in earlier days. He no longer killed
beetles, and had no desire to exhibit anyone else's killings. He was content
now to read about beetles and to look at detailed photographs and dia-
grams, for he had learned the value of life.

He had one son, Jack, who built up tidy overdrafts during each term at
university, then came home pleading poverty. Miles had flipped through
the stubs in one of Jack's famished chequebooks: payments to record
stores, bookshops, restaurants, a wine bar. He had returned the chequebook to Jack's secondhand tweed jacket, replacing it carefully between a
diary and a letter from a besotted (and jilted) girlfriend. Later, he had
asked Jack about his spending and had received honest answers.

Miles knew that his kind did not deal in honesty. Perhaps that was the
problem. He examined the large-paned windows along the quiet street, the
car's interior warming nicely. Through one ground-floor window he could
watch the silent drama of a man and a woman, both on the point of leaving
the building, while by running the car forward a yard or two he might
glance into another lit interior. The choice was his. For once, and with a
feeling of abrupt free will, he decided to drive away completely. He had,
after all, to visit the watchmen.

Somewhere behind him, in the early evening twilight, came the sound of
an explosion.

Miles stopped outside the Cordelia, a popular *nouveau riche* hotel off
Hyde Park. The receptionist was listening to her pocket radio.

"Has there been a news flash?" he asked.

"Yes, isn't it awful? Another bomb."

Miles nodded and headed for the lifts. The lift was mirrored, and, riding
it alone to the fifth floor, he tried not to catch a glimpse of himself. Another bomb. There had been one last week, in a car parked in Knights-
bridge, and another had been defused just in time. London had taken on a
siege mentality, and the security services were running around like so
many ants in a glass case. Miles could feel a headache coming on. He knew
that by the time he reached home he would be ready for a confrontation. It

was not a good sign, and that was part of the reason for this short break in his journey. He wanted, too, however, to make a few phone calls on the firm's bill. Every little bit helped.

He knocked twice on the door of room 514, and the door was opened by Jeff Phillips, looking tired, his tie hanging undone around his neck.

"Hello, Miles," he said, surprised. "What's up?"

Inside the room, Tony Sinclair was busy listening to something on a headset. The headset was attached to a tape recorder and a small receiver. He nodded in greeting towards Miles, seeming interested in the conversation on which he was eavesdropping.

"Nothing," said Miles. "I just wanted to check, that's all. There's been another bomb."

"Where?"

"I don't know. I heard it go off as I was driving here. Somewhere near Piccadilly."

Jeff Phillips shook his head. He poured some coffee from a thermos, gesturing with the cup towards his superior, but Miles waved away the offer.

He flicked through his tiny notebook, which was filled with telephone numbers and initials, nothing more. Yes, he did have a couple of calls to make, but they were not that important. He realised now that his reason for coming here was simply to defer his going home. There did not seem to be any good nights at home now, and mostly, he supposed, that was his fault. He would be irritable, pernickety, finding fault with small, unimportant things, and would store up his irritation deep within himself like the larva of a dung beetle, warm and quickening within its womb of dung. Jack had given him a year's adoption of a dung beetle at London Zoo as a birthday present, and Miles had never received a more handsome gift in his life. He had visited the glass case, deep in the subdued light and warmth of the insect house, and had watched the beetle for a long time, marvelling at the simplicity of its life.

What his colleagues did not know was that Miles Flint had found counterparts for them all in the beetle world.

He felt the pulse of the headache within him. A few whiskies often did that. So why did he drink them? Well, he was a Scot after all. He was supposed to drink whisky.

"Do you have any aspirin, Jeff?"

"Afraid not. Been on the bottle, have we?"

"I've had a couple, yes."

"Thought I could smell it." Phillips sipped his tepid coffee.

Miles was thinking of James Bond, who was a Scot but drank martinis. Not very realistic, that. The resemblance between Miles and James Bond, as Miles was only too aware, stopped at their country of origin. Bond was a comic cut, a superman, while he, Miles Flint, was flesh and blood and nerves.

And headache.

"It's been quiet here," said Phillips. "A few phone calls to his embassy, made in Arabic, just asking about the situation back home and if they had any of this week's newspapers, and a call to Harrods, made in English, to ask what time they close. He went out for an hour and a half. Bought the *Telegraph,* would you believe, and a dirty magazine. Tony knows the name of it. I don't go in for them myself. He also purchased two packets of Dunhill's and one bottle of three-star brandy. That's about it. Came back to his room. Telephoned to the States, to one of those recorded pornographic message services. Again Tony has the details. You can listen to the recording we made if you like. Tony reckons our man got the number from the magazine he bought."

"Who's he speaking to just now?"

Phillips went across to check the notepad which lay on Tony Sinclair's knees.

"To Jermyn Street. Arranging a fitting. These people." Phillips shook his head in ironic disbelief.

Miles knew what he meant. The watchmen seemed to spend half their lives trailing men and women who did little more than buy expensive clothes and gifts for their families back home.

"He's making another call," said Tony Sinclair, the section's most recent recruit. Miles was watching him for any signs of weakness, of hesitation or misjudgement. Tony was still on probation.

"Speaking Arabic again," he said now, switching on the tape recorder. As he began to scribble furiously with his ballpoint pen, Jeff Phillips went to his shoulder to watch.

"He's arranging a meeting," Phillips murmured. "This looks a little more promising."

Miles Flint, attuned to such things, doubted it, but it gave him a good excuse not to go home just yet. He would phone Sheila and tell her.

"Mind if I come along on this one?" he asked. Phillips shrugged his shoulders.

"Not at all," he said. "Your Arabic is as good as mine, I'm sure. But isn't this supposed to be your night off?"

"I'd like to stick with this one," lied Miles. "I'll just make a quick call home."

"Fine," said Phillips. "I'll go downstairs and fetch the car."

CHAPTER 2

Having put his car into the hotel's basement garage, Miles began to unwind in the firm's gleaming Rover.

Miles Flint was a watchman. It was his job to look and to listen, and then report back to his section chief, nothing more. He did not mind such a passive role in life but was aware that others did not share his meticulous pleasure in sifting through the daily affairs of those he was sent to watch. Once or twice, to his certain knowledge, Billy Monmouth had tried to induce his promotion laterally through a word in the right ear. Miles did not want promotion. It suited him to be a watchman.

Billy and he had been invited to join the firm back in 1966, when it was just beginning to recover from a devastating few years of defection, rumour, and counterrumour. It was said that a supermole had confessed to wartime subversion but was being kept under wraps, and that a more dangerous double agent had been active, too, in later years. Much soul and navel searching had been taking place back then, and, really, that sense of suspicion had never blown away, like rotting leaves left too long in a garden.

And now there were new scandals, new stories to be foisted on the same old public. One could choose to ignore it all, of course, and get on with life. Nevertheless, Billy and he had talked about these things over lunch.

The more Miles thought about Billy, the more it struck him how odd he had seemed in the club. He had laughed but not with his usual timbre. Billy had been worried about something but could not bring himself to speak of it. He was a longhorn beetle, the self-sufficient predator of the family. Miles wasn't so sure about his own classification: most of the time he settled for the quiet life of the museum beetle. Jeff Phillips, on the other hand, driving the car with effortless grace, belonged to *Buprestidae,* the splendour beetles. They loved warmth and sunshine, were brightly coloured, and spent their days sipping pollen and nectar. Ah yes, that was Jeff Phillips, with his silk ties and his noisy Italian shoes. Looking across to Phillips now, Miles remembered that despite the splendour beetle's airs and graces, its young fed upon rotten wood and old vegetables. For some reason, the thought cheered him immensely.

They drove slowly. Phillips really was an excellent driver, unshowy but never losing his prey. He had been a watchman for just over a year but was already busy, Miles knew, trying for one of those "lateral promotions" so beloved by Billy Monmouth.

"Turning into the Strand."

The Arab's code name was Latchkey. Miles wondered just who was responsible for these absurdities. Someone had to sit at a desk all day doing nothing else but inventing code names. In the past few months Miles had been detailed to watch a real rogues' gallery: Ivanhoe, Possum, Conch, Tundish, Agamemnon. And now Latchkey, who was perhaps the main assassin for a group of lesser-known oil-producing states in the Gulf. Conceivably, however, he might be merely what his public image and his passport showed: a well-placed civil engineer, in London to advise his embassy on possible contracts for British companies in the Gulf. Some very high-tech refineries were about to be built—were, as Billy had put it, "in the pipeline"—in order to extract every last drop of commercial goodness from the crude natural product. And that was why no toes were to be stepped on, no possible evidence of interference left lying around. Discretion was paramount if the contracts were not to be endangered, and the burden belonged to Miles.

"Taxi signalling and stopping," said Phillips. "I'll drop you and park the car."

Miles slipped out of the car and followed Latchkey into the Doric, one of the capital's grandest hotels, feeling uncomfortably shabby. His shoes were scuffed and unpolished, his trousers just a little too creased. Well, he could always pretend to be American. *In Philly, we always dress down for dinner,* he thought to himself as he pushed through the revolving door. The Arab was gliding into the cocktail bar, smoothing down his tie as he went.

"Would you have a light?"

The girl who barred his way was blonde, petite, and very pretty, with a trained voice and a trained smile. Everything about her looked trained, so that her movements told the prospective customer that she was a professional girl. Miles had no time to waste.

"I'm afraid not," he said, moving past her.

She was not about to waste time herself, time being money in her world. She smiled again, drifting off towards another tired-looking traveller.

The bar was busy with early evening drinkers, not those who leave their offices tired and thirsty, but those who feel it a duty to consume a few expensive drinks before an expensive meal. Miles pushed an earpiece into his ear as he walked, the slender flex curving down his neck and into his top pocket. He found a chair with his back to Latchkey, who was seated alone at a table for two. Having ordered a whisky, miming to the waiter that he was partially deaf, Miles took a notebook from his pocket and produced a silver pen from the same place. He looked like the perfect accountant, ready to jot down a few calculations of profit margins and VAT contributions.

In poising the pen, an expensive-looking fountain model, Miles angled its top towards Latchkey, and through his earpiece came the chaotic sounds of the bar. He cursed silently the fact that there were so many people around. Latchkey, having coughed twice, ordered a fresh orange juice from the waiter—"as in freshly squeezed, you understand"—while Miles, appearing to mull over his figures, listened.

Jeff Phillips would be calling for assistance, though it still seemed unlikely that anything important was about to take place. The really important meetings always took place either in obscure, well-guarded rooms, or else in parks and on heaths, preferably with a storm raging in the background. Nothing that the constantly ingenious technical-support boffins could rig up in their dark chambers was of much help on a windswept hill.

The pen, however, was superb, a tiny transmitter inside the cap sending information to the receiver inside his pocket, and from there to the earpiece. It was as close to James Bond as the firm's scientists ever came, but it was not perfect. Miles was hard pressed to hear what Latchkey was saying to the waiter who had brought him his drink. A couple nearby, thinking themselves involved in the most intimate dialogue, kept interrupting, the woman's voice of just sufficient flutedness to block out the Arab's soft inflections. Miles, listening to their conversation, hoped that they would turn words into deeds and slip upstairs to their room. But then Latchkey wasn't saying anything yet, so where was the harm in trying out the equipment on other couples in the vicinity? None, however, as a quick sweep revealed, were saying the sorts of thing that the fluted woman was saying to her partner.

Miles's great fear was that Latchkey and his contact would speak together in Arabic, for he knew that his Arabic, despite Phillips's protestations, was a little rusty. The meeting had been arranged in Arabic, but with English pleasantries at the end of the dialogue. Tony Sinclair had worked quickly and accurately on the transcription, and Miles would remember that. He tried to ignore the niggling feeling that he had been stupid to come here tonight, stupid to have insisted on playing a role in what was not his drama. He should have gritted his teeth and gone home. His own fears for his marriage had caused him to make an error of professional judgement. That was the most worrying thing of all.

The woman shrieked suddenly, laughing at her partner's lubricious joke, and, looking up, Miles saw that Phillips was standing in the doorway, looking around as though for a friend. Their eyes met for less than a second, and Miles knew that the backup had arrived. At that moment a swarthy man brushed past Phillips and walked across to Latchkey's table. Miles, nodding as a drink was laid before him by the sweating waiter, concentrated hard on the table behind him.

"*Salaam aleikhum.*"

"*Aleikhum salaam.*"

"It's good to see you again. How is the refinery project progressing?"

"There have been some difficulties."

As their conversation continued—in English, praise Allah—it became obvious to Miles that he was wasting his time. The two men discussed what introductions were to be made to what companies. They even spoke about bribes which might be offered to them by certain work-hungry corporations in return for a slice of this or that contract. It was all very businesslike and aboveboard. The contact was Latchkey's man in the City, nothing more. They drank little and spoke slowly and clearly.

It was just after ten o'clock when they rose to shake hands. Both seemed pleased with the monies which would be slipped into their hands sub rosa in the days to follow. Latchkey told his friend to wait for him outside, and then went into the toilet, looking back and smiling as he did so.

"Drinking alone?"

It was the girl again, not having much luck tonight, but determined to keep on trying. Miles tucked the earpiece back into his pocket while she pulled a chair across from where the Arab's contact had been sitting.

"Just finishing," he said, watching her cross her legs as she sat down.

"What a pity," she said, her bottom lip full. "What else are you doing tonight then?"

"Going home to my wife, that's all."

"You don't sound very happy about it. Why not stay here and keep me company? I'd make you happy."

Miles shook his head.

"Not tonight," he said.

"Which night then?"

"A year next Saturday."

She laughed at this.

"I'll hold you to that. You see if I don't."

"It'll be my pleasure."

He was beginning to enjoy this little game, signalling as it did the end of his evening's work. At the same time, however, Latchkey was taking a long time, considering that he had a friend waiting for him outside, and when the door of the gentlemen's toilet opened and Latchkey's dark suit, white shirt, and pale tie emerged, the man wearing them was not Latchkey.

Aghast, Miles recalled that a bearded businessman, a little the worse for drink, had entered the toilet before Latchkey, and that the same bearded businessman had emerged during his conversation with the girl. Something was very, very wrong, for it was that bearded businessman who now wore Latchkey's clothes.

Miles rose to his feet a little shakily, the girl forgotten, and walked quickly from the bar. Phillips was seated in the foyer, flicking uninterestedly through a newspaper. When he saw the look on his superior's face, he jumped to his feet.

"What's wrong?"

"Everything. We've been sold a dummy. There was a bearded man, a bit drunk, grey suit, glasses. Did you see him leave?" Miles felt queasy. It had been an old trick, fairly clumsy in execution. Nevertheless, it had caught him dead.

"Yes, he left a couple of minutes ago, but he looked as sober as the proverbial judge to me."

"I'll bet he did. It was Latchkey. And there's a ringer in the bar just now wearing Latchkey's clothes."

"Hook, line, and bloody sinker. Where would he be going?"

"Well, you can bet he's not off for a late-night fitting in Jermyn Street. Has someone taken the contact?"

"He's being tailed."

"Right, stay here and keep a tab on the one still in the bar. I'd better phone in with the happy news."

"OK. Anything else?"

"Yes. Pray that nothing happens in London tonight. Not a bombing or a break-in or a single solitary mugging, because if it does, we're all in trouble." He looked back towards the bar. "Double bloody trouble."

As the whirligig of his thoughts slowed and began spinning in the right direction, Miles saw how perfectly everything had been underplayed by the Arab. His own error had been in underestimating every single move. Would a younger man have done that? Probably. What he could not deny, however, was that his mind had been on other things throughout. He had been only half interested. And there was something else, something at the edge of his vision. What was it? It had something to do with the girl. Yes, she had approached just as Latchkey was disappearing into the toilet, and Latchkey had turned and, seeming to sum up the situation, had smiled towards him. No, not towards him, directly *at* him. There could have been many reasons for that smile. The most obvious now was that Latchkey had known who Miles was. *He had known.*

And he hadn't even bothered to hide the fact.

CHAPTER 3

All in all, thought the Israeli, it had been a successful if not an enjoyable evening. He did not enjoy mixing with people. They could be such treacherous animals, their claws hidden by smiles and bows, handshakes and pats on the back. A pat on the back usually heralded some conspiracy or other, one's opponent touching one for luck. The alcohol had been very pleasant, however, and Nira had been there, flaunting her beauty as though she were a display case and it her precious diadem. Ah, but she would not believe that he could know such words as "diadem," or have such cultured thoughts. His outward appearance bespoke a large, earthy, and vaguely unpleasant appetite, and this had aided him in his life's work, if not in love. He might be all things to all women, if only they would allow him the opportunity of pleasuring them. He knew the most intricate paths of delight, but to taste them alone was to taste nothing.

The taxi dropped him at the end of his street, so that he could catch a few gulps of brisk night air before retiring. There had been talk tonight both during and after dinner which he should file in his memory before going to sleep, but it could wait until morning. Not an interesting night then, but successful insofar as he had met Nira again, and had spoken with her alone for a few moments, and had registered in the strongest terms his interest in her. She had been embarrassed, of course, and had walked away at the first possible and excusable moment, but it was done. He could afford to take his time over such a challenging seduction, when the prize would be so wondrously sweet.

He was fumbling for the bunch of keys in his trouser pocket when, staggering backwards, he began to choke, his tongue swelling to fill his throat, brain squeezed with blood. The professional within him knew in a final moment of lucidity that he did not have time to resist the cheese wire which now melted through his neck. Spinning toward a blackening vertigo of spirit, he hoped instead for heaven and redemption.

The Arab, job done, did not even smile this time.

Sheila Flint rose early, not surprised to find that she had been sleeping alone. She found Miles still at his desk in the downstairs study, his head lying across folded arms. September sun, milk-warm, poured through the window. Sheila stood in the doorway, watching him sleep, his face puffy like that of a well-fed child, his breath quiet with stealth.

He had always been something of a mystery to her, even in sleep. She had been attracted to him in the beginning because his long silences and half-aware eyes had betokened some kind of inner calm and, even, genius. But he had quickly shown her another face, brawling with other students after drinking binges, fiercely jealous of her other friends. Well, he had changed over the years, had come to have a genius only for passivity, and for a decade and a half she had pretended to herself that she, too, liked the quiet life. Then she had set about educating herself in life, going to night classes, attending the cinema and the opera—alone, or with Moira, her clever, trustworthy, and only slightly too good-looking ally—and enrolling for Open University courses which kept her mind moving. Miles showed little interest. Nothing, it seemed, could push him back into his old self. He was growing old, and oh, God, she was growing old too.

She liked her job in the civil service but hated London. To her continual surprise, it did not hate her back. It seemed to her a city without love or compromise, and she was forever finding examples of both to confound her feelings. The same ambivalence existed in her marriage. Despite a lack of real communication and, at times, even animosity, Miles and she had lasted longer than any of the other couples they had known, and they had a son who had grown into a normal, mistrustful, and unloving young man. People called theirs "the perfect marriage."

Watching Miles now as a trickle of saliva left the corner of his mouth, she was reminded of Jack as a baby, spluttering food and monosyllables, tying her to him with chains of guilt and dependence. She remembered, too, that he was due home in the next week or two, gracing them with his presence for a few days until university term started.

On the wall above Miles's desk was mounted the certificate from London Zoo reminding him that he was the adoptive parent of a dung beetle. Jack's gift had infuriated her, for it showed that even he knew more about Miles than she did. Miles had been delighted with the present. So original, so unusual. I'm original, too, she had wanted to cry, as father and son had burrowed deep into one another's embrace. I want to be part of your bloody little conspiracy. She had a mind, didn't she? She had inspired ideas. Everyone at work came to her with their problems, thinking her a genius at lateral thinking. She would have liked to tell Miles this, to have him see her more clearly, but they never talked about work. Miles bloody Flint and his "internal security." She knew who he worked for; he worked for the Ministry of Euphemisms.

So be it.

She was far too early yet for work, but would not sleep again, and had no intention of waking Miles, so she tiptoed through to the kitchen and made coffee. Waiting for the kettle to boil (percolated coffee would be too noisy), she studied her kitchen. Yes, *hers.* She had chosen every detail, every last cup and spoon. Miles had nodded at every purchase, sometimes not even noticing that he was eating off new crockery. She sat on her stool at the breakfast bar and set her mind to the previous day's crossword. "Finally does creep slowly forward to watch." Three letters. Sleep while you can, Miles. I have my secrets, too, a whole chest full of them.

Reaching for a pen, she folded back the paper and filled in the three empty boxes with the word "spy."

The telephone call from Colonel Denniston served only to bring into the waking world all of Miles Flint's nightmares.

"Flint? Denniston here. There's a meeting in my office in one hour. Be there."

"Yes, sir. Has anything happened?"

"Too bloody right it has. Some Israeli official's been decapitated outside his own house. Sounds like your man Latchkey, doesn't it? See you in an hour."

Lying in his hot bath, stiff from an uncomfortable sleep, Miles closed his eyes for a few precious moments. Of course there had been an assassination, and a crude one by the sound of it. What else could he have expected?

There was a knocking at the door. Miles never locked the bathroom door, but Sheila didn't come in any more if he was there.

"I'm going now," she called.

"I might be back late again tonight," he answered. "So I may as well apologise now. Sorry."

There was silence as she moved away. Then the front door slammed shut, leaving the house somehow colder. As far as Sheila was concerned, Miles worked for internal security, and that was that. Security, yes, but now Miles had evidence of a leak somewhere in the firm, for how else could the Arab have known about him? Then again, what sort of evidence was a smile? It seemed inadmissible.

Looking around the bathroom, Miles seemed to see everything anew. The shapes of sink, toilet bowl, bath seemed strange to him, and even the bathwater felt curiously new as he ran his hands through it. In this reverie, he let his mind go blank, until an internal alarm system reminded him of his appointment, and the world fell back upon him like the last wall of some condemned building.

CHAPTER 4

Colonel "H" Denniston, section chief of the Watcher Service, MI5's surveillance and report unit, liked the simple life. His apartment near to Victoria Street was rented, renting giving so many less complications to one's life. Denniston didn't like to feel tied and disliked the niggling difficulties of life, like shopping, shaving, changing light bulbs. The widow upstairs from his flat, taking pity on him perhaps, would buy a few things for him if he wished, and if he decided to decline her offer, then Denniston would plan his own shopping trips like military manoeuvres.

Denniston had been in charge of the watchmen for only three years but already had built around himself a reputation for severe correctness and efficiency. He used this reputation like a shield, and he was as angry as hell that a dent had been made in it. He sat at his teak desk and studied some papers from a slim folder. In front of him sat Flint, Phillips, and young Sinclair, lined up in a row like schoolboy truants. Sinclair had his hands in his lap as though he might be needing to urinate, while Flint made a show of cleaning his glasses. Phillips, though, arms folded, legs crossed, looked relaxed and a little too confident. His pink tie outraged Denniston, an Army man of thirty-one years with a military dislike of the flamboyant.

"You were the responsible agent at the time Latchkey went missing, weren't you, Phillips?"

Denniston saw his question have the immediate and hoped-for impact. Phillips unfolded his arms and gripped his thighs with his hands, perhaps to stop them from shaking.

"Well . . . no, sir, not really. You see, I . . . ahm . . ."

"You were, at the time, acting under orders given by a senior officer?"

"Yes, yes, actually, I was."

"Hmm." Denniston looked at the papers again, rearranging them, sifting through as though in search of something specific.

Miles Flint coughed.

"What do we know, sir," he said, "about the dead man?"

"We know, Flint, that he was garrotted around midnight, and that the Israelis kept it to themselves until five this morning."

"Do we know when he was actually found?"

"No, but it seems that he was found by his own people, so there were no cries of foul murder in the streets."

Staring past the Colonel's bowed head, Miles watched the windows of the office block across the way. Government offices, too, of course. He saw secretaries hurrying past, weighed down with sheaves of paper.

"We know, too," the Colonel was saying, "that the dead man, though attached to the embassy, was no ordinary aide, though that may be his official title. He seems to have been working on the periphery. Something of an arms dealer in an earlier incarnation. All very discreet, of course, but he was on our files."

"Any links with Mossad, sir?" asked Phillips.

"Again, no." Denniston looked across to Tony Sinclair. "That's Israeli security, you know."

"Yes, sir," said Sinclair in hushed tones. "I know."

"Best outfit in the business as far as I'm concerned."

Denniston was about to go back to his reading when the door opened and the deputy director came hurrying into the room.

"Good morning, gentlemen," he said crisply, drawing a chair over to the desk and seating himself beside a now flushed Colonel Denniston. "Briefing your men, Colonel? Very wise, I should think. There will be an investigation, of course."

"Yes, sir. Of course, sir."

"And the old boy himself wants to see us in fifteen minutes. But I thought I'd say my piece first."

"Of course, sir. Thank you, sir."

Miles hated to see a grown man cry, and that was just what the Colonel was doing. Not outwardly, of course. His tears were directed inward, but all the more pitiful for that. He was crying from the soul.

Employees of the firm, at every level, called the deputy director "Partridge" or, more often, "Mr. Partridge." He seemed to have no known Christian name and no military title. The "Mr.," Miles assumed, came from his gentlemanly dress sense and expensive manners. Butlers, too, were called "Mr." by the menials of the household, weren't they? But Partridge was no butler.

Miles had met him many times before, when being assigned to surveillance cases for which he was the senior watchman. The last of these occasions had been only eight days ago, when "Latchkey" had come into being. Partridge, looking across the table and seeing Miles watching him, smiled quickly, the smile, thought Miles, of the tiger beetle. It was Denniston, however, whom he had termed the department's tiger beetle. He had marked Partridge down, perhaps wrongly, as *Platyrhopalopsis melyi.*

Platyrhopalopsis melyi was a small beetle, not much more than a centimetre long, which lived in ants' nests and was sustained by the ants, who in turn licked a sweet secretion from the beetle's body. Miles had never been able to find out as much as he would have liked about this faintly arousing symbiosis. The first time Partridge and he had met, Partridge had reminded him of the tiny beetle, something in the man's attitude prompting the comparison.

Perhaps, though, this had been a rash decision, for the more Miles saw of Partridge, the more there was in him of the tiger beetle, *Cicindelidae,* a ferocious and powerful predator. Partridge had managed to turn Denniston into a weak, glandular schoolboy. It was quite a feat.

"I suppose you have spoken of the murder, Colonel?"

"Yes, sir."

"And have filled in what we know of the victim's background?"

"Yes, sir."

Turning to the three guilty-looking men on the other side of the table, Partridge placed his hands delicately in front of him as though he were counsel for the defence in a difficult case, anxious to reassure his doomed clients.

"This is a serious matter, gentlemen, of that there's no question. But it's not quite as serious as it might have been. The murdered man's employers want everything kept quiet, or as quiet as possible under the circumstances. There were, it seems, certain visa irregularities which neither they nor we would wish to have to pursue. Moreover, they do not know that we were keeping an eye on Latchkey, which gives us a decided advantage in the matter. I can now tell you that Latchkey did not return to his room last night. He left behind all of his things, including a fairly good bottle of brandy and several new suits. Even his passport was left behind, though I think we can assume it is a forgery and that he will by now have left the country."

Miles saw now that the switch had been very cleverly planned. The phone calls to Harrods and Jermyn Street, the purchase of a bottle of spirits and some reading matter, and even the meeting with the contact— all had been designed to make anyone think that a long surveillance was in progress, lulling the watchmen into a false sense of being *in medias res.* Clever, clever, clever.

"Yes," Partridge was saying, "I'm afraid that, in soccer terminology,

we've been caught a bit square. Their man has scooted past us to score."
He allowed a smile to form on the palimpsest of his face, then to melt away
again as if it had never existed. Nobody in the room had dared smile back.
Their futures were being decided, and it was no joke. "We've got Special
Branch onto the man with whom, as one of us was not quite quick enough
to spot, Latchkey changed clothes. We don't think they'll get much from
him. This was probably a strictly one-off job for him, and he'll have nothing to fear. Likewise, Latchkey's contact, who went back last night to his
fairly substantial apartment in NW1. He's been on our files for some time
actually, though we won't be acting against him at this time. So, gentlemen"—Partridge gave each of them a two-second glance—"we've been
bloody lucky in one respect, in that this is not going to damage our reputation or our standing with a friendly nation. In another respect, however,
we've thoroughly botched a resolutely straightforward surveillance operation, and a man is dead as a result. There will be a full internal inquiry."

Miles wondered how long it had taken Partridge to prepare his speech,
which now ended with a reshuffling of papers. Phillips, Sinclair, and Colonel Denniston, who had been sitting bolt upright, shifted in their seats,
lecture over.

"Well," said Partridge, rising, "I've had my say. Let's see what the boss
has to say, shall we?"

And they followed him in near-reverential silence to the lift.

The Director was, so the office gossip went, close to retirement. Certainly,
as they entered his curiously small office, Miles scented a world-weariness,
an old man's smell, as though oxygen were being pumped out, leaving a
vacuum.

"Sit down, please."

It was not that the old boy *was* old, not particularly, though to the likes
of Phillips and Sinclair he might appear so. Responsibility always made
people look older than their years, and in that respect the Director looked
about a hundred and twenty. He had plenty of hair, albeit of a distin-
guished silver and yellow colouring, and his face was relatively unwrin-
kled. But Miles could sense the ageing process upon the man: his clothes
were old and his movements were old.

He was standing, staring from his uncleaned window onto the street
below. Rather than sitting down himself, Miles felt that he should be
offering a chair to the elder statesman. But then he remembered the old
boy's reputation as a tenacious and quick-witted administrator, and his
links with the all-powerful, and Miles sat down with as much respect as he
could muster.

"When you leave this office, gentlemen, I would like you to go and draft
full reports on this matter, and I do mean full. Security will be along to see
you in due course and will cross-check everything." He turned from the

window and examined them, seeming to photograph them with his clear blue eyes. "This," he said, "has been a bloody farce from start to finish. I had thought of suspending every one of you, of asking for resignations even." He paused, letting his words sink in. It was as if Partridge had set them up for this kill.

"Colonel Denniston," he continued, "you have led your section efficiently for several years. It's a pity this had to happen. There has to be a tightening up of procedure. Do you understand?"

"Yes, sir." Denniston was making a good showing. He had his pride, that was sure. His eyes met those of the Director without blinking.

"Good."

Miles noticed that Jeff Phillips had gone very pale, as if he had just realised that he, too, would have to suffer the caning, and was afraid that he would not accept it with the same strength as his friends. The Director's eyes met those of Phillips and Sinclair, then came to rest on Miles.

"If there's anyone to blame, Flint, it's you." With the slow drama of a Shakespearean actor, the old boy took his seat, placing his hands on the leather-topped desk. "You are to blame. You were careless, sloppy even. We don't expect that of you, and we *cannot* accept it of you. Perhaps you should take a long hard look at yourself and your future here. It may be that you need a change of scenery, who knows?"

"With respect, sir, I like the scenery here."

"Do you?" whispered the Director. He leaned forward confidentially, his eyes filling with a malign humour. "Flint, you're a bloody fool. You should never have been in that hotel in the first place. You should have been at home with your family."

Partridge turned to look at Miles now, as though to indicate that he was in agreement with his superior's words. His eyes were like tunnels burrowing deep underground. You *are* a tiger beetle, thought Miles.

"If it hadn't been me, sir, it would have been someone else."

"And which would you have preferred?"

There was another silence while Miles, looking as though he were considering this, thought about nothing in particular.

"That will be all," said the Director. "Partridge, I'd like a word, please."

When Partridge rose, they all did. Miles, his legs unsteady for the first few seconds, noticed the relief on Colonel Denniston's face. Perhaps the old boy was right. Perhaps Miles did need a change, something to challenge him. He had made an error of judgement, and that very error had already jolted him part of the way back into place. Something was askew, was very wrong about this whole thing, and, with his watchman's mind, he needed to find out—for himself this time—what it was.

CHAPTER 5

With two fingers, and with multiple mistakes, corrections, and additions, Miles worked on his report, wishing that the section had a word processor, and knowing that he would not, in any case, have had the guts to use it. He mentioned the visit to the Cordelia, the scene and situation there, his wish to become involved in the surveillance, and then the scene in the Doric. He mentioned his conversation with the girl, but not his speculations as to her possible involvement in the case. There were one or two things which, for the moment, he would keep to himself. After all, if there were a mole in the firm, then he would need to be more careful than he had been up till now, and certainly more careful than the poor Israeli. Although the office was stuffy, he felt himself becoming encircled by a cold, icy wasteland of his own creation. Silence was his best defence now, silence and surveillance.

Of course he did not mention the Arab's smile. Over and over again he played back that moment in his memory, trying to freeze the frame to see if he had missed something. But already the picture was losing its clarity. The edges were fading away, leaving only the smile, like the Cheshire cat in *Alice in Wonderland.*

Moreover, the Arab's smile led him back to the previous afternoon and his extended lunch with Billy Monmouth, his friend's laughter just a shade off normal. Such subtle shades were Miles's preoccupation now, and he gave the lunch more attention. What had been worrying him? He scribbled Billy's name onto a piece of paper, thought better of it, and decided on a coded series of letters instead. Thoughtfully, he began to assign a letter to every person he could think of who might be the mole, including, after much hesitancy, his wife.

Billy Monmouth bought his lunch at a sandwich bar and carried it back to his apartment, which wasn't far from the office. In the lift, he peeled the wrapping away from what was supposed to be a tuna fish roll. All he could see was mayonnaise.

A piece of string lay on the coffee table in his lounge, meaning that he had had a visitor. He put down the roll and, wiping his hands, went over to one wall, along which was arranged a large and catholic selection of record albums. The stereo itself sat in a corner of the room, cruelly underused. Many of the albums he had never played and never would. He had bought them only for the names of their artists.

He crouched and examined the spines of the record sleeves. The first four albums were by Andy Williams, Paul Anka, Janis Ian, and Tchaikovsky. The message contained in their arrangement was simple: W-A-I-T.

Nothing more, for the record which came after Tchaikovsky's *Nutcracker* was by Miles Davis, and an album by Miles Davis, they had agreed, would mean "Message delivered." He had his instructions.

Skipping lunch, Miles decided to calm himself by visiting his favourite shop, a grimy jazz emporium on the edge of Soho. On the way he encountered a routine London car crash. A Rover had gone into the side of a spanking new Renault 5, and the driver of the Renault was being helped, shakily, from his crumpled car, while the driver of the Rover explained to a bored-looking young constable that it really was not his fault.

A crowd had gathered, as was customary, and Miles embedded himself in it. Having satisfied himself that there was no blood on view, he turned his attention to the crowd itself. What kind of person was attracted to a car crash? There were a few old ladies, a couple of young girls who chewed gum casually as though to say that they had seen it all before, some derelicts who were trying to cadge money from those around them, and then there were the other blank faces, the faces of those anonymous souls who kept locked within themselves dreams of violence.

And, of course, Miles himself, his own dreams of violence kept under lock and key, watching it all with the reserve of an expert witness, should such be needed.

"He's famous, he is," said one old woman. "I seen him on the telly."

"Get away," said one of the girls. "Which one?"

"The posh one talking to the policeman."

The woman made sure that her whispered conversation was loud enough to be heard all around. The Rover driver, trying to ignore the woman's voice, examined his watch testily, late for some appointment. The constable, as was his privilege, began to take things more slowly than ever.

"Is he an actor then?"

"No, it was the news he was on."

"The news?"

"Not so long ago either. Last night, night before."

"Is he a newsreader then?"

"No, he's a politician."

Miles began pushing his way out of the thinning crowd, to whom not even this was newsworthy enough in a city under siege, and made his way the hundred yards or so to the shop, where Dave, the proprietor, was playing some new early recordings by the Miles Davis Quintet.

"He's the boss," he called to Miles, jerking a thumb towards the turntable. "You can say what you like, but Miles is the boss."

Miles was not about to argue with that.

He went off to the racks to browse, finding this a good way to concentrate. With his fingers walking through the packed record sleeves, his mind was free, and time seemed to vanish. He had rejected an offer to lunch with

Jeff Phillips, and wondered whether he might start to gain a reputation for frugality or even downright meanness within the firm. Billy had told him that one or two people in the past had tried to give him the nickname "Skinflint" but it had never stuck.

Miles preferred his other nickname—The Invisible Man. As an undergraduate, he had joined his university's Officers' Training Corps and had enjoyed some of the weekend exercises. He was very good at these for the simple reason that he never got caught, and he never got caught for the more complex reason that, as other trainees told him, he "seemed to disappear," though in reality all he had done was to make himself as innocuous as possible.

Nowadays, he was aware of a beetle which did that too, an expert in camouflage. It was called the tortoise beetle, and its larvae carried lumps of excrement around on their backs, beneath which they could not be seen. Perhaps Miles was a bit like the tortoise beetle. But no, for he had been found out by a smiling Arab, and all because he would not go home to his wife.

He had first met her at Edinburgh University. They were both undergraduates, invited to a certain party where Miles had become roaring drunk and had wormed his way into a fight from which Sheila had rescued him. The following Monday, having put the weekend and his bruises behind him as a lost forty-eight hours, Miles had gone into the lecture hall yawning and ready for the fresh week's work. A girl had slid into the row beside him.

"Good morning, Miles," she had said, squeezing his arm. Shocked, he had tried to recall her face, pretending all the time that of course he knew who she was. He was bemused to find that, apparently, he had found himself a girlfriend without any of the long, painful searching which he had assumed would precede the event.

And that had been that, more or less: Miles's first girlfriend had become his wife.

"I wouldn't have put you down as a jazz fan, Miles."

Miles turned from the rack of records to find Richard Mowbray standing beside him.

"Oh, hello, Richard."

Billy referred to him as "Tricky Dicky" because of his slight American accent, but Miles knew that Richard Mowbray was as English as his name suggested. He had been schooled for five years in the States while his father worked in a university there, and those five crucial years had left him with a slight mid-Atlantic inflection to his otherwise thoroughly orthodox voice.

Mowbray was looking around him. He wore tinted glasses—an affectation—and looked older than his thirty-five years—another affectation. He, too, was a watchman.

"I've heard the news, of course."

"Of course," said Miles. Was this a coincidental meeting? He thought not. Mowbray was supposed to be watching a suspected IRA cell in Forest Hill. He was well out of his territory.

"What do you think of it all, Miles?" Mowbray's face had the sincerity of a President and the teeth of an alligator. Miles could not help asking himself what he wanted.

"What do you want, Richard?"

"I want to talk."

"Shouldn't you be somewhere else?"

"It's not my shift. Besides, it looks like another dead end, surprise, surprise."

"So what is it you want to talk about?"

"The CIA, of course."

Miles looked for a smile, for some acknowledgement that a joke was being made. None came.

"OK," said Miles, as a trumpet strained its way towards climax behind him, "let's talk."

"Great. There's a coffee shop across the road. Advertising execs mostly. That do you?"

"Fine."

And Mowbray led him across the street and into a sweet-smelling café where Jeff Phillips was already waiting for them.

"What is this?" said Miles.

"Milk and sugar?" asked Mowbray, pouring the coffee.

"No, thanks. I think I'll take it black and bitter."

"Suit yourself. Jeff?"

"White, no sugar, thank you."

Miles checked his watch. He was tired of these games of protocol. It seemed that business could not be discussed without a preamble of sham courtesies and responses. Phillips sipped his coffee just a little too appreciatively: this, too, was part of the game. Miles felt his patience ebb, leaving only wrack and salt.

"You mentioned the CIA, Richard."

"Yes, I did. I've got a little theory about our cousins. I'd like to hear your reaction to it. You see, it struck me a while back that the cousins are every bit as interested in our activities as are the Russians. Agreed?"

Miles nodded.

"So," continued Mowbray, "why does it never occur to us that there may be CIA moles inside the firm, eh? Or Israeli moles, or Australian?"

"In fact," interrupted Phillips, "any country you care to mention."

"Madagascar?" countered Miles, remembering some textbook geography. "Mali? Mauritania? Mongolia?"

Richard Mowbray held open his arms, a smile just evident on his face.

"Why the hell not?" he said.

Yes, thought Miles, everything but British moles. He had dropped a teaspoon on the floor at the beginning of this conversation and, picking it up, had checked beneath the table for bugs.

"What do you think, Miles?" asked Phillips now.

"I think it's banal."

"Do you?" This from Mowbray, leaning forward in his chair now, taking on the pose of the thinker. "Then maybe I shouldn't tell you the rest."

"The rest of what?"

"What about if I told you that the U.S. embassy in Moscow has all the parts for a small nuclear device located in different sections of the building? The wolf already in the fold: what would you say?"

"I'd say you were mad."

"Maybe he's not as ready as we suspected," Phillips said to Mowbray.

"Look, Richard, what is all this about?" Miles was concerning himself with Mowbray. Phillips was a wet-ear, hardly out of nappies. He'd go along with anything that might mean a commendation or the chance to make a fast reputation. But Mowbray was different: Miles had no doubt that it was Mowbray's baby in the pram, for it was Mowbray who had looked disconsolate when Miles said what an ugly child it was.

If possible, Mowbray leaned forward even further.

"I'm compiling a sort of list, Miles, a dossier of, well, let's just say the slightly odd, the irregular. You know, those hiccups in certain operations, the occasional slipups which appear to occur for no good reason. I'd like, quite unofficially, to have your version of last night's events on paper. If there are moles in this department, then we—and I would have thought you'd be included, Miles—want to gas them once and for all."

Miles looked to Phillips.

"Jeff is part of my little team. There are others, too. What do you say, Miles?"

"I say you're off your trolley, Richard. Sorry, but there it is. Now if you'll excuse me." He had already risen to his feet, coffee untouched, and now waved back as he went, went back out into the sanity of the unchanged street.

He breathed deeply as he walked. There was madness everywhere. The bottom fell out of a woman's carrier bag and tins of food went rolling across the road. Miles dodged them and kept on walking. He noticed that passersby were wary of parked cars, and rightly so. Any one of them might contain another bomb. People glanced in windows, searching for anonymous packages, or steered well clear of any driverless cars by the roadside. Well, on a day like this, thought Miles, I may as well cut through Oxford Street. Having encountered so much madness, a little more could do no harm. What was Richard Mowbray's game?

The pavements were packed with lunchtime shoppers, seeking those items without which they would not last the afternoon. Insect life. Miles was about to shake his head slowly when in front of him a large window exploded silently into the street, followed a split second later by earth-rending thunder. Silence reigned as shards of glass poured down like silver, and then there were the first screams, and Miles checked himself for cuts. No, he was all right. *He* was all right. But only yards ahead of him was chaos.

Later, he would wonder why it was that he veered away from it all and into Soho, not wanting to get involved. A ten-pound bomb it had been, easy, planted inside one of the garish shops while the pedestrians had been checking out the cars only. Later, he would wonder, too, why he found the go-go bar and paid his money and watched the show for ten minutes, why he went to the peep show and crouched in the rank cubicle, where he could watch from a slit not much bigger than the mouth of a postbox. The peep show was of circular design, and instead of watching the parody of lust, he had concentrated on the pairs of eyes which he could see past the two girls. Dear God, they looked sad. He thought that he might even recognise one pair of eyes, but, too late, the slat came down like a judgement upon him, and only the reality of the cubicle remained, replacing for a time that much greater and much more incomprehensible reality: Oxford Street had been bombed.

A young boy, running past, screaming with joy, brought Miles awake. He was in Hyde Park, seated on a damp bench beside an old woman sur-rounded by black plastic bags. The bags were tied with thick string and were arranged about her like a protective wall. She was staring at Miles, and he smiled towards her.

Slowly, it came back to him: the car accident, meeting Mowbray and Phillips, and the bomb, dear God, the bomb. It was half past five, and his lunchtime had turned into another afternoon off. A sort of panic had overtaken him this afternoon, so that he had felt less in charge of his life than usual. Yes, he remembered a similar sensation from his student days: those weekend blackouts, the anger and frustration, the fights . . . But in those days he would not have walked away from an explosion, would he? He would have stayed to help the injured, the survivors. But not now, not now that he was a watchman.

The old woman rose slowly from the bench and began to gather together her bags. Somehow she managed to heave them onto her back, and Miles felt a sudden impulse to help her.

"I can bleedin' manage!" she growled at him. Then, moving away through the park, "Watch out for yourself, dearie, just you watch out."

Yes, that reminded him, there was a puzzle he had to solve. He hadn't got very far, had he? Well, he knew just the cure for that now: send in a mole to catch a mole.

Everybody who knew him thought that Pete Saville had just a little too much love for his computer. He seemed to be at his desk before everyone else in the mornings, and he was always—*always*—the last to leave. Didn't he have any social life? A girlfriend? But Pete just shrugged his shoulders and told them that they should know better than to interfere with a man who loved his work. So no one paid him much attention nowadays, and no one asked him to the pub or out to a party, which was just fine by Pete Saville.

It meant that he could forge ahead with Armourgeddon 2000.

Armourgeddon was going to make Pete Saville's fortune. He had only to iron out a few bugs, and then the whole package would be ready. It was hacker-proof, it was easy to learn and to play, and, above all, it was addictive. Yes, Armourgeddon 2000 was the computer game to beat them all. . . .

"Hello, Pete."

He almost leapt out of his chair. Recovering quickly, the first thing he did was switch off the screen.

"Sorry, did I startle you?"

"No, it's just, well, I didn't hear you come in, that's all."

"Ah."

Miles walked around the room, inspecting the individual consoles, while Pete watched him.

"Working late again, eh?"

"Yes."

"You work late a lot, don't you?"

"Yes."

"Lots to do, I suppose, being a processor?"

Approaching Pete's desk, Miles crouched slightly, gazing into the blank screen. Reflected there he saw his own face, and, in profile, the face of one very anxious young man.

"Am I disturbing you, Pete?"

"No, not really."

"I couldn't help noticing you switch off the screen when I came in. Something top secret, I suppose?"

Pete smiled.

"You could put it like that."

With a quick movement, knowing exactly which button to press, Miles brought the screen back to life. A green space zombie was obliterating the Orgone commander.

"Haven't you added the sound track yet?"

Pete Saville was silent.

"Have you found the bug yet?"

What colour there was in Pete Saville's face fell away. Miles was smiling now. He began his tour of the room all over again.

"I'd like a favour, Pete."

"How did you know?"

"It's my job to know. Everything. I've stood here behind you and watched you work. What's it called again? Armageddon 2000?"

"Armourgeddon," Pete was quick to correct. "It's a pun."

"Is it now?" Miles nodded his head thoughtfully. "Yes, I can see that. But I'll tell you what else it is. It's an abuse of your position here. R2 is not your toy to play with."

"So what are you going to do?"

"Peter, I'm only here for a favour, and I want to know if you will do me that favour, that's all."

"How could you stand behind me and watch me work without my seeing you?"

"What's my nickname, Pete? What is it they all call me?"

Pete remembered, and swallowed hard.

"What's this favour?" he asked through dry lips.

"I need to look at some personnel files and a few other bits and pieces. Nothing sensitive or classified . . . well, not *really.*"

"It's no problem then—"

"But I don't want to leave any record on the computer that I've been through the files. That is possible, isn't it?"

"I'm not sure." Pete thought again of Armourgeddon. All he needed were a few quiet weeks, perhaps three more months at the outside, and then he could leave this place forever. "I'm not sure it's been done before," he said, "not on this system. So I'm not sure that it *can* be done. Tampering with the memory . . . getting past the codes . . . I don't know."

"If anyone can do it, Pete . . . I have faith in your ability to worm your way inside the system. Will you have a go?"

Pete's head felt as light as helium. He touched the computer screen, touched the place where the Orgone commander had been standing.

"Yes," he said, "yes, I'll give it a try."

"I thought you might," said Miles, pulling a chair over towards the desk.

CHAPTER 6

No one had been killed, that was the miracle. But over the next ten days everyone became more cautious than ever. An empty shoebox could not sit for long in an open rubbish bin without one of the bomb disposal teams being summoned. It was a busy time for them. A busy time, too, for Miles Flint, sifting through what information he could find. He asked discreet questions of a few uninvolved colleagues, tracked as far as was possible the daily affairs of those closest to the Latchkey case, and was himself interviewed on three occasions by men from internal security.

He had been assigned to the Harvest surveillance, working with Richard Mowbray and his team in Forest Hill. This gave Miles the chance to apologise to Mowbray, then to pick his brains about what dirty dealings he thought he had uncovered. Most of these were simple paranoia.

Then one day, having driven the Jag home, Miles opened the door of his study and saw, jumping across his desk, the largest beetle he had ever set eyes on. Astonishment turned into panic when he noticed that the beetle was a joke-shop affair, with plastic tubing trailing from its rear to a point beneath the desk. Looking down, he saw a man there, bundled up like a foetus so as to squeeze into the space beneath the desk.

The man was grinning, and, letting go of the rubber beetle, he began to extricate himself from his cramped position. For a moment Miles wondered, Who the hell is it? And he even considered the possibility of some outlandish execution, before realising that the tall young man was Jack, who now rubbed his shoulders as he stretched.

"Christ, Dad," he said, laughing. "The look on your face!"

"Ha bloody ha!"

Miles hesitated, wondering whether or not to reach out and shake his son's hand. The dilemma was resolved when Jack came forward and gave him a brief hug.

"So, what brings you home? Broke again, I suppose?"

"Summer hols, you know." Jack walked around the room like an investigating policeman, or, thought Miles, like a caged big cat, impatient, larger than his surroundings. "I just thought I'd give you the benefit of my company for a week or so before I head back to Edinburgh."

"What have you been up to all summer?"

"The usual." He studied one set of beetles, trapped behind glass. "I worked for a few weeks in a café during the Festival, and before that I was on the dole. I took off up north for a while actually, wandering about the Highlands. If it weren't all cliché, I'd say it was a consciousness-raising experience. You know, you can start walking across the hills up there and never see a soul from one day to the next. No houses, no electric pylons even. Lots of birds and animals, but not another human being. When I got back to Edinburgh, I nearly went mad. I was seeing everything differently, you see."

Yes, Miles could see.

"How did the exams go?"

"Fine. A cinch, actually."

"I don't suppose Edinburgh's changed?"

"You'd be surprised. New hotels and shopping complexes. A big drug problem in the housing estates. High incidence of AIDS. Child-murderers running around everywhere."

"I meant the university."

"Oh." Jack laughed. "It's the same as ever. Nothing happening. Departments full of drunks and half-wits."

"Do you mean the students or the lecturers?"

"Both."

Miles had been surprised—pleasantly so—when Jack decided to go to Edinburgh University, while the majority of his school friends had stuck to Oxbridge. But Miles could guess the reasons why Jack had not followed them: he was independent, stubbornly so, and he was just a little proud of his Scottish roots.

Miles had not set foot in Edinburgh for fifteen years, but he had a vivid memory of the city and its people, and he remembered the weather above all else, the relentless wind which chilled to the marrow, and dark winter afternoons which drove one indoors to study. Sheila and he had gone back just that once. It had been enough.

"It hasn't been too quiet down here of late, has it?" said Jack now.

"You mean the bombings?"

"Yes. The IRA, isn't it?"

"Apparently. It hasn't affected us though. Life has to go on, et cetera."

Of course Miles had told no one of his proximity to the Oxford Street bomb. He would have been unable to justify his running away. That was what it had been after all—running away. He told no one, and found flakes of glass in his hair and his clothes for days afterward.

"Have you seen your mother?"

"How else could I have got in?"

"Don't you still have a key?"

"I lost it last term. God knows how. I thought it was on my key ring, but then one day it vanished. I'll get another one cut."

I'll have to change the lock now, thought Miles. It was better to be safe than sorry. One could never tell . . .

"I *will* replace it." Jack said this in such a way that Miles knew his thoughts had been showing. He smiled.

"It doesn't matter," he said. "Come on, let's have a drink."

"Is there any tequila in the house?"

"Certainly not. Why?"

"Slammers are all the rage up north. What about bourbon?"

"You'll drink best malt whisky, my lad, and you'll thank me for it. Do you know what they add to bourbon to give it that flavour?"

"No."

"Neither do I. That's reason enough to stick to whisky, don't you agree?"

They were laughing as they entered the living room, where Sheila sat with an Open University textbook on her lap and a pencil gripped hard between her teeth. She had been listening to their laughter as it left the study and came toward her, rumbling like some ancient beast. Her teeth bit through wood toward lead, and she could almost taste blood in her mouth. Did she want anything to drink? No, she did not want anything to drink. They seemed massive, father and son, filling her space and her peace and her thoughts with their bulk. When they turned their backs to her at the drinks table, she stuck out her tongue at them, and felt better for it. Then they sat down, expecting no doubt that she would put away her work and listen to their conversation, rising only to make tea and sandwiches. She held the pencil fast, sucking back the saliva which threatened to drip from the sides of her mouth. She was the wolf, hungry, angry, and she watched as they sat in their woolly smugness, cradling their glasses as though protecting the tribal fire.

Then Miles asked her a question, and she had to choose whether to ignore him, answer with a grunt, or take the pencil from her mouth. She grunted.

"Yes," said Miles, raising the glass to his lips, "I thought you'd agree."

"What OU course are you doing, Mum?" asked Jack. She slipped the pencil from between her teeth.

"A bit of everything," she said.

He nodded, and turned back to his father. Their questions were politeness, she knew. The sort of things one would say to a child so that it wouldn't feel excluded from the general conversation. She felt more isolated than ever. Then she remembered her secret.

To his eternal chagrin, Harold Sizewell had not been born in England. His father had been a professor of history and, while on a sabbatical teaching year in Paris, had found his wife to be rather more fecund than the expensive doctors back in London had diagnosed.

So Harry Sizewell was born French, and educated outside Windsor, and though he had never, so to speak, had a French thought in his life, it was hard—devilish hard—to throw off the tag.

For one thing, the media could always use it against him. Not that this bothered him particularly; there was little which could, to an MP, be termed "bad publicity," even the nickname "Harry the Frog." He had entered politics solely because his father had forbidden him to do so, and it was his misfortune to have been left an orphan before he gained his seat in the House. Still, he had it now, and his father would have been appalled by his quick and unhindered success. Appalled, the old socialist. The thought pleased Harry Sizewell, and he toasted himself with his breakfast tomato juice.

The morning mail—heavy as usual—gave little succour. Once, he had employed a secretary to open his mail for him and to send out the acknowledgements of receipt, but that had proved unsatisfactory: one could never be sure how open to misinterpretation or potentially incriminatory one's mail could be. And so he had decided to start opening his own mail, most of which, however, consisted of bills.

The damage to his Rover was estimated at nine hundred pounds. Nine hundred pounds for a couple of dents and a scraping of paint. That bloody fool of a Renault driver, hurtling away from the lights like that when all he had wanted to do was squeeze through his own red light so as not to be late at the House.

The day ahead promised little; Parliament was still in recess and the conference season had ended. He loathed conferences and spent too much time shaking hands with complete strangers and listening to tittle-tattle.

"I hear you're on this committee that's looking into defence funding," someone had said over a cocktail at some grandee's party.

"How did you hear that?"

"A little birdie told me. Well, one just *does* hear, doesn't one?"

Yes, one did. It was surprising just how many strangers had known so much about him. Who were they all? Defence was a touchy subject these days. He would rather as few people as possible knew of his involvement, especially when one considered what else the committee was investigating. Political dynamite, it was.

"Oh yes, Sizewell, of course. I knew your father at university."

"Did you, sir? You must be older than you look."

"Flattery, Sizewell, flattery. Your father was known for it too. A bit of a success with the young ladies when we were undergraduates together. I suppose you are too, eh? Chip off the old block."

A success with the ladies . . . Hardly. The PM had dropped a hint, by way of an equerry, that marriage would improve Harry Sizewell's standing within both the community and the party. It had not been a threat, just a suggestion. . . .

Ah, but there had been other threats to deal with, real threats, not just the rumblings of disgruntled constituents. Yes, real threats, lucid, cogent, to the point. The telephone rang, and, his mind elsewhere, he answered it.

"Remember this, Sizewell," the voice hissed. "I'm going to have you if you don't listen to me. I really am going to have you."

In horror, Harry Sizewell slammed down the receiver and stared at it, then lifted it off the hook quickly and set it down on the table. But the voice was still there, loud and clear as though from the next room, spitting out from the earpiece.

"You can't hide forever, Sizewell. You can't hide from me."

"Go away!" screamed Harry Sizewell, running into the next room, slamming the door shut. "Just go away."

CHAPTER 7

Pete Saville had a recurring dream, and in this dream he was trapped within Armourgeddon 2000, really trapped, twisted up in circuitry and flashing lights. The screen was there, real to the touch, and through it he could see the outside world, operating as normal. No one noticed that he was trapped within his console, that the game held him while the auto-play mode sent him reeling around his own set of maps and scenarios, trying to stop the ultimate war.

He never won.

Today's dream, however, had a twist, for someone was sitting at the console playing the game. This was worse even than auto-mode, for the player made mistakes that sent Pete roaring out of existence or careering around the most deadly battle zones. Dragging himself up to the screen during a lull, he looked out onto the smiling face of Miles Flint, then collapsed.

He woke to utter exhaustion. It seemed to him that he was sacrificing his sanity for a game. It was all he lived for, night and day, day after night.

The phone rang, and he stumbled through the cold hallway.

"Hello?"

"Is that Peter Saville?"

"Speaking."

"Peter, some of the security chaps would like a word."

Pete felt his life crumbling like a crashed computer program. He held on to the telephone with both hands, his voice becoming a whisper.

"Oh yes?"

"Nothing very important, I dare say. They'll be along about eleven."

"What, here?"

"Of course not." The voice seemed amused. "They'll send for you at your office. You are going in today?"

"Yes, oh yes."

"Good."

And the telephone went dead. Only then did it occur to Pete that he had not asked who was calling; had not the faintest idea whose voice had brought him to this standstill. One movement, he felt, and he would flake away to nothing but dust, like a wall with dry rot. He was worried now all right, worried and mentally exhausted. It was a bad combination.

Miles and Jack made a weekend of it. On Saturday they watched Chelsea playing in a friendly. It was years since Miles had been to watch a football match, and he yelled with gusto, enjoying the catharsis. Jack watched in amazement as his father swapped banter with the fans next to them and gave vent to raucous indignation when Chelsea's penalty claim was refused.

On Sunday they visited the zoo. It was wet, and not many people were about. A nice change, thought Jack, from football. He had taken along a couple of apples and some old vegetables from the kitchen, which he fed to the pigs in the children's area.

Later, following his father into the underpass, Jack thought about how the years had brought them closer together. He understood nowadays, as he had not when he was younger, that his father had achieved the right temperament for his own lines of work and life. Friends in Edinburgh might have attributed some Zenlike quality to Miles's attitude. And Sheila? Well, too much Yin, they would have said, too, too much.

"Not brought any excreta for your offspring, Dad?"

Miles had smiled but seemed preoccupied. He was thinking not of beetles but of moles. Moles and bugs, to be precise. A zoo seemed the perfect setting for his metaphors.

"I would think there would be enough of that lying around here already, wouldn't you?"

Jack, sniffing the air, his nose wrinkled, nodded agreement.

Miles had made two visits to the hotel and had not happened to meet the girl, which seemed to point to her complicity. His investigation was proceeding slowly—when it was proceeding at all—and he was becoming less sure of his suspicions. The smile had all but vanished now, as had the Latchkey case. He had been interviewed three times, Phillips and Sinclair twice. Miles, of course, was more suspect than they, for he had had no reason to be there, and it was he who had let Latchkey slip out into the night. There had been another meeting with Partridge and the old boy. The investigation's findings had been read out, and, while pointing out that human negligence had resulted in a death, there were no recommendations regarding further action or reprimands. Even the media had walked over the whole thing without seeing it.

And that had been that. So why didn't he just let the whole thing drop? Because his own trust in his intuition was at stake. It was as simple as that.

On a wall in the insect house was posted a list of adopters and their adopted, and there was his name. Jack chuckled, patting his shoulder, and then they made for the glass case itself. There were around four thousand species of beetle in Britain alone, and this specimen was all his. The dung beetle, or dor beetle, dor being Anglo-Saxon for "drone"—the noise the beetle made in flight. Miles took off his glasses to study the case. Well, a ball of dung was there all right, but there was no sign of life. Miles knew that the beetle would be in there. No one would see it until it wanted to be seen. He nodded thoughtfully and turned away, while Jack tapped at the glass, attempting to coax the creature out of its darkness.

Back home, two messages awaited Miles on the answering machine.

Sheila had gone out for the day with Moira. They were visiting an exhibition. Miles traced Sheila's likes and dislikes by going around after her, examining what she had just been reading or otherwise studying. She had taken an interest in Francis Bacon, bird-watching, and Marxism, and in all these things she was aided and abetted by Moira, her old school friend. Moira was actually cleverer than Sheila, as well as being the more attractive. She was a bit of a splendour beetle, and whenever he was in her company Miles felt like some old museum beetle again, bedded down in stuffed animals and relics of the past.

Sheila visited exhibitions often when Jack was at home. It was no coincidence. She did not shun him physically but placed a sort of veil over herself when he was around, treating him like the son of an acquaintance rather than her own. She would give him everything except the acknowledgement of kinship. They had fallen out once five years ago when he had been in the midst of an adolescent fit. They hadn't spoken to one another for days afterward, and their relationship had never really recovered.

"This is Partridge here, Miles. We'd like to see you tomorrow if that's convenient. King's Cross, platform 4. Get yourself a platform ticket. See you at ten-thirty sharp."

Partridge: that meant trouble, but of what sort? And why King's Cross? Was Partridge going somewhere? And who might that "we" include within its wide parameters? It was all very mysterious, very cloak and dagger.

The second message was from a less than sober Billy, asking if they might meet for lunch tomorrow. Jack, entering from the kitchen with two mugs of coffee, a packet of biscuits between his teeth, was motioned to listen.

"Billy here, Miles. Hate these bloody machines. Inhuman. Can't talk to them."

Technology worried Miles too. It used to be the case that when someone died, for example, all that was left were memories and perhaps a few faded photographs. But now there were tape recordings and video recordings, and so memory became less important to the process. That was a dangerous phenomenon, for machines could be manipulated, could go wrong, could forget.

Just as the Arab's smile was slipping away from him forever.

His private line, the messages always came by way of his private line. Ever more regularly, and despite two changes of number, they came. A trace had been put on the calls, but they were always too succinct.

"I'm going to have you, Sizewell, really I am."

Partridge had sent some fool round to interview him. Did he know who could be responsible for the calls? No, of course he didn't. Did he know why someone should want to "get him"? Oh yes, he knew that all right, but he wasn't about to say anything to anyone about it. Except perhaps to Partridge himself.

The telephone rang again and was answered by the man whose job it now was to do so. Harry Sizewell was no coward. He had brought in Partridge and his men not out of weakness but as part of his strategy. He was trying to show his tormentor that he would not give in to threats, that he would be strong. But what if the man wouldn't play any longer? What if he *did* have something from Sizewell's past? Everyone had skeletons in their closet, didn't they? Everyone had something which would be best left to rot away in secrecy and in darkness.

I'm going to have you, Sizewell, really I am.

It was the bully's pointed promise to everyone who would not stand up for themselves. Well, he, Harry Sizewell, would not shrink from such a challenge. Bullies were there to be beaten; it was their only purpose in life. And when Sizewell suspected that Partridge and his gang were not taking the whole thing seriously enough, he made a complaint which sent Partridge himself scurrying out of the woodwork.

"What else can we do?"

"You tell me, Partridge. I thought that was your job." Sizewell was standing, Partridge seated. The latter's appearance of total calm made Sizewell angrier still.

"We could change your number again."

"You've tried already. He still bloody well gets through."

"Yes, that *is* interesting."

"What do you mean?"

"Well, it cuts down the number of possible culprits. Not everyone has immediate access to VIP ex-directory numbers. We're making inquiries in that direction."

"Good of you, I'm sure."

"If we could do more we would. Don't you believe that?"

"I'm not sure if I do."

Partridge smoothed his hands over his knees.

"How long have we known one another, Harry?"

"Look, it's quite simple. All I'm asking—"

"How long?"

Sizewell glanced toward him, then away. He crossed to the window and stared out through the heavy net curtain. The curtaining came with the job. It was bomb-resistant, there to catch shards of glass and trap them. But *he* was not bomb-resistant. He turned.

"Look, Partridge, I happen to be friendly with the PM, and—"

Partridge had already risen to his feet and was approaching the telephone. He bent down towards the wall socket and pulled out the connector.

"Satisfied?" he asked with a smile.

Sizewell strode over to him.

"No, I'm bloody not, and if that's your attitude—"

Harry Sizewell's cheeks were a strong colour of red already, partly natural, partly from anger and frustration. They grew even redder when Partridge, seeming hardly to move at all, struck him with first the palm and then the back of his hand. Sizewell's mouth opened, and his eyes grew foggy like a botched piece of double glazing.

"You're acting like a child," Partridge said. "For God's sake, that's no way for someone in your position to behave. We *all* have to deal with these sorts of thing. Now if you'll excuse me, I have more pressing matters."

"I'll report this, Partridge, don't think that I won't!"

But the door was already closing. Sizewell touched his face with his fingers, feeling the soft red of the slap and behind it the fierce burning of humiliation.

"Don't think I won't," he muttered, reconnecting the telephone.

CHAPTER 8

King's Cross on a Monday morning had the scowling face of a spoilt child. Partridge liked railway stations for their human-interest value. Low-life scoundrels rubbed shoulders with haughty businessmen, while Pavlovian clusters of travellers sipped grey tea and watched the flickering departures board.

A ragged creature shuffled his feet to a tune played on the harmonica, while his free hand jostled for money from the restless commuters. He was not having much luck and moved along quickly with a sideways, crablike motion, while the conspiracy to ignore his existence held fast.

While Partridge watched this circus, the old boy watched the trains themselves. It was a hobby he had held dear for over forty years. He was standing at the very furthest tip of the platform, beside two other spotters, one a teenager, unhandsome and dressed in the perennial duffel coat, the other a man in his thirties, who looked like an off-shift station employee. The Director seemed to know this man, for they had swapped notes at one point, while Partridge, halfway down the platform and looking for all the world like a civil servant, watched. Partridge had taken up train spotting only after having discovered that it was the one real passion in his superior's life. He checked his sleek watch now. It was ten-seventeen.

"Miles," Partridge said affably, "good of you to come. The old boy would like a word."

The dung beetle comes of a very good family, *Scarabaeidae,* amongst which sits on high the Sacred Scarab. The ancient Egyptians worshipped it like some deity. Silent, black, the scarab seemed to hold within itself the power and the meaning of the universe.

And for this reason Miles liked to think of his most superior officer as the Sacred Scarab, most honoured of all the beetles.

"Good morning, sir."

Miles's greeting went unanswered as the Director busied himself jotting down an engine number.

"I only collect the engine numbers, you know," he said at last, as the train pulled to a stop. "Some enthusiasts collect carriage numbers, too. But there's such a thing as being overenthusiastic, don't you agree?"

"Yes, sir."

"Some spotters, well, they always need to know more. Their curiosity can never be satisfied. Then there are others like me, like Mr. Partridge here, who are interested in only the one part of the hobby, and we stick to that. Do you see?"

"Yes, sir," said Miles, not seeing at all.

"Miles, I'm not famous for circumlocution. You've been doing some hunting within the department. I want to know why."

"Well . . ." began Miles.

A woman was having trouble opening the door of her carriage, and Partridge rushed forward to help her. She seemed impressed, and glanced back at him as she walked up the platform, a heavy bag hanging from one arm. Partridge came to rejoin them, seeming pleased with himself. More than ever he reminded Miles of *Platyrhopalopsis melyi. Mel,* Latin for honey. Partridge's smile oozed from his face.

"Well, sir," Miles began again, "I was just a little worried by the Latchkey business, that's all."

"Worried?" said Partridge.

"Yes. You see, there was something about that operation which struck a wrong chord."

"Your own bungling, perhaps?"

"All right, I fell for a very old trick, but it's more than that. I'm not just trying to cover up my mistakes."

"Then just what exactly are you trying to do?" asked Partridge.

"I merely wanted to be sure that my own mistake had been the only one made."

"And that involved checking on Mr. Partridge and myself?" The old boy was fingering his dog-eared notebook. It looked for all the world like a coded series, all those columns of numbers.

"It was routine, sir. I was looking at everyone."

"We know that," snapped the Director. "You'd be surprised what we know. But you have to admit that your investigation has been anything but 'routine.' You must realise that?"

"Yes, sir."

"Good. Now let's get some tea and talk about cynegetics."

"You were a classics man, weren't you, Flint?"

Miles watched the Earl Grey being poured, while Partridge stared from the window of the hotel's morning room. A few turnings had lifted them out of the immediate squalor of King's Cross and dropped them in this backwater of tranquillity. Miles felt that this would be where the interrogation really started.

"I was, yes."

"Then you've probably heard the word 'cynegetic'?"

"I know that *kynegetes* means hunter."

"Quite so. There is, and this is for your ears only, a very small unit within the department. Someone somewhere decided to call it the Cynegetic Section. Someone with a classics degree, perhaps." The Director smiled to himself. "Anyway, Cynegetics is involved with the rooting out of, well, let's just say of anyone who might be acting in a suspicious manner. Especially, it is interested in those who appear to be hunting within the department."

"I see."

"As you were doing," added Partridge, turning from the window to add just a touch of milk to his tea, stirring it slowly. "Very ably, I might add."

"And," said the Director, "as others seem to be doing. You met with Richard Mowbray recently?"

"I've been assigned to the same case."

"Yes, but before that. He followed you to a record shop. Cynegetics were following *him.*"

"I've got nothing to do with Mowbray, sir."

"We're aware of that," answered Partridge. God, thought Miles, what a double act they make. Such timing.

"But it does seem rather a large coincidence," the old boy said on cue. "Doesn't it?"

Miles decided not to answer. Through the morning-room doors he could see a whispered commotion in the lobby. A suitcase had been left unattended, and the staff didn't want to touch it.

"Miles," began the Director solicitously, "I'm retiring soon. Perhaps as soon as the end of this year. And I don't want to find, as some of my predecessors have found, any blemish staining the last days of my public career, or of my ensuing retirement come to that. You understand? A fairly substantial honour is not too far away."

Miles understood.

"So," the old boy continued, not looking so old now, his eyes as hard as diamonds, "I would be . . . perturbed if anything were to come to light, especially without my knowing about it. You've read the newspapers lately, you know that Fleet Street has more than a few daggers drawn against us. We need to be . . . what's the phrase again? Ah, yes, we need to be a 'clean machine.' An American friend of mine is very keen on that phrase."

"At the same time," Partridge interrupted, his voice low with sincerity, "if I should happen to be promoted to Director—"

"As seems likely," explained the Director.

"—then I should not want to find *my*self faced with a first duty of investigating my own service. Nor should I like to think that I were being spied upon by my own officers. There has been too much of that in the past by the—what do the press term them?—the "Young Turks." Too much of it, Miles, and too much of it of late. The service is secure, Miles. Believe that. The service *is* secure."

What could he say? Could he tell them that, no, the service was not secure, all because of a smile which might not have been directed at him? Their faces bespoke the sublime, like monks who know no sin. In their most upper echelon of the firm, ignorance was indeed bliss. Cynegetics had been set up to keep the place nice and tidy, as though for an inspection. Push all the dust under the carpets. Miles realised that, quite simply, these men did not want to know, and if they did not want to know, then to all intents and purposes there was nothing *to* know. No knowledge could exist unless they accepted it.

"I see," he said, lifting his cup. "Is that all?"

"Well," said Partridge, "I for one would like to know just what your suspicions were."

"Yes, good point," said the Director.

Miles sipped his tea. He paused for a moment, then swallowed.

"Whatever it was," he said, "it's history now."

They seemed pleased with this, like schoolboys whose fag was not going to report a roasting at their hands.

"I *am* enjoying this tea," said the Director brightly. "It's rare to find a good cup of tea these days, even in London."

"I quite agree," said Partridge, smiling at Miles.

The fracas in the lobby seemed to have ended. Someone had come forward and claimed the case as his. Miles caught a glimpse of a young woman as she walked past the reception desk. He wondered where he had seen her before. Then he remembered. Only two weeks ago, in the cocktail bar, with Latchkey grinning towards him. Here she was, delivered into his hands in one of the firm's "safe" hotels. Coincidence? Miles thought not. He was beginning to believe in kismet.

When the occasional customer, all social conscience and guilt reflex, asked Felicity why she did what she did, when she had—in their tired old phrasing—"so much going for her," she usually just shrugged, and they would let it rest. Of late, however, she had given the question some thought. The money was good, of course, and often she would be involved in little more than escort work. Her clients were businessmen, desperate for success, and a pretty, intelligent companion for the evening was, to them, a sign of that success. She tried not to think about the other nights, the tough ones, when she took on the lechers and the heavyweight drinkers. She cried after those engagements, and bathed, soaking them out of her system. It was hard work, too hard sometimes.

The hotel management never troubled her. If they became suspicious, well, her appearance and her accent were usually enough to see them off, and there were other ways, too, of course. She did it for the money. She was saving up to open her own boutique, or—last month's notion—a bookshop. She had changed her mind so often. But she had a good bank manager, who advised her on possible investments and never asked about taxes and such. She was just waiting for the day when he, too, would become a customer. There was a sordid glimmer to his smile. But one day she would put all this behind her and become a celebrity. Her shop, whatever it was, would be *the* place to be seen. Her photograph would appear in the magazines, and she might even be seen on TV . . . seen by all her old clients, who would recognise her. And then one of them would sell the story of her past life to a newspaper, out of spite. Sheer spite . . .

"Hello, miss."

And she had saved her money so well and had fought off the competition. (God, some of those girls were tough.) She had not given in to the many pimps who had tried to threaten her. She was not stupid. She would not have succeeded if she were. Her mother had taught her all she had needed to know about survival. All those dark, cold nights of fireside horror stories about how life could suck you as dry as a beached bone. All those lessons . . .

"Excuse me."

"Yes?" She looked up from her reverie into the smiling eyes of a small, middle-aged man.

"We've met before," he said. "At least, I think we have. Yes, I'm sure of it. Though I'm a bit early for our appointment."

"Appointment?"

"Yes, we met two weeks ago. In the Doric. Just off the Strand. You asked me if I had a light, and then we met again in the cocktail bar. I said we could arrange to meet there again in a year's time."

Felicity laughed.

"I remember now," she said. "You ran away from me. I have to tell you that men don't often do that. I was a bit startled."

"Well, that evening, I was a bit unsettled myself."

"Won't you join me?"

She was seated at a small table in the reception area. Miles had watched her for a minute or two, Partridge and the old boy having left for the office. As he sat down, Felicity thought to herself, He's actually quite tall. Why did I think he was short?

"You remember that night?" he asked.

"Oh yes. You seemed to be just about the only unattached person in the place, apart from me. Birds of a feather, I thought, but I was wrong, it seems."

"That was why you approached me twice?"

"Yes." Her voice was steady, but Miles detected something. It had been a while ago now, and she had allowed herself the luxury of forgetting all the details. But something about that evening had just come back to her, and she was trying to think about it at the same time as she spoke to him. He decided to attack.

"Who put you up to it?"

"I beg your pardon?" The blood began to colour her already flushed cheeks. She was pretty, there was no doubting that. Even Partridge had given her more than cursory attention before leaving.

"I asked who put you up to it. The whole thing was a setup, wasn't it? I can see it in your face, Miss . . . ?"

"Felicity," she whispered.

"Look, Felicity, it was a long time ago, wasn't it? But you do remember? It's hardly going to hurt you now to tell me who it was, is it? Who put you up to it, Felicity?"

"I . . ." She was just a little frightened now, and Miles did not want to frighten her.

"Do you know what it was all about?" he said. "I'll tell you, it was a joke arranged by some friends of mine. I was waiting there for them, you see, and I think they put you up to it, so that they could have a laugh when they finally did come along and find us together. Is that it, Felicity?"

"Well, he never said exactly . . ." She stopped, but had already said too much. It would be easy now to prise the rest from her, now that she had taken the first, irretrievable step.

"Yes?" he prompted.

"But you told me when you left that you were on your way home."

"I was lying." The smile never left Miles's face. "I'd rumbled you, you see. So I went off elsewhere."

"Did you find your friends?"

"Yes, but neither of them would own up to the joke. That's why it's been niggling me."

Felicity nodded her head. What the hell, it was nothing to do with her. She was free to talk about it, wasn't she? This was a free country. She made herself more comfortable in her seat. Business, she thought to herself, that was what this had become.

"I don't usually give away that sort of information, you know. It's bad for my reputation. I do have my reputation to consider."

Miles was ready for this. He reached for his wallet and produced two ten-pound notes, hoping it would not seem derisory. She stared at the cash, then lifted it swiftly and stuffed it into her clutch purse, black and shining like a beetle.

The duty manager was in front of them like a shot, his voice colder than his eyes and his eyes as cold as icicles.

"Out, please, both of you. I've been watching, and this is *not* that kind of establishment."

Miles, despite the laughter he could feel rising within him, saw that this was a dangerous situation. Felicity, flaring her nostrils, was ready for remonstrance and, perhaps, physical action. The manager would not tolerate that, would telephone for the police. A couple at reception were already watching the scene with interest. Miles could not afford this, could not afford to be noticed. He grabbed Felicity's arm.

"Come on," he said.

"How dare you!" Felicity shouted to the impassive figure, as Miles steered her towards the door. "Just what the hell do you think—"

But by then they were outside, and the fresh air seemed to calm her immediately. She giggled.

"Now then," said Miles, "what was it you were about to tell me?"

"I was about to tell you," she said, her bottom lip curling, "that twenty pounds will get you more than conversation."

But conversation was what he wanted, and she gave him five minutes' worth. It wasn't much, but it was just about enough. Afterward, he coaxed her telephone number out of her by suggesting that he might one day want to give her some escort work. The number was scribbled in his notebook, a 586 prefix: northwest London. He could find her address easily enough back at the office.

What was important was that she had substantiated his fragile theory. He *had* been set up. A man had motioned to her from the door of the hotel and, when she was outside, had given her a description of Miles. Could she describe this man? Tallish, good-looking, a bit suave even, nicely spoken.

And that was it. She had been paid to talk to Miles, probably to distract his attention ever so slightly. Well, it had worked like a charm. The question now was, who was it? Phillips seemed the obvious choice, but Phillips had been smartly attired, and the man who had approached her had been casually dressed.

He thought to himself for the hundredth time, So what if there *is* a conspiracy? Who cares? It's over, nobody wants to know about it with the possible exception of Richard Mowbray. So why bother? Why not just go back to square one?

Because, he knew, if he did not solve the mystery, there could be no "going back." It was as though the first square had been removed from the board.

"Dad!"

Jack came loping towards him, a pair of headphones clamped to his head.

"Where the hell did you spring from?"

Jack slipped the headphones down around his neck.

"Oh," he said, switching off the tape, "I've just been wandering about. I was supposed to meet someone for lunch at that little Greek place near the British Museum. They didn't turn up."

"Oh, Christ, what time is it?" Miles looked at his Longines, left to him by his father. It was ten past one. "I'm supposed to be meeting Billy at one. Damn." He turned to Jack. "Would you like to join us?" Miles hoped that his tone would hint that this was politeness only, that Jack would not be welcome. Jack smiled, touching his father on the shoulder.

"Thanks but no, thanks," he said. "Things to see, people to do. You know how it is."

"Well," said Miles in mitigation, "we must arrange to have lunch together in town before you leave. A proper lunch, just the two of us."

"Yes," agreed Jack, already moving away. And with a wave he was gone, putting distance between them.

Miles watched him go, then made for a nearby pub, the King and Country. He would telephone Billy at the restaurant. Billy would understand.

It was two when he arrived, but Billy had contented himself with four or five drinks meantime and was now in a malleable state.

"Bloody glad you could make it, Miles."

"I'm just sorry I'm late, Billy."

A businessman, dripping gold, led a quite stunning young woman to one of the restaurant's better tables. At once, Billy's antennae caught the scent, and he stared at the woman even after she had settled down with the menu.

"Christ, Miles, isn't that superb?"

Checking in the mirrored wall behind Billy, Miles was forced to agree.

"Yes," said Billy, "I wouldn't mind, I can tell you."

Miles thought again of the longhorn beetle, with its long and sensitive antennae, antennae which could pinpoint a female thousands of yards away. Billy could actually *sense* when a beautiful woman was nearby. It was quite a talent. At the same time, though, it seemed to Miles that Billy, for all his bravado, was afraid of women, taking lovers the way Mithridates had taken poison: sip by sip to make himself immune against them.

"So what's been happening, Miles?"

"You know bloody well what's been happening. You're a magnet for office gossip."

"Well, I know *some* of it, but probably not all. You lost Latchkey?"

"The very evening I'd been having a drink with you."

"Yes, a curious coincidence."

The waiter came then, and they ordered, Miles sticking to dishes he knew: minestrone, fettucine.

"I take it there has been an inquiry?" said Billy after the waiter had gone.

Miles fingered his soup spoon, wondering whether to drop it. He decided no, what the hell. Let them listen.

"Of sorts. It was all very low-key."

"Funny," said Billy as the first course arrived, "I was thinking of Philip Hayton the other day. Do you remember him?"

"No."

"He was one of the older boys. A headhunter. He was on my first interview panel, I recall."

"Of course, yes, Philip Hayton. He was killed in an accident, wasn't he?"

"Over in Ireland, yes. A boating accident. Except, of course, that there were rumours to the effect that he had been executed."

"Oh?"

"Mmm. By the IRA, I suppose, though there wasn't much of an IRA back then. Funny business . . ."

There was no more talk of the firm until they were sipping nicely bitter espresso coffee and Billy was debating whether he could manage another portion of cheese with his last crumbly biscuit.

"I was wondering," he said, "what you thought of this Latchkey business?"

"What do you mean?"

"Well, who's to blame?"

"I'm to blame, of course."

"Oh yes, well, as far as the record goes, but you said yourself that you've had your wrists slapped and that's about it. No retribution, no demotion, nothing."

"They want it kept quiet."

"So as not to rile the Israelis? Yes, I can imagine."

"And I've been punished in another sense."

"Oh?"

"Yes, they've sent me to work beside Richard Mowbray."

Billy smiled. He knew Mowbray, whom he irritated by insisting on calling him "Mauberley."

"The Mauberley Barmy Army, eh? Now there's a man who has his sights quite firmly fixed on nothing but the top slot. He wants the old boy's job, and one of these years, God help us, he may just get it."

"It's a frightening prospect."

"So you're working on Harvest, eh?"

"That's right."

"It looks promising. Are you day watchman or night watchman?"

"Richard has a rota."

"I'll bet he has. Be careful of Mauberley, Miles. He could drag you down with him. Have you heard his latest one?"

"About the cousins having a bomb in their Moscow embassy?"

"No, I'd not heard that. I was referring to his theory that the *Belgrano* was torpedoed by an American midget submarine."

"That's crazy."

"In F Branch they have a new name for him: Meltdown Mowbray."

Miles, feeling the lightness of the wine inside him, was beginning to laugh at this when a large, well-dressed man approached the table.

"Billy Monmouth!"

"Andrew." Billy rose from his chair, holding on to his napkin with one hand and shaking with the other. "Where have you been hiding?"

"I've been in France. A company-funded shopping trip." The man called Andrew smiled down on Miles, full of self-satisfaction and wanting others to share in it. Miles wondered why, being so full already, the man needed to eat at all.

"Andrew, this is Miles Flint, a colleague of mine."

They shook hands. Andrew's hand was warm and slightly damp. He radiated well-being and charm, and could probably afford another Rolex should he lose the one he was wearing.

"Andrew is a salesman," explained Billy.

"That's right, and a damned good one. What do you do, Miles?"

"I'm just a civil servant."

"Same game as Billy here, eh? Well, don't think *I* don't know who wields the power in this country. I've watched 'Yes, Prime Minister.' In fact, I do a lot of dealing with the civil service. Hard but fair, would you agree?"

"What's fair about us?" said Billy, causing all three to laugh.

"Well, I'd better be getting to my table. We must get together for a drink, Billy, really we must. Keep in touch. Nice to have met you, Miles." And with that the man was off, walking to the corner table and joining his friends. He kissed the beautiful woman on the hand, laying custodial fingers on her neck, motioning across towards Billy and Miles. The woman smiled at them, then pecked Andrew on the cheek while he picked up a menu.

Billy, who had smiled back like an addict to his fix, now said from behind his smile, "What a shit," and decided on another portion of Brie to go with his whisky.

"He's a slight acquaintance," he said. "We see one another at dinner parties, where we inevitably get drunk and end up promising ourselves this mythical get-together."

"He seems nice, though."

Billy laughed.

"Come on, our man Flint, Andrew Gray is a proper little jumped-up shit and you know it. Your voice may be without irony, my friend, but your eyes betray you." Billy paused. "You know, Miles, you're quite cunning in your way. I mean, you sit there all silent, watching, and people tend to forget that you're there at all, but you are. Oh, you are. I admire that, though I also find it just faintly disturbing."

As before, there seemed an unspoken meaning behind Billy's words. Miles was wondering why Philip Hayton's name had been brought into play, and remembered that Billy was on his list of suspects. In fact, he was at the top.

"I suppose I am faintly disturbing, Billy," said Miles. "It's one of my most appealing features."

And Billy laughed loudly this time, catching the attention of the beautiful woman. He smiled at her, antennae twitching, a hunter intent on the chase.

CHAPTER 9

Sheila, listening to Mozart in the living room, thought of Miles. Although she abhorred physical violence, a pleasant shivery feeling came to her when she remembered the way he had fought for her as a student. He had been wild as a teenager, trying to prove something to himself and to the world. No longer . . . They had enjoyed themselves back then, but now they had grown so far apart. It was like being married to an amnesiac.

The base of her neck prickled as the *Requiem* washed over her, full of its own violence. She had seen the film *Amadeus* with Moira, and they had fallen out about whether or not it was farfetched. It never did to fall out with Moira. She was such a good friend, useful for all sorts of things, and she knew so much. Miles liked her too. Sheila could see that, for all his subtlety. He would risk a glance at Moira whenever he felt safe, taking in her legs with one sweep, maybe her breasts at a later opportunity. His concealed admiration bordered on the perverse. Why didn't he just come out and say he found her attractive? Sheila wouldn't mind; she wouldn't be jealous. One afternoon last week, walking past a building site, a crowd of workmen had whistled at her, and she had smiled back at them rather than giving them her usual snarl. Did she miss praise so much that she had to accept it from strangers?

Yes, she thought to herself, smiling again.

"Hello, Mother."

She had not heard Jack come in, had not even heard him closing the door. He had been noisy as a youngster, banging doors shut with a healthy disrespect for them. But nowadays he cultivated his father's habits of stealth and secrecy. She felt the conspiracy ripening between them, unspoken but definitely there.

"What's this?" Standing in front of her, Jack shouted this aloud, his thumb held toward the stereo.

"Mozart," she said softly, turning the record down. "What are you doing home so early?"

Jack shrugged, then lifted a peach from the fruit bowl. Once he would have asked for her permission, which she would always have given.

"What are *you* doing home?" he mimicked.

"I took a half day. I've got a lot of leave still to take. Have you eaten lunch?"

"No, actually. I was supposed to meet a friend, but she didn't show. Then I bumped into Dad, but he had a prior engagement."

"Oh?" Sheila thought she could see the slightest chink in Jack's armour. "I've not eaten myself," she said. "Why don't we have something together?"

Jack, finishing the peach noisily, looked at her, trying to find some barb, some catch: there was none. So, smiling, nodding, he graciously accepted her invitation and suggested that they open a bottle of wine for starters.

Turning into Marlborough Place that evening, Miles wondered how Partridge and the old boy had found out about his use of the computer. Pete Saville must have left something for them to find, something he should not have left. They had probably questioned him, and he would have talked straight away. He had no defence, after all.

Whoever it was who had talked to Felicity on that night, he was a goliath beetle. Miles was clear enough about that. Goliath beetles were very fragile indeed, and therefore very hard to collect. They flew through their forest terrain at great height, rarely alighting on the ground, where predators and collectors awaited them. This was the figure of the enemy: hard to catch, soaring above the mundane world and, when captured, brittle as spun sugar.

He opened the door to his house, wondering again, with slight vertigo, how much it must be worth. Sheila and he had bought it in the sixties, and even then it had been an expensive ruin, albeit an expensive ruin in St. John's Wood. A fortuitous inheritance on Sheila's part had ensured that they could buy two floors' worth, and Sheila had loved it from the first tentative visit. Dry rot in one of the walls a few years ago had cost a thousand pounds to fix, and Miles feared more incursions, more deterioration. It was in the nature of buildings to fall down; all one ever did was shore them up.

There were voices in the living room, loudly conversational. He listened at the door for a moment.

"Come in, Miles, for Christ's sake," called Sheila. "Why do you always have to skulk at the door? I can always hear you, you know."

Inside, Sheila lay along the sofa, a glass of tawny wine in one hand. From the tawniness, he guessed that one of his better clarets had been opened. But, to his dismay, he saw on the floor not one but three empty bottles: the last of his '70. Sheila smiled towards him with catlike superiority. Jack, legs dangling over the arm of his chair, let a long-stemmed glass play between his fingers. It was empty.

"Good evening, Miles," said Sheila. "Is it that time already? It seems like only half an hour since we finished lunch, doesn't it, Jack?"

Jack merely nodded, enough of his wits left to know that to speak would be to betray his all too evident condition.

"Mind if I join you?" Miles made to sit on the sofa, and Sheila shifted her legs helpfully. Clearly, she thought that some kind of victory had been won over Miles, and that she could now claim Jack as an ally in her struggle. They had eaten lunch together. Miles could see the whole sequence unfold, compounded by his own earlier rejection of his son.

He felt sick in his stomach. It was impossible these days when there were three of them in the house. He wondered why Jack bothered to come home at all. There could be no halfway house, no no-man's-land. Always it had to be two against one.

"Oh, by the way," said Sheila, "Jack thinks there's wet rot in the larder."

"Oh?"

"Yes," said Sheila. Lying half along the sofa, her legs curved towards the floor, she was like an insect, her body divided into abdomen, thorax, and head. The aroma of her drunkenness was all around, cutting Jack off from him, bringing the conspiracy to fruition.

"Maybe we should sell the place then."

Sheila shook her head loosely.

"House values continue to rise," she said with absolute clarity, "at a higher rate in areas like this than anywhere else in Britain. If we wait just a few more years, Miles, we can sell up and buy a palace elsewhere. We've been through all this."

Jack laughed, as Miles had hoped he would.

"What are you laughing at?" asked Sheila, annoyed.

"Listen to you," said Jack. "The best part of three bottles of wine, and you can still spout economics like Milton Keynes."

"That should be Milton Friedman," corrected Miles. "Or do you mean Maynard Keynes?"

Jack looked at him, a little puzzled.

"Why?" he asked. "What did I say?"

"You said Milton Keynes," said Sheila, bursting into laughter and throwing herself forward.

"Is there any wine left?" Miles asked now, sure that his wife and son were less of a combined force than he had at first feared. Sheila was still laughing, and Jack studied her in stilted horror.

"Loads," said Sheila. "Get another bottle. And watch out for that rising damp."

"Wet rot," Jack corrected quickly, his voice stabbing the air.

"Well, whatever," mumbled Sheila, all laughter gone.

"Right," said Miles, examining the quietened room, "let's have ourselves a little party, shall we?"

But the room remained silent after he left. The party had already finished.

He wondered whether Sheila could really always hear him outside the door. Until recently, he had thought himself infallible. Now he knew differently.

He brought another bottle of wine into the room. Sheila was reading, while Jack still played with his empty glass.

"Here we are then. You could well be right, Jack. There does seem to be a patch of rot in the floor timbers. We'll have it inspected."

He opened the bottle and poured three generous glasses, then set his own aside for the moment, allowing the young wine at least a slender chance to breathe. Jack gulped his own down without tasting it.

"Sorry about lunch, Jack. I had to see Billy Monmouth. It was all shop talk."

"That's all right."

"What was Billy saying, then?" Sheila turned the page of her book.

"You know Billy. Gossip mainly."

"We haven't had him round for a while, have we?"

The fact was, they had no one round these days. Their friends—the married couples—had disintegrated like old houses.

"No, we haven't," said Miles, and the conversation stopped there. Dead.

CHAPTER 10

He was being followed, and none too subtly. Already in a bookshop a man had approached him asking for a light, though no smoking was allowed. Then another man—different face, same eyes—had asked him the time. So Pete Saville was moving now, weaving through the narrow streets of the city, trying to lose the men. He didn't want the streets to get too narrow though, or too quiet, for that would be asking for trouble. He had enough trouble as it was.

He didn't recognise any of them, but that didn't mean anything. Their accents were English, but that meant nothing either. He had counted four of them so far, four or just maybe five. Oh, God, what had he done? He was sure that it had something, everything to do with Miles Flint. Mr. Partridge had warned him. Miles bloody Flint and his bloody snooping. He dived into another street, seeking a telephone box, not knowing whom to ring. Perhaps he should turn and confront them. Yes, why not? Every reason in the world.

Pete Saville was scared.

This was no game, no Armourgeddon. It was real, and it was dangerous, perhaps lethal. He glanced back. Two following on one pavement, two on the other. Walking briskly. Hands by their sides. Almost casual.

What had he done?

He turned corner after corner. Saw a bus and made a run for it, but it moved off ahead of him, leaving him flailing at the wind. There were people about, some of them giving him curious looks. He could tell them, but tell them what?

Oh, he was scared, how he was scared.

So run, and keep on running. But they had decided to make their move. They were gaining effortlessly, coming nearer, nearer. And now a fifth man was calling out his name, patiently, as though paging him in a hotel. Pete Saville didn't feel as though he were in a hotel.

The smell of the abattoir was in the air.

Pete's heart was melting with the heat in his lungs. His brain was singed. He could taste cordite on his tongue. He stopped, leaning his head against a car. But when they were a few yards from him, he took to his heels again, willing himself on with the last of his being. He rounded a corner and was confronted by policemen. They were cordoning off an area of pavement, unravelling a length of red and white tape with which to make the road impassable. A small crowd had gathered on the other side of the tape, watching. It was being broken up by several uniformed policemen. Damn, it was a dead end. But the men would do nothing, not with the police here. No, Pete was safe.

He was safe!

He heard his name called again, and pushed his way past some onlookers, slipping under the cordon. Someone shouted at him, a different voice this time, then someone screamed. He thought he heard the word "bomb" and stopped in his tracks. He was outside a small restaurant and saw for the first time the soldiers, who were everywhere. And beyond them, his pursuers, watching with the rest of the crowd, smiling at him, not about to follow him past the cordon.

Bomb? Oh, God, what had he done?

The police stood at the tape and told him to come back from the building. But no, he couldn't do that. The building was his sanctuary. He could pass through it and out of the other side, could lose the men that way.

Making up his mind, he headed into the restaurant, vaguely aware of two
Army men working at the back of the tables.

There was a sudden suction, a huge, dusty gust of hot wind, and the roar
of jet engines, of thunder overhead. When the dust cleared, and the
screams abated, and people were blinking and shaking fragments from
their clothes, Pete Saville wasn't there anymore, and neither were the two
bomb disposal experts. Even the hunters seemed to have disappeared, leaving behind them only the police and the civilians, most of them in shock,
and the man called Andrew Gray, standing at a safe distance beside a
lamppost, watching.

CHAPTER 11

"You know about it then?"

"Cynegetics?" Mowbray laughed. "Of course I do."

"Why am I always the last to hear about these things?"

Mowbray shrugged, looking more transatlantic than ever in tinted
glasses and a sheepskin jacket. He was supposed to look like an estate
agent who showed people around the large Forest Hill house which the
firm had procured for Harvest. Harvest was supposed, so Billy Monmouth
had said, to bring forth a "bumper crop" of IRA sleepers, soon to be
activated now that a full-scale campaign was under way. Three more poor
bastards had been blown up, one a civilian. Nobody knew who he was. He
had just run into a cordoned-off area at the wrong moment, and a bomb
had gone off prematurely. There was nothing solid enough left to identify.

The Harvest cell had been under surveillance for weeks, three Irishmen
and a woman in a house across the road from the watchmen. The occupants were, variously, an unemployed electrician, a park keeper, a mechanic, and a secretary on a building site. If they were sleepers, then they
were sleeping soundly. It looked like yet another waste of time, but Miles
knew that no one could afford to become complacent.

"There isn't even a bloody telephone in the house," said "Mad Phil."
"There's *never* been a cell that didn't have a phone in the house."

"Mad Phil" enjoyed complaining and liked to think that he excelled in
it. He was neither mad, nor was his name Phil, but those were the letters
after his name: Graham Lockett, MA, D.Phil. Billy had coined the nickname, and it had stuck, just as "Tricky Dicky" and "Mauberley" had
stuck for Richard Mowbray.

"Doesn't it worry you, Richard?"

"What?"

"That Cynegetics are on to you."

"Not in the least. What is it I'm doing that's wrong?"

"Have they been to see you?"

"Yes, several times, and Partridge has had a word, too, but I repeat, what am I doing that's wrong? If the firm is clean, then why should anyone worry about my little dossier?"

Suddenly Miles could see the beauty of Mowbray's tactics: those who opposed him must have reasons for doing so, and so were suspects themselves, while those who aided him would be thought clean.

"You're right, Richard."

"Of course I am, Miles."

"Shift's nearly over," said Mad Phil, checking his watch. For once, there was not a trace of complaint in his voice.

Jack had left London, off to visit friends in Oxford before heading north. Miles had slipped him fifty pounds as he left.

" 'Bye then," he had said, and that had been that. They had not managed to agree a time for their lunch together, and so it had never taken place. It hung between them in the air, just another broken promise.

"Thank God," Mowbray said to Mad Phil. "What are you doing tonight?"

"Nothing much. I thought I might try that new wine bar in Chelsea. The Lustra. Have you heard of it?"

"I haven't, no."

"Then I'll probably finish up at the Cathay, since I'm in the area. Best Chinese food in London."

"Sounds good. What about you, Miles?"

Miles had thought of going back to the office but knew now that his every move would be subject to Cynegetics' scrutiny. He had not been in touch with Pete Saville, but a call to Billy had brought the gossip that Saville had been moved on, though nobody knew where.

"What do you suggest, Richard?"

"I suggest we go along with Phil here to this Lustra place. Sounds kinda fun."

"It's a bit of a distance from here," said Miles.

"A few miles," said Mad Phil grudgingly. He was seated at the window, a pair of high-powered binoculars in his hands. Everyone was at home across the road.

"I suppose I could phone my wife," said Miles. Anything to keep him away from the house.

"That's the spirit," said Mowbray. "It's settled then, Phil can drive us in the company car."

Mad Phil didn't look altogether happy. Perhaps, thought Miles, he likes to drink alone. Well, for this one evening, Phil would have an audience for his complaints against life.

The Lustra turned out to be everything Miles had expected, and it appalled him. There were mirrors everywhere, half hidden by various pot plants and creepers.

"Great place, eh?"

The clientele were opening-night vampires, the chic underbelly of London whose sole intention in life was to "get noticed." It was not the place for an "invisible man." The clothes were loud, the music marginally less so, but everything was drowned out by the shrieking, vacuous voices of the young things. Miles's whisky had been drowned, too, scoop after scoop of the barman's ice shovelled into it. It now resembled an iceberg looking for a disaster. Disaster, in fact, was all around.

"Great place, eh, Richard?"

"Absolutely, Phil, absolutely."

Mowbray, slapping one hand against the table out of time with the music, looked almost as out of place as Miles.

"My round," he said now, heading off to the distant bar. Mad Phil pointed to a figure somewhere at the back of the lounge.

"She's a celebrity," he said, "though I can't remember why."

"Doesn't that disqualify her from the title?" asked Miles, loosening after the first two drinks.

But Mad Phil hadn't heard him and was surveying the crowd again.

Mowbray returned, his large hands cradling three tumblers. Miles was not surprised to see that they were doubles, and said nothing. Mad Phil did not seem to notice that the drinks were larger than his own round or Miles's had been, and he polished off a sixth at one gulp. Miles waited. Mowbray's kind could never remain quiet about their acts of generosity, for it was not generosity in itself but rather a keen desire to impress; which was, in fact, the opposite of generosity.

"This," said Mowbray, on schedule, "is what I call a drink. Cheers, Miles."

"Cheers," replied Miles, stifling a schoolboy smirk.

"You know, up in Scotland they serve fifths or even quarter gills. No wonder they're a nation of alcoholics."

"They're not, actually, a race of alcoholics, Richard. And they possess the most civilised licensing laws I know of."

Miles sounded hurt.

"Sorry," said Mowbray, "I keep forgetting you're Scottish. It was just a joke."

"That's all right."

"This is quite a good place really," said Mad Phil, turning to them both.

Miles left the Lustra early, feigning tiredness, and walked to South Kensington station, changing onto the Jubilee Line at Green Park. He caught the midevening hiatus, and only a few washed-out businessmen sat in his carriage. Mowbray had started his speech about circles within circles, infiltration, double agents and double double agents, and Miles had felt a need to leave.

"Jeff Phillips believes me," Mowbray had said. "So do others in the firm. If anything goes wrong on a case, one of *our* cases, we're suspicious."

"Then I would have thought, Richard," Miles had said, "that I would have been on your files as a potential double agent."

"But you *are* on our files, Miles. You're under suspicion."

Well, good luck to them. Good luck to the Mauberley Barmy Army and its witch hunt. Perhaps Mowbray thought this a speedy and efficient way to make his mark on the firm and, more importantly, on its overseers. But it was also going to make him an awful lot of enemies. He was staking all or nothing on plucking a fine, sharp needle from the haystack. Perhaps Miles should remind him that needles have a way of making people go to sleep for a very long time. . . .

Darkness was falling, early and cool. His car was parked a distance from the house, not for security reasons but because parking spaces were so difficult to find. A bird had left a large token of its esteem on the roof of the Jag. His father had always said that bird shit was lucky. His father had nurtured some curious notions.

He was still a distance from his house when he saw a man emerge from the gate and walk confidently away in the opposite direction, toward Abbey Road. Through the dusk, Miles was uncertain for a moment whether it had been his gate or not, but as he neared the house he felt sure that it had been. The man had looked familiar, too, even from a distance. He had disappeared now, and Miles walked thoughtfully to his front door, opening it quietly, standing in the hall for a moment, sensing its warmth, seeking a scent, a presence.

He went to the living-room door and listened, then, remembering Sheila's words, opened it quickly. The room was empty. There was a bottle of wine on the floor, and, quite correctly, a single glass beside it. The bottle was half empty, and a little of the missing half was still in the glass. Nothing was out of place. Leaving the room, he gave the hall scant attention, moving up the staircase silently. He could hear Sheila now. She was in the bedroom, humming a tune. But first he went to Jack's room. Here, too, everything was as it should be. There were posters on the walls, curling, faded memories of adolescence, and paperback books on the floor and packed into a secondhand bookcase. Miles had studied this room before, curious as to its secrets. Nothing was wrong.

Except the fact that the low single bed was still warm with a slight musk of body heat.

Downstairs again, sweating, Miles opened the front door and slammed it shut. He opened the living-room door, looked in, then closed it again.

"Miles? I'm up here."

He took the stairs two at a time and entered the bedroom. Sheila was packing some clothes into a small case. Miles felt his insides jolt, as though they wanted suddenly to be his outsides.

"Hello there," Sheila said, folding a cardigan.

"What are you doing?"

"This? Oh, I'm throwing a lot of my old clothes out. There's a jumble sale at the church, and I thought they might be glad of . . . Miles? What's wrong? You look ghastly."

"No, no, I'm all right. Been a busy day, that's all." He sat down on the stool at the dressing table.

"This doesn't mean that I'm about to embark on a spending spree, you know," said Sheila, as though this might have been what was worrying him. But, great God, he had thought for a second that she was leaving him, he had really believed it.

"You're back early," she said now.

"Am I?" He checked his watch. "Yes, just a little, I suppose."

"What was wrong? Company not to your liking?"

"Something like that."

"That's always been your problem, Miles. You've never learned to adapt. You'd never make a diplomat."

"And what have you been up to?" he asked quickly, giving her the chance to recall that someone had just left.

In reply, she picked up a green coat from the heap on the bed and studied it.

"Do you remember this, Miles? You brought it home one day, said you'd bought it on impulse. The only coat you ever bought me. It's well out of fashion now."

"You never liked it."

"That's not true."

"I can't remember you ever wearing it."

Sheila just shrugged, perhaps thinking him a little drunk and edgy, and folded the coat into the case. The case was now full, and she pulled the clasps shut.

"Shall we go downstairs?" she suggested.

In the living room he mentioned the wine.

"Well," said Sheila, "if you can go slinking off to barrooms with your friends, what the hell, I can drink by myself."

"Fair comment."

"What was the pub like, anyway?"

"It was a wine bar."

"Pardon my mistake. Why are you so snappy?"

"Snappy?"

"Yes, snap, snap." She clapped together her hands as though they were an alligator's jaws. "Snap, snap."

"Well, the wine bar was bloody foul."

"Is that all?"

"No."

"What then?"

He paused, swallowed, mumbled something about needing a glass of water. Sheila reminded him that there was plenty of wine left.

They finished the wine between them, listening to Shostakovich. Miles checked the kitchen, on the pretext of making a sandwich, but found no more evidence, no washed-up wineglass or recently emptied ashtray. At last he excused himself and went to his study. He remembered Jack's practical joke, the beetle. It was in a drawer of his desk and he brought it out, making it jump at his command. Thank God there was something in his life he could control.

That Sheila had made no mention of a visitor was damning enough in itself, but then there was also the bed, still warm. He thought of all the revenge tragedies Sheila had read, all the dark tales of cold, furtive couplings. Inch-thick, knee-deep, o'er head and ears a forked one. The beetle jumped. He heard Sheila begin to climb the stairs, calling down to him that she would see him up there.

"I won't be long!" he called back.

Surely, he reasoned, Sheila was intelligent enough not to let a man come here. But, having thought this, he thought, too, how ideal the situation had been, with Jack out of the house again and he, Miles, out drinking. He knew that his telephoned excuses to her often resulted in a long night away from home. Everything had been perfectly set up for a deception, for a long-deferred meeting. For everything. The warm bed, which grew hotter in his memory, would be cold and neutral now. Just as the Arab's smile had faded away to nothing. They seemed part of the same process of disintegration.

There was something more, though, something which bothered Miles much more. For he was in no doubt now that the man who had walked away from him had walked with Billy Monmouth's gait and was wearing Billy Monmouth's clothes.

CHAPTER 12

Jim Stevens was sucking mud. It was not a pleasant sensation. He should have taken the morning off, should have visited a dentist.

He was drinking coffee, trying to trickle the grey liquid into the good side of his mouth, the side where it didn't hurt. Coffee dribbled onto his tie and his shirt, while the other customers in the café looked at him blankly.

Where was the man he was supposed to meet? He was late, that's where he was. That was London for you. Time went to pieces here; the more you watched the clock, the later you were. Stevens had been in London only thirteen months. It really pissed him off. His new editor did not allow him

much freedom, certainly not as much as old Jameson up in Edinburgh
had. He had become a cog. They didn't want him to use his initiative.

Take the murder of that embassy man, the Israeli. Everyone shrugged
their shoulders. Just a robbery gone wrong. But then why was everyone
being so careful to skirt around it? That was what interested Stevens; it
was as if an unspoken D-notice had been slapped on it. He wasn't sure
what he could smell, but he could smell something. Perhaps it was the
poison in his mouth, but then again . . .

There were the phone calls, too, anonymous but regular. "Keep at it,
there's a story there, and while you're at it why not take a look at Harold
Sizewell, MP? A little birdie tells me he's hot." Stevens called the voice on
the telephone his "Deep Throat." He kept its existence secret from everyone around him. Maybe they all had something to hide.

The enemy tooth bunched up its fist and slammed it hard into the
quivering root. Stevens threw half a cup of cold coffee over his trousers
and clutched his jawbone, cursing.

"Mr. Stevens?"

"Yes, damn it."

"I telephoned you."

"Great, sit down. Do you have any aspirin?"

"No."

"Fine."

He looked at the man, younger than his voice, deferential in manner. A
civil servant smell about him, but very junior. Still, they knew stories, too,
didn't they? They were crawling out of the woodwork these days with their
tuppence worth of spite.

"So what can I do for you, Mr. . . . ?"

"Sinclair, Tony Sinclair. That's my real name, I swear, but please call
me Tim Hickey from now on."

"That's fine by me, Tim. Well, what is it I can do?"

"It's more a case of what *I* think I can do for you."

It was a cliché perhaps, but there was none sweeter to Stevens's ear.
They always liked to think of themselves as doing you a favour. It saved
them feeling guilty about spilling the beans. God, Jim, there goes another
cliché. All they were doing in fact, of course, was seeking revenge, sometimes out of spite, sometimes justifiably. Not that motive was any of his
concern. Maybe it would be a tale of some philandering cabinet minister, a
private secretary with paedophilic leanings, an administrator with occult
powers and a coven in the Cotswolds. Surrogate revenge, thought Stevens,
that's what I am.

"Go on," he said, stabbing at his cheek with a finger, goading the pain to
life.

"Well," said the lean young man, "you see, I'm a spy."

Walking down a nervous Whitehall, Stevens recalled that when he had first arrived in London a young graduate named Compton-Burnett had been given the job of acquainting him with the city. Since he had not known any decent pubs, he had been of little use to Stevens, but he still remembered their first meeting in the editor's office, the young man laughing behind his executive spectacles.

"No relation, I'm afraid," Compton-Burnett had said, as though Stevens were supposed to get some joke. He had looked towards the editor, who had looked away, baffled. Compton-Burnett had then walked him down Whitehall, pointing out the various government buildings.

"What's that one, then?" Stevens had asked.

"Ah, that's the MoD."

"And what about that one?"

"Ah, I think that's the MoD too."

"And the ugly one?"

"Milk and fish."

"Milk and fish?"

"Agriculture and fisheries," Compton-Burnett explained, laughing again, pushing his glasses back up the slippery slope of his nose.

"And that one?"

"Not sure. MoD possibly." But on closer inspection the tiny building, towered over by its colleagues like a tiny dictator by his bodyguards, had turned out to be the Scottish Office. Nowadays, Stevens knew the identities of most of these buildings, and none of them interested him except the tiny little Scottish Office. He empathised with it, seeing something of his own situation mirrored there, and tried to look the other way whenever he passed it.

At the entrance to Downing Street several thuggish-looking policemen had replaced the usual crew of friendly "bobbies." It was a bad time. Bombing campaigns were bad news for everyone, but then bad news was just what the press thrived on.

His tooth reminded him again that there were plenty of dental surgeries in the area. And he had wasted the whole morning. Nervous little Sinclair aka Hickey had wanted only to bite and scratch, having been kicked out of his little job, ready with his tiny fists to beat against the door of that which had been denied him. But Stevens had shut his eyes and his ears, had told Sinclair that there was another investigative journalist in London who would listen to him with a clearer notion of what he was talking about.

This had not pleased the young man. He had a story to tell. (Stevens wondered now whether he had said "tell" or "sell.") It was a tale of injustice, of underhand dealing. It was a great big zero in Stevens's book, a zero with not the faintest hope of any corroboration. Take it to Australia, pal. Write it up as a novel, sell a million.

"Take me seriously, you bastard!" And with that Tim Hickey aka Tony

Sinclair had risen to his feet and walked out of the café. Which was just what Jim Stevens had wanted him to do.

He had problems of his own after all, didn't he? And a column to write through the pain.

He met Janine in the Tilting Room. Happy Hour. His tooth no longer hurt. He had swallowed his fear, marched into the surgery, and, hissing that this was a national emergency, had been led into the little torture room.

And so, tooth numb, mouth half frozen, he found himself trying to drink whisky and spilling it down his trousers. Nothing had changed. Only his pocket was lighter.

"Hi," said Janine, squeezing in beside him.

"You're late."

She ignored this.

"What have you done to your face?" she asked.

"Don't ask."

She was a bright young girl with bright looks and a bright figure. Stevens was aware that they cut unlikely cloth as a couple.

"What have you got for me?"

She was already searching in her briefcase, drawing forth a red file. She opened it and began to read to herself, her usual ploy before telling him her findings. She said it was an exercise for her short-term memory. To Stevens, it was a long-term pain in the arse.

She was a bright girl. She wanted to work in the media. The media hadn't existed in Stevens's youth. But she was learning the hard way, because her family, though decent and hard-working, were nobodies, and so there was no ready-made niche for her in her chosen career. A friend had pleaded with Stevens to take her on as a lackey, and Stevens had agreed.

"Not much up that particular avenue," she said. "It seems that Sizewell has shares in a dozen companies apart from those of which he's a director, but there's nothing to suggest that he has been involved in the manoeuvring of contracts towards any of those companies."

"You're telling me he's clean. What about his personal life?"

"What do you want me to do? Sleep with him?"

"Not a bad idea," Stevens said, regretting it immediately as Janine threw him a ferocious look.

"This case needs some dirty work if it's to uncover any dirt on the Right Dishonourable Gentleman."

"Well, count me out," said Janine, smiling a superior smile. No fillings in *her* mouth.

The Sizewell investigation seemed to be leading nowhere. How could he ever have imagined it would, based as it was on crank phone calls and one sighting of the MP entering an exclusive gay club? It was never going to be front page, not unless he started beating up old queens or hiring rent boys. But the caller's voice wasn't the voice of a hoaxer. It was calm and articulate, and very sure of itself. It had told Stevens that Sizewell visited that club, the Last Peacock, now and again, and that "he has been a very naughty boy."

He'd give it just a little longer, just a week or so more.

"Hello, you're a nice girl."

It had been Janine's idea, all Janine's idea. They had left the Tilting Room and, ignoring the call of fast food to Stevens's nostrils, had taken a cab (expenses! expenses!) to some new wine bar, the Lustra. This was well out of Jim Stevens's territory but seemed to please Janine with its wall-to-wall Porsche key rings and inherited fox stoles.

"You are a *very* attractive girl."

The voice was new money, and there was money in the smile and money in the clothes: tasteful no, but moneyed yes. The man, blond, half-permed, slid into the seat beside Janine. She smiled, enjoying the attention.

"Yes, far too nice for the likes of him. Your uncle, is he? Or a friend of your grandfather's perhaps?" Janine giggled at this, and Stevens felt betrayed. "Well," continued the oil monkey, "say goodbye to the nice old man and hello to your sugar daddy, babe."

"Butt out, pal." Stevens was only mildly surprised to find his voice becoming ridiculously Scottish all of a sudden.

"No offence, Jock, old boy." The man looked across to Stevens for the first time, his grin full of good teeth. That was almost the final straw. "You don't mind, though, if I have a chat with your niece, do you?"

"If you don't butt out, pal, I'm going to butt in—your teeth." Oh yes, Jim, the macho act. This won't help your position with Janine. Wit perhaps, some cutting riposte which would leave the opponent reduced to rubble. He was a journalist after all, he should know a few comebacks. He racked his brain: none. His fists began to squeeze themselves into little bon mots beneath the table, and his temporary filling throbbed with a whole glucose drip's worth of adrenalin.

"It's OK, Jim," said Janine, trying to reason with the incoming tide. Stevens knew that if he used force he would lose her, lose any kind of chance that he might ever have with her. But then what chance did he have anyway?

When Golden Boy put his hand on her knee, three things happened rather quickly. One was that Janine swiped the hand away expertly, with the minimum of fuss and the maximum of contempt. The second was that Jim Stevens leaned across the table, pulled Golden Boy across it by his skinny leather tie, and chopped him on the back of the neck as he fell, hoping that he had laid some kind of rabbit punch upon his opponent's pale flesh.

The man crawled a little way across the room, then got to his knees, and finally, rubbing his neck, to his feet. His friends were there beside him, and money began changing hands, as though after a bet. The bar was quiet: some kind of "happening" had just occurred, and everyone was humble with awe before the participants.

It was only then that the third thing registered upon Jim Stevens: someone had taken a flash photograph as he had tugged at the man. He stared at the crew before him. Although he did not recognise the blond, the others were definitely reporters. Reporters. Of course they were, or he was Bruce Lee.

"Thanks, people," said Golden Boy, still rubbing his neck. "Let's go." And with that the entourage left the bar, one of them packing away his camera and lenses as he went.

"What was all that—" began Janine, reddening as the clientele continued to stare at her. A bouncer of professional wrestler proportions was striding towards their table.

"Don't ask," growled Stevens, "and don't, for Christ's sake, buy a tabloid tomorrow."

"So you know about it then?"

"Cynegetics?" Billy Monmouth laughed. "Of course."

"Why am I always the last to hear about everything?"

For once, it was Miles who had insisted on lunch, and he had insisted, too, that he should pay. Billy had shrugged, smiling, briskly alive to the beginning of October, autumn seeming to bring out the hunter in him.

"Well, it's not the sort of thing I would gossip about normally. How did you find out about it?"

"Luck really," said Miles. "It doesn't matter."

They had eaten at a restaurant close to Holborn.

"How many are there working on Harvest?" Billy had asked.

"Seven altogether," Miles had lied.

"Seven, eh? A sort of combine-Harvester, would you say?" Billy had laughed at his joke.

"Yes," Miles had said, his mouth dry despite the Pomerol, "and I for one don't want to come a cropper this time."

"A cropper, that's very good, Miles." But Billy had stopped laughing, faced with the steel in Miles's voice and in his eyes.

"What do you know about Cynegetics?" Miles asked now, waiting for the coffee and Billy's brandy.

"Oh, not very much. Rumours mostly. Nobody's really sure who's in it, you see, but the whole thing is probably run under Partridge's direction."

"Partridge?"

Billy nodded. He was being cagier than usual.

"It was set up under his directive, apparently. It's Partridge's pear tree."

"But why?"

"Paranoia, Miles. You know the firm."

During lunch, a litany of facts about beetles played in Miles's head. He thought of the deathwatch beetle, ticking like a time bomb, and of the whirligig beetle, skating across the surfaces of ponds. Miles felt like a whirligig beetle, dizzy yet exhilarated. But he felt like a deathwatch beetle, too.

"What was that, Billy? I was miles away."

"I said that Jeff Phillips is rumoured to have been transferred to Cynegetics as from last week. Lateral promotion."

"Good God. But Phillips is in on Richard Mowbray's little scheme."

"Then maybe the gossip is wrong. It sometimes happens."

"But not often."

Billy smiled again, swirling the brandy around in his mouth before swallowing. He cleared his throat to speak.

"There's an exhibition on around the corner from here. I was thinking of paying a visit. The gallery's run by one of our old girls. Do you fancy it, or are you in a hurry?"

Miles was in no hurry whatsoever.

It was a small gallery, brightly lit. The exhibition was of "Vorticist Painting, 1912–1916." Both Billy and Miles bought the catalogue, Miles hoping to surprise Sheila with this evidence of culture, but then pulling himself up sharply when he remembered why he was here.

While Billy hung back to have a few words with the overdressed old lady by the door, Miles entered the Vorticist world. He found the paintings forbidding and waited for Billy to catch up.

"Oskar Kokoschka used to live around the corner from us," he told Billy, realising, too late, how fatuous the remark must seem.

"Really?" said Billy. "Well, well."

They stopped at a line drawing of Ezra Pound.

"That's where I got the name for Mowbray," said Billy. "Mauberley is a character created by Pound."

"Oh?"

"Yes, old Pound was a bit of a fascist. Mad, too. Wrote some of his best stuff after the Allies had declared him insane."

"That probably says quite a lot about poetry," said Miles.

"I agree. What is it Shakespeare says? 'The lunatic, the lover, and the poet / Are of imagination all compact.' Something like that."

"Speaking of madmen and lovers," said Miles, "I know about you and Sheila."

Billy, studying the catalogue with preternatural interest, glanced up at a large canvas which appeared to contain millions of tiny nuts and bolts, twisted together into a vaguely human shape.

"Ah," he said at last, "so that's what this is all about. What do you want me to say?"

"Nothing."

"What did Sheila say?"

"Sheila doesn't know. And I'm not going to tell her. You are." Billy looked ready to protest. "I've already moved a few things out of the house. I'm going to stay away for a while, to give us all time to make decisions."

"But, Miles, it wasn't like that," hissed Billy. "I mean, there's no need for—"

"I don't want to hear it, not any of it, not now." Miles checked his watch. "There's just one more thing—I think you are the most complete bastard I've ever met. Knowing you, you'll take that as a compliment. It's not meant as one, believe me." He made to move away, but Billy clawed at his sleeve. Miles turned back towards him.

"Oh," he said, "and I forgot this."

The catalogue was heavy, and it hit Billy Monmouth's jaw with a deafening crack. He staggered against the nuts and bolts painting, several visitors looking on in horror as blood began to ooze from his lip and his gum. Miles was walking away, and he did not look invisible at all now. He looked like the watched, not the watchman, while Billy Monmouth fumbled for a handkerchief and some self-esteem.

PART TWO
Billy's Jaw

CHAPTER 13

He detested avocado dip, always had, always would. The very colour was an insult to him, and so many parties these days seemed to find a bowl of such sludge de rigueur. What else was there? The smiling minion who had thrust a plate and a napkin (paper) into his hand hovered behind the table, awaiting his selection. The plate, he noted, had one of those plastic rings clipped onto its rim. He was supposed to keep his glass of vile white wine in this venerated halo, and didn't all the guests look such complete pricks as they did so, not trusting the dreaded ring enough not to leave one hand hovering close to it? This meant that they had no free hand anyway, and so the ring did not fulfil its one and only function. Bloody thing. Sizewell ripped his from the plate and threw it, with a plop, into the avocado dip, where it sank majestically. The waitress, only observer of this, looked at Sizewell in horror, while he smiled at her, happy with life once more, and asked her quite politely for a piece of the spinach quiche and a vol-au-vent or three.

He was ravenous, having just come from a lengthy and painstaking sitting of the committee, where just about all they had thrashed out were their legitimate and nonlegitimate claims for expenses incurred thus far. But the Smythsons' party had promised lots of food, and so he had not bothered to eat beforehand. For his sin, he was consigned to function on a stomach half full of pastry.

"Harry, old boy."

"Tanya!"

"Good to see you."

"Tanya, how *are* you?"

"Can't complain, you know."

No, she couldn't complain. Only those landed with her interminable company could complain. Tanya Smythson, the unmarried (and unmarriable) elder daughter of the family, had a way of seeking Sizewell out and carving a territory between the rest of the world and them so that no one interrupted and no one came to save Sizewell from his misery.

Tanya, formidable, buxom Tanya. To be honest, he had taken quite a shine to her on their first meeting. She had seemed game for anything, but now, of course, he knew why: men were her game, and she was becoming frantic as the years progressed and they would not let her into their magic circle. One quick session, he thought, one session with a young thorough-bred would see you straight, would rearrange your metabolism and make you a calmer, less formidable figure. But where was the young man who would give Tanya what she wanted from life? He was nowhere. Certainly he was *not* Harry Sizewell.

But now, and to Sizewell's astonishment, someone was coming toward them, holding out a hand of friendship, smiling.

"Hello, Mr. Sizewell."

"Mr. Partridge, how very good to see you. Tanya, meet Mr. Partridge, one of the Home Office mandarins."

Tanya looked ready to breathe fire and brimstone. Nevertheless, she produced a smile from somewhere deep within her.

"Tanya," began Partridge winningly, "would you excuse us for just one minute, please? I have to discuss something with Mr. Sizewell."

As Tanya moved off, peering into Sizewell's soul to try to fathom just how put out he was by this interruption, he shrugged his shoulders and promised to see her again later.

"Thank you, thank you, thank you," he whispered from one side of his mouth. "You've made an old man very happy."

"Well," said Partridge, his face soft but his voice as hard as steel, "I did want to have a word actually."

"Oh?"

"How's the committee progressing?"

"Slowly, of course, how else would a committee progress?" Sizewell bit into the spinach quiche, feeling it drip water onto his plate. Defrosted then, rather than fresh. He should have known.

"Good, good. And that other matter?"

"Hmm? Oh, the threats. Well, he's been fairly quiet."

But Partridge's attention had already been diverted.

"That man over there, do you know him?"

"The bulbous chap? Seen him around. Why?"

"Well, before I came to your rescue, I couldn't help noticing that he was keeping an eye on you."

"Or on Tanya?"

"I shouldn't think so, would you? No, our man was definitely keeping an eye on *you*. Do you have a name?"

"A name?"

"For him. The bulbous man. Does he have a name?"

"Probably, but I'm damned if I know what it is." Sizewell seemed already to have forgotten that he was speaking to the man who had saved him from the agonies of Tanya Smythson. He was irritated by Partridge's forceful questions. One just did not treat an MP that way, and he would say so.

"Look here—"

But Partridge stopped him cold.

"How can we protect you from threats if you don't tell us everything there is to know?"

"You mean about that chap over there? I know nothing at all about him."

"I mean about this mysterious committee of yours."

"Oh." The spinach lost whatever flavour it had possessed, and Sizewell seemed to be remembering the slap he had been given by Partridge.

"I mean," continued Partridge, "I hear your committee isn't just looking into defence spending but into security spending, and, moreover, into security links between the NATO countries, and their possible strengthening."

"How the devil do you know that?"

"We must know everything, or else how can we protect you? If we don't know who your enemies are, we can't hope to act against them. Bear that in mind."

Partridge moved off, slowly, elegantly, and Sizewell felt suddenly obese and clumsy, sweat shining on his forehead and nose, hair sleek and unfashionable. He was deciding to leave the party then and there when the squat man began trundling towards him, a hand shooting out before him like a spear.

"The Honourable Harold Sizewell?" asked the man, shaking Sizewell's hand as a candidate in a safe seat would shake that of a sceptical voter.

"Yes," said Sizewell, "Mr. . . . ?"

"Andrew Gray," said the man. "A friend of mine is one of your constituents. He thinks you're doing a good job, just thought you'd like to know. His name's Monmouth. Do you know him?"

"No, I don't, but thank you."

"Not at all, not at all. I know how hard you people work for so little recompense. The public thinks of politicians as leading rich, glamorous lives, but we know better, don't we?"

"I agree entirely, Mr. Gray. Are you involved in politics yourself?"

"Only as an interested outsider. I deal in futures."

"I see. And how is the market behaving?"

"Couldn't be better. Everyone wants a future after all, don't they?"

Sizewell joined in the man's laughter, and Gray patted him on the shoulder as he moved away, back into the throng. Sizewell's laughter stopped as soon as the man had disappeared, and, in panic, he looked around for Partridge, but he had disappeared too. Damn and blast, and just when Harry Sizewell needed him.

For he was sure that the squat and pugnacious man had owned the same voice which had, with anonymous conviction, been threatening him over the telephone these past weeks.

While Mad Phil slept, Miles kept an eye on the Harvest home. It was late. He should have wakened Phil to swap the watch, but he found that he didn't need much sleep these days and nights, and besides, Phil looked so peaceful, almost childlike, in his sleeping bag.

The house across the way was quiet: everything was asleep except the city's nightlife. Foxes, hedgehogs, and cats on the prowl, all the night creatures who hid from the city's daytime chaos. Miles, too, was in hiding. Nobody had minded when he moved his things into the house. He had a little room of his own, with a sleeping bag, radio and pocket-sized television, and a camping stove. He had bought a couple of cheap pots and a kettle. The house had running water and even a supply of electricity. What more could he want? He felt like a boy again, embarked upon an adventure.

A week had passed since his meeting with Billy. It was cold at nights now, but he kept warm in his sleeping bag and did not think of Sheila too often. He became immersed in Harvest, reading and rereading the case notes and watching, day and night, watching.

Forest Hill was a far cry from St. John's Wood, but there were two good cafés along with a late-opening off licence. What more did he need? He would drink a can or two of beer while watching the tiny television screen. Late at night he watched chat shows, but during the day he preferred the children's cartoons. There was one he liked in particular: "The Amazing Adventures of Spiderman." Jack had been an omnivorous reader of comics, and Miles, having taken an interest in his son's reading, still remembered Spiderman, a meek college student who, bitten by a radioactive spider, found himself with phenomenal powers.

More than the TV, however, he was interested in Harvest. The woman interested him most. She was a clean and tidy-minded twenty-eight-year-old, with short dark hair and the pinched 1930s look of so many Irishwomen.

He had a good view of her bedroom. He had watched her walk past her window in a towelling robe, brushing her hair with short, vicious strokes, entering the bathroom, and, through the obscured glass, had watched her drop the robe onto the floor and step into her bath. He had watched one of the men, the mechanic, interrupt her in her room, bringing her cups of tea, trying to charm his way into her bed. Miles hoped that the mechanic was cold at night in his narrow bed, as cold as Miles was himself.

In the guise of a television repairman, one of the firm's sparkies had gained access to the deserted living room and had planted a couple of neat bugs. It had been a beautiful operation. A jamming device had ensured that one of the men called the TV rental company to complain, and the company notified the sparky, who went in and did the job. But little had been learned from the devices. There had not even been a hint of political dialogue in the house. It was as clean as could be.

If it were a cell, then it was the best Miles had ever seen. But it could still be a cell. They were highly trained these days, trained more or less to forget about their ultimate meaning. Certainly a mechanic and an electrician would be of incalculable use to a terrorist cell, as might someone with access to a building site (where detonators and even dynamite would be available). But what about the man who worked steadfastly and sombrely as a park keeper? Could he be some kind of screen, putting the watchmen off the scent? Could he be hiding some specialisation? Or might they be planning such a crude bombing that the matériel they would need was weedkiller?

"Fancy a beer, Miles?"

Mowbray handed him a can, pulling one open for himself.

"Thanks," said Miles.

"You're welcome. How's things?"

"Fine. They're all watching television."

"I meant regarding your own situation."

"Oh."

Mowbray, like the others, had been very circumspect about Miles's sudden occupation of the house. "I'm sure we all understand," he had said. Miles had wondered.

"What's the word back at HQ, Richard?"

Mowbray shrugged his shoulders. The one thing Miles missed about Billy Monmouth was his vast knowledge of office gossip. It had occurred to Miles recently, though, that Billy knew just a little *too* much. He was like a huge filter for drips from every level.

"Not much," said Mowbray. "Jeff Phillips is off on some kind of course."

"Oh?"

"Without a word to me."

"What else?"

"Well, you asked about Peter Saville, but I can't find out a thing. He seems to have been transferred. I think someone called it a 'lateral promotion.' "

"Who did? Who said that?"

"Hell, I can't remember, Miles."

"Was it Billy Monmouth?"

"Of course not. He and I are barely on speaking terms. There was one thing though. You know Tony Sinclair, don't you?"

"He worked on Latchkey with me. He was on probation."

"He's out, gone. Resigned."

Now this was news, and Miles narrowed his eyes as he tried to focus on its meaning.

"Tony Sinclair?"

"Mmm. It seems he wasn't enjoying the work. What was he like?"

"He loved the work. That's what he was like."

Jeff Phillips transferred, Tony Sinclair "resigned," Peter Saville vanished. Curiouser and curiouser. Did it have something to do with the Israeli? It seemed like that. Anyone who had anything to do with the Latchkey case and its aftermath was being moved on.

"Bit of activity over there," said Mowbray, peering out of the window.

The park keeper and the electrician were leaving for the pub, which left the randy mechanic alone in the house with the secretary. Miles made a note of the time and the circumstance. A couple of the lads downstairs would keep tabs on the pubgoers.

"What are you reading, Richard?"

"Graham Greene." Mowbray studied the cover of his book. "Quite credible really. Only cost me a quid, but it's falling to pieces."

"It's a spy novel, right?"

"Sort of. Not our stuff though. The other place: cloak-and-dagger games with the Russkies."

Miles, nodding in shadow, wondered what sort of games the mechanic was playing tonight, and thought back to his early days with Sheila. He remembered a drunken friend making repeated passes at her during a noisy all-night party and the way he had brawled with his friend in the middle of the dance floor. In those days he had fought to keep Sheila. And now . . . ?

The lights went out in the living room, then came on simultaneously in the bathroom and the woman's bedroom. She walked to her window and stared up at the sky, asking herself questions perhaps, or just dreaming. She played with her hair, twirling it so that she looked ruffled and feminine. The light went off in the bathroom, and, as Miles and Mowbray held their breath, the mechanic appeared in the doorway behind the girl and sought her permission to enter. She heard him but kept on staring out of the window. Her face alone gave away her intent. With slow deliberation, she closed the curtains, and her silhouette was approached by the man's, until they merged and moved back into the room, out of sight.

"Lucky swine," muttered Mowbray, returning to his book. Then, a little later, "Would you believe it? There are two pages missing. Two pages." And he threw the book into a corner in disgust, where more pages fell away.

"I should think that's us for the evening, Miles."

"Yes," said Miles, "I should think so." He felt lonely all of a sudden, and chilled to the bone.

CHAPTER 14

THE HELL RAISER OF FLEET STREET!

Stevens, at his desk, stared at the clipping for the thousandth time. There was the photograph, the two sentences of journalese beneath it, and the bloody headline. They had been looking for some action and, finding none, had caught sight of Stevens and a photogenic young lady. Bets had been laid, and the manager, who had promised them all a photograph and a story, had attempted his seduction. Everyone got an early night; they had their picture and their bare words of captioning.

THE HELL RAISER OF FLEET STREET!

They'd be laughing their heads off back in Edinburgh. Look at what happened to our golden boy, they'd be saying. Sons of . . .

He picked up the ringing telephone.

"Hello?" he said. And heard the same measured voice, a poetry-recital voice, the kind of voice people paid money for. But *was* it the same voice? He would puzzle the day away thinking that one over, once he had heard the message. Straight off, however, he prepared himself for a few more words of wisdom from "Deep Throat," ready to tell the man that he needed more to go on . . . But his thoughts short-circuited when he heard what the voice had to say.

"That's for starters," it said. "Lay off Sizewell, or there'll be more, much more. See you, hell raiser."

And with that the telephone went as dead as Jim Stevens's tooth.

"Jim!"

It was Macfarlane, his editor, calling from the inner sanctum. Rising from his chair, numb with shock from the call, Stevens had little time to wonder how many times he had walked this walk from his desk to an editor's office.

"What can I do for you, Terry?"

"Close the door for a start."

Stevens did so, muffling the sounds of the outside office.

"This isn't a social call then?" he asked.

Macfarlane, seated behind his ancient desk, relic of the newspaper's earliest years, pushed back his thinning hair.

"Jim, I'm going to tell you what they told me—lay off."

"Lay off what?"

"I don't know. They said *you'd* know."

"Who are *they?*"

"Too important for names, Jim. Over my head."

Jim Stevens sat down.

"Well," he said, "who gave you the message?"

"Do you really want to know? God gave me the message. God himself, calling from one of his half dozen country houses. Your boss, my boss, this paper's boss."

"I'm impressed."

"You better be, or you can type your job out, stick it in an envelope, and post it to the moon."

"Over and out, eh?"

Macfarlane rubbed at the flesh on either side of his nose. He looked not only tired—he always looked tired—but somehow beaten into submission by life.

"Look, Jim, I'm loath to say this. I'm a reporter too, remember. I don't like it when someone pulls the blinkers over my eyes and then leads me through a field full of shit. But the world works that way sometimes. There are jockeys riding us, and sometimes when you peep out from behind the blinkers you see what's better left alone. End of story."

"That's very nice imagery, Terry, but it doesn't add up to much."

"Then let me take it a stage further. You, Jim, are one step away from the glue factory."

Stevens rose from his chair.

"Thanks for the warning. I haven't a clue what it's a warning about, but I'll keep on my toes, Terry." He opened the door. "You might even say I'll keep on trotting."

He closed the door behind him, but softly, and walked back to his desk. What was that all about? Sizewell was the obvious answer. He hated arguing with Macfarlane. It was rumoured that the guy had something seriously wrong with him, that he worked through a lot of pain. Didn't we all? He recalled their last falling out. He had been sent to cover a suicide. Some bank employee had jumped from his sixth-floor office, leaving behind a young wife. Stevens had filed the story, only to be growled at by Macfarlane: what about the wife? Was she attractive? No, not especially. Well, why not say so anyway? The story's too dull, almost dead. So you want lies? Jim Stevens had asked. And Macfarlane had nodded. Go for the sordid jugular, then alter the facts by cosmetic surgery. Why bother? he had thought. Why try to tell the truth when the truth isn't wanted anymore?

Journalism these days meant stakeouts, infrared lenses, false identities, bugs. It was all change, desperate change. These days, news was twisted around into a corkscrew with which to extract the twenty or thirty pence from each punter's pocket. He should have listened more patiently to Sinclair aka Hickey, should have gone by the old rules, but he had grown weary of trying to turn babbled stories into good copy.

The telephone rang again. Despite himself, he answered it.

"Crime desk, I suppose."

"Mr. Stevens?"

Recognising the voice, he brightened up.

"Hello, Mr. Hickey. It is Mr. Tim Hickey, isn't it?"

"That's right."

"Listen, I'm glad you called. In fact, I was just thinking about you. I'm sorry about our last meeting. I had a raging toothache, not in the best of moods, sorry. But I'd like us to meet again." He was working now, pen in hand. Someone up there had given him a second chance, and he would kick like a mule until Macfarlane's "jockeys" had all been unseated. "I'd like to hear your story. Really I would."

Miles Flint had spent a rare free morning in the reading room of the British Museum. He had not been given this time off; he had been ordered to take it, ordered by Richard Mowbray, who said that he was worried about Miles's ability to function after so long on the surveillance. "Take some air, Miles. Don't let us see you for a day." So he had trekked into the city and caught up on some articles about beetles in the recent journals.

Leaving the museum, he bumped into Tony Sinclair.

"Tony!"

"Hello, Miles." Sinclair seemed surprised, and not very pleased to see him. "What are you doing here? Keeping tabs on me?"

"Why should I do that, Tony? No, it's just my day off. I was doing some research. And you?"

"Killing time."

Miles nodded.

"I heard you'd moved on."

"There was no volition in it. I was pushed out. Didn't you know that?" Sinclair was eyeing him warily, glancing at the passersby.

"No," said Miles. "This is news to me. I'm a bit out of touch, I'm afraid."

"You had nothing to do with it, then?"

Miles shook his head, and Tony Sinclair seemed to relax.

"I was never even asked for a report on you," Miles said.

"I don't understand it, Miles, really I don't." Sinclair's voice was becoming elegiac.

"Well, neither do I, Tony."

But Miles *had* wondered about it, oh yes, he had wondered.

"Look," said Sinclair, checking his watch, "I really must be going. I've a meeting with someone."

"Which way are you headed?"

"Charing Cross Road."

"Fine, I'll walk there with you."

There were way too many questions in Miles's head for any order of importance to be ascertained, and so he ended up asking none. He had wanted to meet Tony Sinclair, yet now that he had he was reticent, not knowing if he wanted to know any more than he already did. Knowledge was weakness sometimes. He knew that now.

At the corner of Oxford Street they parted. Miles had refrained even from asking for Sinclair's telephone number. So that was that. He watched him disappear, to be swallowed up by the midday crush, then started along the obstacle course that was Oxford Street. Some workmen were putting in a new window to replace the one which had been blown out. Miles shivered, remembering that day. People had fear in their eyes: any one of these windows might be treacherous. They walked past almost on tiptoe. As he made to move into the road, a hand grabbed his arm.

It was Tony Sinclair, his teeth brightly displayed.

"Latchkey stinks to high heaven," he snarled. "You already know that, so why aren't you doing anything about it? *I'm* going to do something, that's a promise. I'm going to find out why."

And with that he was off again, forcing his way past the protesting office workers, a man beating against the tide.

Well, good for you, thought Miles, good for you, Tony Sinclair. You've reminded me of something I was longing to forget.

All the same, the way things were going he did not give Tony much hope of success. He felt a wintry gust, and it was as though he were already in the funeral parlour, staring into the open coffin.

The phone rang and rang but she wasn't answering. Where the hell was she? Out doing research? In bed with some athlete? Stevens didn't care. But he needed her help. It had been an unprofitable lunch; Sinclair aka Hickey had known a bit after all. So the Israeli's assassin had been followed and lost by the spies, and the murder itself had been hushed up by the Israelis. It was front-page news, but Stevens wanted more.

"Answer, Janine, for Christ's sake," he said into the mouthpiece.

He knew now that he had something and that his hunch about the murder had been correct. Here was something more for Janine to work on. Well, if she wouldn't sleep with Harry Sizewell, she'd have to earn her pennies the hard way. He touched at his temporary filling. There was something rotten behind it all. That went for the tooth, too.

"Hello?"

"Is that Janine?"

"Oh, hello, hell raiser."

"Don't start."

"OK, OK, just joking. What's got into you today?"

"Where do you want me to begin? The world caving in on me or the terminal disease?"

"Like that, huh? And I don't suppose you're phoning up for sympathy?"

"I'm phoning because there's some ferreting I want you to do."

"OK, just show me the rabbit hole."

"My, we are sharp today, aren't we?"

"Is it Sizewell?"

"Not this time. Different story, same pay."

"Pay? Is that those coins you give me every Friday?"

"You just got demoted to a three-day week."

"On parity with you now then, eh? I'll tell my union about you."

"Look, Janine, I yield to your wit, OK? Now, you are a beautiful young woman, intelligent, charming, and you're going to go places. And the first place you're going to go is the Israeli embassy in Palace Gardens."

The order came down by way of Partridge.

"Mr. Partridge said that?" asked Mad Phil, a complaint forming within him.

"Yes," said Mowbray, "Mr. Partridge said that."

Harvest had been declared dormant, and Miles would have to seek other accommodation, leaving the unfolding story of the mechanic and the secretary. He knew now how Mowbray had felt on that night when he had discovered the gap in his novel. He supposed a hotel would be the answer now. He knew of a good, cheap place near Russell Square. It had been used by the firm in the past for various purposes but was now, so far as he knew, dormant too.

"You'll be moving your stuff, won't you, Miles?" Mowbray asked, making it sound like the order it was. "This place will be going back on the market tomorrow afternoon."

"I'll move out in the morning, if that suits."

"Well, the property chaps won't be along before lunchtime," said Mowbray faintly. He was staring out of the window. "Three months. For close on three goddamn months we've been watching that place, and for what? A great big nothing."

"As usual," said Phil, not allowing the opportunity for a quick grumble to pass.

"Yes," agreed Mowbray, "as usual, eh, Miles?"

There was a long pause while Mowbray realised that Miles's last case had not exactly ended in a whimper.

"Sorry," he said.

"That's all right, Richard," said Miles. "It's nice to have had a quiet mission for a change. Peace and quiet. It's been a nice break for me."

And he gave a smile which seemed to unnerve his companions more than it cheered them.

That night Miles was alone as he watched from the window in the darkness. The house was silent, and he was left to his thoughts. The living-room curtains flickered with blue light from the television set, but there was no listening apparatus now, and an engineer would visit the house tomorrow to retrieve the bugs.

The girl was in the house alone, which was unusual. Miles had passed her in the street and in the local supermarket, had smelt up close the perfume she wore, had heard her voice. He rubbed at his chin, feeling a day's stubble. His thoughts were nervous companions, flickering like the television. He knew that it was not uncommon for a watchman to come to empathise with his quarry, to feel a bond of something like friendship. But he was a senior, trained to near perfection in his art. He should not be allowing these emotions such free rein.

But he did.

So it was that he found himself in the garden of her house, wandering freely beneath the street's sodium glare, picking his way towards the living-room window, the flashing blue of the curtains, and her, the woman, somewhere within. The garden was overgrown but not yet too far gone. He did not make a sound as he moved, the grass underfoot wet and yielding. Some condensation on the windows showed that she was alive, was breathing only feet away from him. He was absorbed, not thinking, hardly daring to breathe himself, just watching.

So he did not notice, in this new scheme of things, when the blue of the television became a sharper, brighter blue, the blue of a police car, which sat outside the house as the two officers approached him slowly and asked him to accompany them to the station for questioning. She stared out from behind her curtains as he was led gently away, and a neighbour across the way shouted out something which, mercifully, he did not catch. . . .

The room had been freshly painted, and he liked its simplicity, the way it said, I am a place of detention, not to be imprinted with the personalities of my occupants.

"We can't even get a name out of him," he heard someone say.

"Never mind that. We've checked the stuff in his wallet. He's quite an important fish, as it happens. Something in the Home Office. Somebody's coming from there to pick him up."

"What? At this time of night? He *must* be important."

The officers seemed like humanoids made out of nuts and bolts, creaking their way toward the dawn like tired old machines. The station itself was run like a garage. Who would fetch him, Mowbray or Denniston? Had he blown another case? He supposed he had. But why should a bunch of terrorists need a park keeper, and why did a park keeper let his garden go to weeds?

"Do you want a cup of tea or something?"

"Yes, please. Milk and no sugar."

The young constable had become less frosty upon hearing that Miles was such an "important fish." The tea was placed before him, a spoon sliding against the rim of the mug. Old stains mottled the circumference, as if the machine which washed the crockery was running down.

"All right, sir?" This was a detective, suited and with rather an awkward brown and green tie hanging limply around his neck. He seated himself opposite Miles, spreading sheets of paper before him, paperwork to be checked and filed.

"You don't pay your parking fines very often, do you, sir? But then you don't need to. It's better than diplomatic immunity, what you buggers have got."

"I specifically asked for sugar in my tea," Miles said calmly. "This tea doesn't have sugar in it."

"Constable, fetch our guest here another cup of tea, will you?"

"But, sir, he didn't—"

"Just do it, laddie."

Peeved, the constable picked up the mug and left, much to Miles's satisfaction. He studied the detective now.

"Are you Scottish, officer?"

The detective nodded, lighting a cigarette for himself and offering one to Miles, which, after debate, he declined.

"How did you know? I didn't think I had much of an accent left."

"I'm sure you don't. It was your use of the word 'laddie.' "

"Yes, of course."

"I'm Scottish myself. From the east coast."

"I'm from the west." The detective was growing edgy. The conversation was slipping away from professional matters. He shuffled his papers together and cleared his throat. "What were you doing in that garden?"

"That's classified," said Miles.

There was nothing for him to fear, nothing save the grilling he would receive from his own people. But he could invent excuses enough for the purpose. He had seen something suspicious, and, having no contact with base, had decided to move in closer. Arrested by mistake. It had happened to watchmen before.

"Classified?"

"Under a Home Office directive." But of course they knew who he was anyway: *It's better than diplomatic immunity, what you buggers have got.*

"I see," said the detective.

"There's a phone number I can write down. You could pass it to Special Branch."

The detective nodded, seeming bored all of a sudden. He shuffled his papers again. They were playing a little game now, weren't they, a waiting game, of no consequence.

Just then the door opened. There was someone outside. The detective seemed relieved, smiling at Miles as he left the room. The door closed again and Miles was alone with himself. He felt mildly drunk, as though coming out of a heavy session. He knew that he had messed things up. Something had snapped inside him in that empty house. He had become feral.

He had slipped up.

Again.

It was not lost on him that this might just be what the old boy needed in order, politely of course, to get rid of him. He was becoming a thorn in the old boy's side, and a public one at that.

The door opened again. Billy Monmouth was standing in the doorway.

"Come on, Miles," he said matter-of-factly, "let's go."

CHAPTER 15

It was one of the firm's cars, another Rover, or perhaps the same one that had taken Jeff Phillips and him to the Doric. Billy seemed preoccupied with the perils of night driving in London. Unmarked police cars jockeyed for position in outside and inside lanes, trying to intuit the villains and the drunks. Security bells rang out all around like old-fashioned alarm clocks.

"There's been another bombing," said Billy finally.

"Oh? Where?"

"In an underground car park. We think they were trying to hit a knight of the realm."

"I see. I didn't get you out of bed, did I?"

"I was in the office when the message came through. I asked to be the fetcher."

"Why?"

"I'm not sure now. It seemed like predestination." He laughed a quick, haunted laugh, a reconnaissance into the no-man's-land between them. "How are you, Miles?"

"Oh, I'm fine, just dandy, thank you for asking."

"Sheila and I haven't met, you know, not since . . . Well, it's all over. But listen, Miles, nothing happened between us. All she wanted was someone who would listen to her. I was the listener. That was all. Oh, I dare say that in time we might have . . ." Seeing the look on Miles's face, Billy shut his mouth. Miles had noticed that his speech was a bit stiff, as though the blow from the exhibition catalogue had done some lasting damage.

"But you told her?"

"I telephoned. Cowardly, don't you think? I telephoned that night and told her."

All she wanted was a listener. Sure, but why Billy Monmouth?

"We're going to a small hotel near King's Cross," Billy said at last.

"I think I know the one," said Miles. "For debriefing?"

"It's routine in cases of arrest or identification. Do you want to tell me what happened?"

"Do you want to tell *me* what happened?" asked Miles, sensing Billy flinch from the question. A palpable hit.

"Miles, what do you want me to say?"

"I don't know. What do *you* want *me* to say?"

"For Christ's sake, Miles!"

A car flashed past them, pursued by a brilliant orange and white police car, its blue flashing light reminding Miles of the garden and the soft voices of the policemen coming to him from far away.

He had experienced a short, sharp night of the soul, but he had come out of the other side in one piece, hadn't he? He did not want to drill a hole in Billy's head, and he did not particularly want to hit him. He was torn between wanting to understand and wanting simply to put the whole thing behind him and make a "new" start.

"Who'll be debriefing me?"

"I've no idea. It may even be wonder boy Phillips."

"I thought he was Cynegetics?"

"The title covers a multitude of sins."

The car turned into Bloomsbury. Office cleaners were waiting to gain entry to their buildings, and a few scattered souls had begun to queue at bus stops. Another dawn, another dolour. The sky was grey like a dead face, the city's flesh caught in its final posture.

"There hasn't been much happening," Billy said. He was parking the car outside the same hotel in which Miles, Partridge, and the old boy had taken tea, and in which Miles had encountered Felicity. Ah, he had forgotten about her, forgotten, too, that she had confirmed his suspicions about Latchkey. He had to remember that. *He had to.* It seemed curious, though, that she should be allowed to operate in one of the firm's hotels. They were usually so circumspect about things like that. . . .

"Billy," Miles began, "you're not by any chance a double agent, are you?"

He watched Billy's reaction. The car was parked now, and he was taking the key from the ignition. His face was flushed, but his eyes met Miles's, and what Miles saw was not panic but a mixture of emotions not the least of which was surprise.

Billy opened the car door and placed one expensively shod foot on the road before turning back towards Miles.

"Come on," he said. "We can talk inside."

"We can talk here," said Miles, not moving. "No fear of little interlopers here, after all."

"I'm not a mole, Miles," said Billy, smiling his most sincere smile and making his exit.

"Drink?"

"It's a bit early for me," said Miles, checking his watch.

"Yes," agreed Billy, "I try not to drink before breakfast, but when one has been awake all night . . ."

"Of course."

Billy poured himself a whisky from his hip flask and added a drop of water from the hand-basin tap.

"Cheers then," he said, tipping the cup back as though it contained doctor's orders. He examined himself in the mirror.

"I'm no spring chicken," he said, still peering into the mirror. Then he turned and gave Miles a scolded schoolboy's smile. But Miles was busy trying to perceive Billy from a woman's point of view. He saw skin which was beginning to sag irremediably, hair which was thinning, keen eyes which seemed to hint at a force of intelligence trapped within its cell of a body bag.

"Neither of us is," he said. He was seated on one of the room's twin beds. It sagged luxuriously beneath his weight.

"So, what can I tell you?" Billy sat down on the other bed.

"You mean about Latchkey?"

"Latchkey?" Billy seemed genuinely puzzled. "No, I meant about Sheila and me."

"Oh."

"I mean, I can tell you about the first day we met, purely by accident at a Hayward exhibition. About how we talked, and how we met once or twice more, also to talk. It's not a very exciting tale, Miles. What's so ironic is that we were on the point of calling it a day anyway. I went to the house only that once, and then only because Sheila was upset about Jack."

"Upset?"

"Well, he'd just left, and there was still a gulf between them, wasn't there? She was just trying to understand."

"And she needed you for that?" Miles remembered the warm bed and thought, No, I can't believe any of this.

"Miles, blame me. I was attracted to Sheila, not her to me. I pushed our relationship. She thought our second meeting was chance, too, but it wasn't. I'd set it up.

"All that time we lunched together, drank, gossiped, parted with a handshake and a smile, and all the time, all those months, you were . . . you . . ."

And then it happened, not at all the way he had wanted things to happen. He wanted venom or icy, muted snubs; anything except this stupid blockage in his throat, full of weakness and sentiment. He began to cry, his body jerking in little spasms. And, daring to look up, he saw that Billy, old Billy Monmouth, with a skin like that of a swamp alligator, was crying too, his body as still as marble.

"Jesus Christ, Miles," Billy said softly. "I'm sorry, sorrier than I can say."

Miles was blowing his nose when the door flew open.

"Good God," rasped Colonel Denniston. "What's been going on here?"

Stevens was doing it by the book. It was just that no one had bothered to write this particular book. Janine found him the man he needed at the embassy, a fairly expensive go-between who was able to substantiate—on tape, though he did not know it—that the assassinated man had been a private trader; in other words, was his own operator for most of the time but did odd jobs for the security service. There was Hickey's word for it that MI5 had bungled their surveillance operation and so had allowed the assassin onto the streets. But the Israelis seemed not to know this. So, lowly Jim Stevens had his lever with which to crack open the spies. He knew something they wouldn't want the Israelis to know.

What else did he have? He had something which only Janine's charm and looks could have inveigled from a parliamentary official: the Honourable Harold Sizewell, MP, was sitting on a hush-hush committee which was investigating the funding of the secret services and international cooperation between the various intelligence communities.

The dirt was there, he was sure of it. And the spade he needed with which to do his digging was Sinclair aka Hickey. Jim Stevens had his story.

He told Janine he'd buy her lunch but hadn't let on that they would be eating at her favourite restaurant. He had arranged to meet Macfarlane there, too, and over a long afternoon he would tell his editor the story, with Janine's help. Macfarlane couldn't turn this one away. The blinkers were off.

"Jim! I'm not dressed for this place." Janine had stopped at the door and was refusing to cross the threshold.

"OK," said Stevens chirpily, "take off what you're wearing and we'll go in."

She slapped his chest.

"Pig," she said, smiling, as they entered the restaurant.

Stevens had found a tie in his wardrobe—unused for years—which was absolutely stainless. Hardly able to believe his luck, he had put it on, only realising later, upon meeting Janine and her horrified gaze, that the pink tie was hardly a match for his light brown shirt.

It wasn't one of the better tables, but what the hell. And it *was* a bit more pricy than Stevens's credit card had bargained for, but it was a special occasion. They ordered aperitifs, and Stevens wondered where Macfarlane had got to. A waiter brought a telephone to the table.

"For you, Mr. Stevens."

"Hello?"

"Jim, it's Terry. Listen, sorry I can't make it. Can you come in this afternoon? I've got some bad news."

"Oh yes?" For Janine's sake—radiant, youthful Janine—Stevens tried to sound calm.

"You're fired," said Macfarlane. "None of my doing. The official line is that it's to do with the hell-raiser photograph."

"And unofficially?"

"No comment," said Macfarlane. "Sorry, Jim. Hope I didn't spoil your lunch. 'Bye."

"Lobster bisque, I think," Janine was saying, "and an entrecote for afters. Must watch my figure, mustn't I? Jim? Is everything OK?"

"Fine, Janine. Everything's just dandy."

He was determined, hardened more than ever now. Sod them all. He'd break this story if it was the last thing he did. Somebody would publish it, somebody must. He'd show them all. There came a time when the truth had to push its way up through the mire. Didn't there?

CHAPTER 16

When they finally did make love it was in glorious Technicolor to the music of the Beatles, Miles Davis guesting on trumpet. He felt the luxury of the mattress and the alcoholic glow in which they were both swimming. Everything was all right now, and though he couldn't be sure who his partner was, whether Sheila or Billy or the Irishwoman, he knew that he was home at last and that he would never stray again.

The voice close to his ear told him that it was fine, and always would be. Did it matter that some uninvited guest watched from behind the shutter of a peep-show booth, smirking? No, not really.

"Miles?" The voice seemed to come from the booth, where the eyes had grown feverish. "Miles?"

"Miles!"

He opened his eyes. Those of Richard Mowbray were on him, and a hand rested on his shoulder.

"Wakey, wakey, old chap."

"Richard, I must have dozed off."

"I admire that in a man, Miles, the ability to stay calm when all around are clinging to the wreckage."

"I had no sleep last night." He glanced around his office, having for a moment expected to find himself in the hotel room.

"I came to sympathise," said Mowbray. "Is it true?"

"Is what true?"

"That you saw something suspicious and went over there to investigate?"

Well, that was the story which Denniston, listening like an attentive tiger beetle, had soaked up. Miles had added some nice touches, like the living-room light being turned off and then on again. Denniston had snatched at that one with his mandibles.

"A signal!"

"That's what I suspected, sir."

And Denniston had sat back, pleased with himself.

"Yes, I saw something, Richard," Miles said now, scratching at his face.

"Uh-huh." Mowbray seemed unconvinced, and Miles remembered that it was Mowbray who had come closest to witnessing his dark ebb and flow of the previous night, and of all other nights. Tact was needed.

"It seems strange," he said, "that the very day we move out something like that happens."

Mowbray thumped the desk with his fist.

"That's just what I was thinking, Miles. It's as though they *knew* the operation had been wrapped up."

"Of course, it could be coincidence."

"If I have to make the choice between coincidence and conspiracy, I'll plump for conspiracy every time."

Miles thought of Billy Monmouth, conspiring against him and against Sheila.

"You're probably right, Richard. But then what stops us from ripping our lives apart looking for the watchmen who are watching us?"

"Come on, Miles. What about your act with the restaurant cutlery and the way you check your car? I know all about your little rituals. Would you call them paranoia?"

Miles was suddenly aware of having humoured Mowbray a little too much, and it had led to this, his own discomfort. Did everyone know everything about him? Sheila could hear him at the living-room door. Mowbray was telling him that his little restaurant game was common knowledge. It was a sobering thought. How many people laughed at him behind his back? Everywhere he turned these days he bumped into people who knew too much about him, and all the time it was he who was supposed to be on the watch, on the hunt.

Hunting what?

Hunting his own fantasy of a goliath beetle, a double agent? What kind of beetle was Richard Mowbray anyway? To his enemies in the firm he would be a Colorado beetle. The Colorado beetle had led a harmless existence until settlers took the potato to North America. The beetle loved the new crop, became mesmerised by that first forbidden taste. Yes, that was Mowbray, safe within the firm until he had begun to investigate it for himself, and then coming to enjoy that investigation so much that he wanted to taste more deeply.

But Mowbray would never find a single double agent, for the simple reason that he was wandering aimlessly and in all the wrong directions.

"If there's any paranoia to be found around here, Miles, it isn't in your head, and it certainly isn't in mine."

Mowbray's eyes were like candles, but Miles knew that he was fumbling in the dark.

In the film that evening, John Wayne played a policeman sent across to London to take charge of a criminal wanted in the United States. The film's real entertainment came from the sight of the Hollywood legend stalking the streets of the dull old city. It was nice to watch one of the good old boys in action.

Miles was thinking back to his unheroic undergraduate days, days spent following Sheila, mooning outside her digs, wondering if she had any secret lovers or secret life. He would make a scene if he saw her speaking to other men, and she would laugh at him. God, he had been quick-tempered in those days. The firm had calmed him down.

"Hello."

The voice was just about empty of emotion, but hesitant.

"Hello," he answered.

This was it then. She had entered the living room, was removing her coat. He kept his eyes on the television.

"I'm just going to make myself a coffee. Would you like some?"

"Yes, please," he lied, not wishing to sound intractable.

"Fine."

And she left the room again, while the film played to a score of gunshots and screeching wheels. Miles took a deep breath. Only seconds of this fragile peace remained. He sat up straight in the chair and clasped his hands, the way he had seen actors do when they were supposed to be anxious for resolution. He was no hero, but he could act as well as anyone.

Was it as easy as that then? No, of course not. But they made some kind of effort at a beginning, sitting together on the settee, sharing a bottle of wine, watching television.

Or rather using the flickering pictures as a partial means of escape, so that the conversation never really had a chance to become too volatile, too involved. The television acted like the third party to an argument; neither Miles nor Sheila wanted to make too much fuss in front of it.

And although it was dark, they left the curtains open, to remind themselves how tiny their drama would seem against the perspective of the world. The programmes on TV grew softer as the night progressed, and so did the conversation. Everything conspired, so it seemed, to make their own dialogue easier. The old marriage was over, on that they were agreed.

Did they want a new one to begin, or were they content to see the old one perish and go their separate ways?

"What about you?"

"I asked first."

And both smiled, wishing to try the former path.

"But there has to be give, Miles."

"Agreed."

Sheila was rubbing at her forehead, her eyes moist, and Miles examined her closely. She was the same woman to whom he had lost his virginity, the same woman he had married. Love overwhelmed him, and he put an arm around her, pulling her in towards him. She hugged him silently, her hands sliding over his back. He felt an almost adolescent excitement. Love was a strange and a timeless gift; one never lost the knack.

Over a supper of microwaved pizza and another bottle of Rioja, they spoke softly together, as though afraid of waking their parents in an upstairs room. They giggled together, too, thinking back on the good times, acting like old friends. Perhaps it was important at this fragile stage not to act as husband and wife. Miles mentioned that he had read a lot of Sheila's books.

"You never told me that."

He shrugged his shoulders. So then they talked about books for a while. Sheila applauded silently.

"You *have* been a bookworm, haven't you?" She was smiling. "But, Miles, if you'd told me, we could have had such good discussions, couldn't we?" He agreed that this was true. "Miles, let's go to the theatre sometime together. Let's make it soon."

Miles felt the life flooding back into him. It seemed that the firm, over the years, had sucked the life out of him and replaced it with little coils and bolts of mistrust and fear. But he could change, couldn't he? Starting now, with Sheila giggling and looking so very young, and he trying to impress her and make her laugh. Yes, the life was there again.

They had not mentioned Billy Monmouth yet. Leave the pain to some other time, their eyes said. Everything can be faced in time.

Sheila felt confused, though she tried smiling her most open and encouraging smile. Was this what she had wanted all along? Was this what the fling with Billy had always been leading toward? And had it been a "fling" anyway? She didn't know, not yet. Perhaps if Miles had not found out about Billy she would have told him herself. Yes, she tried telling herself that she had been using Billy, nothing more. No, nothing more than that. Oh, God, she had worried away the past few nights by herself, wondering where Miles was, even going so far as telephoning Jack in Edinburgh, swallowing her embarrassment and asking if his father was there. But not there, and now here, his arms feeling more muscular than she remembered, his back thicker, but having lost weight from his paunch. And it felt so good lying here, without questions, without answers to those questions.

And when the telephone rang, they lay still for a moment in the bed, both with a strong desire to ignore its magnetic plea. But both failed, and there was a giggling race to be first downstairs. Sheila won, and her arm, stretching toward the telephone, pushed it inadvertently onto the floor.

"Whoops," she said, and then, scooping up the receiver, "hello?"

"Can I speak to Miles, please?"

She handed over the telephone in resignation, sticking out her tongue. Miles grabbed the receiver gleefully, breathing heavily.

"Hello?"

"Miles, it's Richard here. Listen, there was a terrible clunking sound when you answered. Be careful. I think you may be bugged."

"Oh, I see," said Miles gravely, smiling and winking at Sheila, who had settled beside him on the parquet floor. "Well, I'll certainly be careful, Richard." Sheila began to ask silently who was calling, but Miles only tapped his nose with his finger, and so she pushed him and caused him to topple. He dropped the telephone, then, having pushed himself back up off the floor, picked it up again.

"There, did you hear it?" asked Mowbray excitedly.

"Yes, I did, Richard, most certainly I did."

"Good God. I wonder who's bugging you, Miles?"

Miles knew exactly who was bugging him at that moment.

"I don't know, Richard. Was there something you wanted to say?"

"Yes, I've got a message. But I'm not sure I should deliver it over such a nonsecure line."

"Well, give it to me anyway, as discreetly as you like." Miles watched Sheila rise to her feet and pad toward the kitchen. She had mimed the drinking of coffee, to which he had nodded eagerly. Watching her retreat, he smiled.

"There's a meeting this evening."

"This evening?"

"A bummer, I agree. Mr. P wants to see us. Something to do with an offshoot of our recent Harvesting activities."

"A sort of a seedling, eh?"

The humour was lost on Mowbray, who spoke past it as though explaining to an idiot the principles of addition and subtraction.

"To do with our recent *Harvesting*, Miles. This evening. Six-thirty at the office of Mr. P."

"Yes, Richard, of course, Richard. I'll try to be there."

"Try? You'd better do more than that, Miles. You're not exactly the favourite nephew at the moment, if you get my drift."

"Like a snowstorm, Richard."

"Where have you been today, for example? Not in your office."

Miles watched Sheila coming back into his line of vision. She wore only her thin satin bedrobe.

"Oh," he said, "I've been around, Richard, believe me, I've been around."

CHAPTER 17

He had to brush late autumn leaves off the bonnet and the windscreen of the Jag. It had lain dormant for some time. The front bumper had been dented slightly, perhaps by some car trying to squeeze out of its tight parking space. No one, however, had put a brick through the front window, and no one had strapped a radio-controlled nasty to the wheel arches or the underbelly.

The drive, however, was not enjoyable, and this thought sent Miles jolting away from one particular set of traffic lights. He had always enjoyed driving his car, *always*. But something about the relationship seemed to have changed. Oh no, not you too, he wanted to say. The sounds of the engine, the change of the gears, the fascia, the leather which supported him, all seemed involved in a conspiracy of estrangement. He was just not right for the car anymore. Divorce was the word that came to mind. He would sell the car and buy something more austere, or—why not?—would travel everywhere by public transport. Too often he had used his car as if it were a womb or a protective shelter of some kind. Well, he was ready to face the world now.

And he was ready, too, to face whatever awaited him in Partridge's office.

The car behind was too close. If he braked at all it would bump him. Why did anyone risk that kind of accident? Maybe the driver was Italian. The car wasn't: it was German, a Mercedes. And it had been behind him for some time.

Pass me if you want, he said to himself, waving one hand out of the window. But the car slowed to keep with him, and Miles, his heart suddenly beating faster, took a good look in his rearview mirror at the driver. Maybe foreign; hard to tell behind those unseasonable sunglasses. Oh, Jesus, it's a tail. Of course it was a tail. What was happening to him? Slow, Miles, far too slow.

He pushed the car up to thirty-five, forty, forty-five, passed a couple of vehicles with an inch or two to spare, heard them sounding their horns, but his concentration was on the mirror and the Mercedes. It was like a shark after its prey: content to sit on his tail, to ride with him until he grew tired or panicked himself into the wrong action. Fifty, fifty-five: near suicide on these central city roads. He took a roundabout too quickly, and suddenly there was another car in the chase, its headlights on full, siren blaring. Miles didn't know whether to laugh or cry. The Merc signalled and turned into a side street, leaving the police car to do its duty. Miles signalled and pulled into the pavement. The car wedged itself in front of him and stopped.

Never mind. He had the telephone number ready.

A gun pointed at him through the window, ordering him to come out slowly. Four of them, none uniformed, all with handguns. Miles opened the door as though it were a surgical operation. He stepped out slowly, turned, and placed his hands on the roof of the car. He didn't want them to make a mistake and pull a trigger.

"Is this your car?"

"Yes."

"We have a report that this car has been seen in the vicinity of a bomb explosion."

"That's ludicrous. I haven't used the car for two weeks. It's been sitting outside my house in St. John's Wood all that time."

"I'm sure we can sort it all out, sir. Driver's licence?"

"Look, officer," said Miles, thinking, This is a clever one, whoever's behind it, "just do yourself and me one favour."

"What would that be?"

"Just telephone Special Branch. I'll give you the number. I've been set up, God knows why. Please, telephone Special Branch."

The gun was still aimed at his head, still only needing a squeeze of the trigger. This would be a bad way to die, a wrong way to die. Miles willed the man into dropping the gun.

"Very well," he said. "We'll do it your way."

Complete confidentiality, that was what Jim Stevens had promised Tim Hickey. From now on, only code names could be used, for Stevens was beginning to work his way deeper and deeper into the case. He told Hickey that the story was so big he had gone free lance, that he had a ready buyer. Hickey looked nervous. He didn't like change. But Stevens was his only horse, so he nodded agreement.

An ex-colleague, one of the few left whom Stevens had not bad-mouthed out of existence on his final afternoon in the office, set up a watch on the comings and goings of the hush-hush Sizewell committee. It met twice a month in an anonymous building just off St. James's Street. The location was curious in itself, but then the committee was engaged in difficult and interesting work: work which would interest many separate parties, not all of them scrupulous about waiting in line with everyone else to hear the ultimate findings.

The other members of the committee were checked out. All were experienced, none came from the security services themselves. Stevens could imagine that MIs 5 and 6 would dearly love to know what was being decided behind the heavy and ornately carved doors of the committee room. The room itself was ultrasafe, swept each and every day for naughty little devices. This much the newspaper's parliamentary correspondent, an alcoholic but hardworking pro of forty years' standing, was able to substantiate.

On the assassination side, things were slower, almost to the point of dead stop. Janine had done her bit, but the Israelis were cagey operators (with good reason) at the best of times, and this was hardly the best of times. Stevens's mysterious telephone caller had rung him at home twice and seemed pleased at the direction the investigation was taking.

"Yeah, well, we'd be going a whole lot faster, mate, if you'd pull the finger out of your posterior and come across with some facts—*hard* facts."

"Such as?"

"Such as the connection between S. and a certain murder, a garrotting, I believe, in London recently."

The voice had exhaled noisily.

"You're progressing, Mr. Stevens, believe me," it had said before ringing off.

The next time, Stevens was planning to threaten that he would pull the plug on the whole thing if he were not given some help. He had worked hard on cases before, of course, but this one was like drawing teeth. It was an apposite image: his back tooth had given up the ghost.

He prodded his mouth now. He had wormed some names out of Tim Hickey too. Cryptonyms, most of them, but there was one which Stevens felt confident about. When someone had been screwed around, they were usually ripe for the confessional. This man must be ripe.

And there couldn't be too many Miles Flints around. Even if he were ex-directory, there would be rates to pay, bank accounts, taxes. Stevens would find this guy Flint and he would speak with him. It seemed they might have quite a lot in common.

"As you are aware, of course, Harvest was always merely part of a much larger operation, which has been sustained for over a year now."

"A sort of seedling, eh?" said Richard Mowbray, smiling at his superior, while Miles sat in injured silence, his mouth straight as a glinting needle. He was still shaking from his run-in with the police, though they had been polite and sympathetic after checking his credentials.

Partridge did not smile either. He sat behind his desk, hands on the flat surface in front of him, as though talking to a television camera, perhaps to advise his countrymen that they were now at war.

"The Director would have been here himself to tell you this, but he has a prior and more important engagement." Partridge paused, making it sound as though their boss had been summoned to Buck House, but Miles was in no doubt that King's Cross was a more likely bet. Here was proof of the gradual handing on of responsibility. Partridge looked and acted every inch a Director. It was his calling and his destiny. "From other segments of the operation—overall code name Circe—several sources of potential irritation have been pinpointed."

Cough it up, man, thought Miles.

Partridge, however, was enjoying the sound of his words and relished having this particular audience captive before him. Perhaps there had been just a touch of melodrama about his wish to see them together. Well, the melodrama was not about to stop there. He had something to say which might just cause them to shift a bit in their seats. He hoped that they would sweat.

"One of these is about to be dealt with. Special Branch has been controlling things up till now, and it will be Special Branch, along with the RUC, who makes the arrest."

"RUC?" This from Mowbray, his eyebrows raised a little.

"It stands for Royal Ulster Constabulary," said Partridge with exaggerated patience.

"I know what it means," snapped Mowbray, "sir."

Partridge nodded, pausing, taking his time. There was plenty of time.

"I don't have to spell it out, do I? An arrest is going to be made in Northern Ireland. Very soon."

"And?" said Miles, suddenly interested.

"And," said Partridge, "we need an observer there, just to register our presence, our interest. I thought," his eyes sweeping the two men, "that one of you would be best suited to the job, having worked on Harvest at this end."

"Having worked up a *dead* end," corrected Mowbray.

Partridge just smiled.

"Circe is a much bigger operation than Harvest. We are here this evening, gentlemen, to decide which one of you should have the honour of representing the firm in the sun-spoilt paradise of Belfast. Now, who's it to be?"

Partridge made them coffee at his own little machine in a corner of the room, which was suddenly filled with the aroma of South America, of wide spaces, sunny plantations, a harvest of beans. The room itself, though, was small and stuffy, and Partridge had opened the window a little to let in some of the chilled evening air and a few droplets of rain from the burgeoning shower.

Miles gulped down the coffee, listening to a siren outside and being reminded of the horror of that gun appearing at his window. His soul had prepared itself for death, and it was still pondering the experience.

Partridge had gone over the details of the mission with them, insisting with a mercenary grin that it was really a sightseeing tour, nothing more.

The real work would be done by the RUC's Mobile Support Unit and the officers of Special Branch.

Special Branch, thought Miles, God bless them.

"Call it lateral promotion," said Partridge, but Miles knew that it was more a case of the last-chance saloon. Both Mowbray and he were thorns in the firm's side; neither would be lost with regret.

"It's just our presence that's required," Partridge continued, talking into the vacuum created by the silence across the table. "Otherwise it looks as though we don't care, looks as though we just sit around in oak-panelled rooms drinking coffee while the others get on with the real labouring. Do you see?"

Miles saw. He saw exactly what Partridge and the old boy were after. They were seeking the resignation of whoever got the job, and they presumed that that man would be Miles Flint. Miles had more ground to make up than did Richard Mowbray. Partridge was guessing now that Miles would feel forced to accept the mission and then would resign rather than go through with it.

"How many days?" he asked.

"Two or three, certainly no more than three."

"Overseeing an arrest?"

"Nothing more."

Miles had seen that look on the face of every quiz-show host.

"This is all bullshit!" spat Mowbray. "We know your game, Partridge. We know you're after the top job, and you'll sacrifice any number of us to get it."

Partridge shrugged his shoulders. He was still smiling at Miles, as if to say, Your opponent's out of the contest, it's just you now, all it needs is your answer to the golden question.

Two minutes later, and with no applause, no cheering, the prize belonged to Miles.

"Thank you, sir," he said.

"I don't believe it!"

And she couldn't, couldn't believe that he was going, that there was so little time, that he was leaving her again right now when everything was balanced so finely on the wire of their marriage.

"It's the truth."

"Are you doing this to spite me, Miles?"

"Of course not. Why do you say that?"

"Well, that's the way it looks to me. One minute we're talking of rebuilding our whole relationship, and the next you're off to Northern Ireland. It doesn't make sense. Why you?"

"It's something the office has been working on for a while, a new initiative. I know more about it than most."

"You've never mentioned it before."

"Only a couple of days."

"Oh, Miles." Sheila came forward and hugged him. "Can no one go in your place? Whatever happened to delegation of responsibility? Tell them you've got personal problems, tell them anything."

"Only a few days," he repeated lamely. Sheila drew back from him.

"Do you trust me for that long?" she asked. She was thinking, I've used Billy Monmouth as a weapon before, I can use him as a threat this time. Miles drew her to him again.

"I'll always trust you, Sheila, and you have to trust me."

"When do you have to leave?"

"Tomorrow." He felt her stiffen but held her fast. "The sooner I go, the sooner I'm back."

"We haven't even had a chance to talk about Billy yet," she said into the fabric of his shirt, her face hot against his shoulder.

"Say it now. It doesn't matter what you say. This is something new. But say it if you want."

Say what? Say that Billy was nothing, merely a cipher for her frustration? Say that he had congratulated her on her dress sense, admired her hair, taken her to the theatre? Say that he had been busy using her as she had been busy using him?

"Be careful, Miles, won't you?"

Again, Miles wondered how much she really knew of his job. Her eyes were shiny with a liquid which would recede soon. Her cheeks were burning to the touch, a fine down covering them.

"Be careful," she repeated in a whisper.

Yes, he would be careful. He could promise her that.

"Let's go to bed," he said.

CHAPTER 18

Billy Monmouth always started the day, if he were awake early enough, with a sauna, swim, and occasionally a massage at his health club. If anybody's body needed toning, he reasoned, it was his. By arriving early, he missed the majority of the cooing, made-up middle-aged women with their flapping eyelashes and breasts. The pool was unused before breakfast, and he could swim without being embarrassed by his puffing, red-faced splashes.

Lying in the sauna, which had not yet quite revved up to its full fierceness, he let his mind drift back towards sleep. He pretended he was back in his mother's womb, pretended the interior was blood-hot. Plunging into the icy pool outside could be the trauma of birth.

From the safety of his womb, he could think, too, of poor Miles and poor Sheila, caught in a marriage where incompatibility and love trod the same awkward line, tentatively holding hands. It had been a game to her. He realised that, of course, but had hoped that her feelings might change. Acting as a player in a new game, she had become hooked for a short time. And he, too, had enjoyed their secret meetings, their passing of messages, the counterfeit trips together. It had made him feel like a spy. The pity was, in the game, Miles was his enemy.

And however hard Billy tried, he could not regret having deceived his friend. He would do it again. For he had played the game a little too intensely this time.

He loved Sheila, God help him.

The door opened, letting in a cool draught of air, breaking Billy's concentration. The betowelled man sat down, breathing heavily, then poured water onto the coals, releasing a lung-bursting gulp of heat.

"Good morning, Andrew."

"Morning, Billy. How's tricks?"

Andrew Gray scratched at his chest and his shoulders, then studied his fingernails, seeking grime. He seemed to find some, for he cleaned the offending nail on the edge of a tooth, then spat into the coals.

"I can't complain, Andrew. Yourself?"

"Just fine, Billy, just fine." Gray was a heavy man, heavy not with any excess but with a sense of well-being. He exuded a confidence that left Billy looking shy and frail by comparison. He eased himself back onto the wooden spars of the bench, then swivelled and slowly lay back. The breaths he took were big, too, filling the cavern of his chest. Billy closed his eyes again, hoping his day was not about to be spoilt.

"Who was that woman you were with at lunch, Andrew?"

"You mean the day you had lunch with your friend Miles? I don't remember her name. Miles seemed like a nice chap."

"Yes."

"So, anything happening at work?"

Billy did not reply. To talk to Gray he needed to be in a certain mood, and whatever that mood was—indifference, perhaps, or cynical torpor—Billy did not feel it this morning. His mind, after all, had been on personal things, secret feelings and emotions, things he very seldom revealed to the brutality of the outside world. But Gray had come in on a chill of wind to remind him that the world was always there, waiting, and that there were other games to be played. Lies, damned lies, deceit and the manipulation of history: that was the role of intelligence. Just for a moment Billy felt real dirt on his skin. Gray would doubtless say that such sentiments were bad for business. Gray himself was hardened. One had only to look at that monstrous rib cage to see that the man was impervious, rock solid, unloved and unlovely. There, Billy had the edge on him perhaps. Not that this would have bothered Gray.

Andrew Gray was a businessman whose business was death.

Billy had never plunged into the pool with such relief before, and he wanted to stay submerged forever, his body chilled to everlasting. Instead he showered, the water scalding him, then went to the massage room, where the Organ Grinder, his arms as thick as thighs, was reading the daily tabloid.

"Mr. Monmouth, sir. Long time no see."

While the Organ Grinder folded his newspaper, Billy hoisted himself onto the table.

"Do my back, will you?" he said.

"My pleasure, sir."

The Organ Grinder was already rubbing his hands with preparatory glee.

Under the slow, circulatory pressure of the hand strokes, Billy began to drift again, but by now it was too late: Gray had entered all his dreams. Each scene contained, somewhere in the shadows near the back, waiting to walk on, the malcontent figure of Andrew Gray, his chest expanding and contracting like a machine.

"Thought I'd find you here."

When Billy opened his eyes, Gray was sitting on the table next to him, swinging his legs, dressed only in the silky bottom half of a track suit. He was rubbing at his chest again, scratching occasionally, finding nothing of interest beneath his fingernails.

Billy said nothing, just tried to give himself up to the massage. The Organ Grinder, despite his name, was by far the gentlest man in the room. Billy remembered the crack Miles had given him with that exhibition catalogue. Miles had not been gentle then. It had been a time bomb of a swipe, too, not hurting at the time but requiring treatment afterward. He'd not forget it in a hurry.

"Mind if I try that?" asked Gray. "It looks interesting."

Somewhere above Billy, roles were exchanged, a few cursory instructions given—don't hurt, don't prod, just go smoothly. And then the Organ Grinder was seated before him on the table, while Andrew Gray's hands fell upon him, working their way into his flesh.

"So, nothing's happening at work, huh?"

"Andrew, what do you want?"

"Nothing much." Gray had started to finger-slap Billy's shoulders. "It's just"—slappety-click—"well, just something I heard this morning. A phone call from a friend"—click-slappety—"about *your* friend Miles Flint."

Billy sat up, pushing Gray away. He stretched his back, feeling some clicks that should not have been there.

"Go on," said Billy. "Tell me about it."

There was no reply. Damn, damn, damn. Billy went back into the changing room and opened his locker. He would dress quickly, try the number again, then go to the office.

Andrew Gray was manipulating his silk tie into an extravagant knot.

"You're sure it was to be today he was leaving?"

"My source is, as they say, Billy, impeccable."

"I don't suppose you're going to tell me who your source is?"

"A little birdie—but not Partridge, if that's what you're thinking." Gray smoothed down his shirt collar and smiled at himself in the mirror.

Billy Monmouth heaved himself into his clothes, not bothering too much whether his tie was askew or his shirt neatly tucked in.

"Does it all connect, do you suppose?" mused Gray, making a final examination of himself.

"What do you think?" said Billy, panting now as though he had tried too many lengths of the pool.

"It remains to be seen, I suppose," said Gray.

"Tell that to Miles Flint."

"I hope you're not going to be rash, Billy." Gray's voice was as level and as deceptive as thin ice.

"I owe him this much," said Billy, walking out of the room with his shoelaces undone but his resolve strengthened.

Andrew Gray nodded to himself in the sudden silence. It had always been his most cherished edict: neither a borrower nor a lender be. Barter, sure, buy and sell, certainly. But Billy Monmouth spoke of "owing" something. There were traps aplenty for the unwise borrower and the unwary lender. He would have to speak to Billy about that sometime. Never have friends, that was the golden rule. Never ever have a friend.

It was becoming more bizarre still. Miles read again the note from the old boy, scrawled as though the writer had been in a rush to catch a train or, more likely, to catch the engine numbers of several trains. It appeared that Miles was to have a cover for his trip across the water, an overelaborate cover at that. He was to be a member of a chartered holiday group, flying out of Heathrow with half a dozen others.

"Why, for God's sake?" he asked Partridge over the telephone, while Sheila sped through the house with newly ironed shirts and handkerchiefs. Miles walked with the telephone to the study door and closed it with his foot.

"Security, Miles. You can't be too careful. The IRA has rather a good little intelligence operation going for it these days. It covers seaports and airports. They're always that little bit more wary of individuals who enter the country, just as our people are."

"But all these people I'm supposed to travel with . . ."

"A seven-day tour of Ireland. Special offer from a national newspaper. Your fellow passengers will be met in Belfast by the rest of the party, who will have travelled by boat or by plane from Glasgow. It'll be easy enough for you to slip away unnoticed. We'll see to that."

"But they'll notice I'm missing."

"Be anonymous, Miles. The more anonymous you are, the less chance there is of that. Besides, the courier will inform them that Mr. Scott has been taken unwell and may rejoin the tour at a later date."

"That's another thing."

"What?"

"That bloody name."

"Walter Scott? I rather think it a nice touch. You are Scottish, after all."

"How am I supposed to remain anonymous with a name like that?"

"Oh, come on, Miles. It's just some pen pusher's joke, that's all. It'll only be your name for a couple of hours at most. I think you're being a bit too serious about the whole thing."

But that was just his point! It was not Miles who was being serious but the firm, and this strange brew of the serious and the farcical was making him very nervous indeed.

"When does your flight leave?"

"Three hours from now."

"We'll have a driver there to take you to the airport in plenty of time."

"Well, my wife thought that she might drive me—"

"No, no, leave that side of things to us. All the best, Miles. Bring me back a souvenir, won't you?"

"What did you have in mind?"

"A decent showing, no cock-ups. Goodbye."

Self-righteous bastard, thought Miles as he went upstairs to wash.

When the telephone rang again—in the hall this time—it was Sheila who answered.

"Hello?"

"Oh, is that you, Sheila? Can I speak to Miles, please? It's Billy."

Sheila stared at the receiver and saw her knuckles bleached white against the red plastic. She was silent, waiting to hear something more. She heard background noise, men's voices.

"Hold on, will you?" she said finally, placing the receiver down gently on the notepad beside the telephone.

Billy Monmouth stared out of his window and into that of another office, where someone else was on the telephone. He wondered if it were a momentary revelation of some parallel universe, a universe where Sheila and he were together. Her voice had unnerved him, and then her silence had pushed him toward rash speeches, pleas, God knows what indiscretions. He had always been afraid of women, but not of Sheila. He missed her. And now Miles was leaving for a few days. . . . And he had telephoned to give him a specific warning. . . . To warn him that he might well be—

"Hello, Billy, what can I do for you?"

In the parallel universe, the telephone caller put down the receiver and greeted a female colleague who had just entered the room. He was rewarded with a peck on the cheek.

"Hello, Miles." Billy suddenly felt very warm, his face growing hot to the touch. He let his fingers graze his jaw, which was still stiff though no longer painful. "I just heard a rumour that you're being sent to Ulster. Is it true?"

"Yes, it is."

"What for? Why you?"

"I drew the short straw, that's all."

"How many straws were there? Just the one?"

"No, two. Listen, what's wrong?"

"Who arranged it, Miles?"

"Look, Billy, I'm getting ready. If you have something to say, say it."

Billy swallowed, his eyes on the window across the way.

"Be careful, Miles, that's all."

"Look, if you know something I don't—"

But the phone had gone dead on him. Damn. Why did people do that? It was such an absurd gesture, and rude, too. Damn. What did Billy mean?

"Have you finished in the bathroom?" Sheila called from upstairs.

"Yes, thanks."

For Billy to call him at home, after what had happened, well, it had to mean something. And Sheila had answered the telephone. What had they said to one another? What was going on? He should be at home saving his marriage, and instead he was flying off to Northern Ireland under the name of Walter Scott. But he had no time to think about it, no time to do anything but act.

Sheila was in the kitchen, preparing herself a sandwich, and Miles was already on the plane, when a ring of the doorbell interrupted her reverie. She peered out through the spy hole and saw a fairly grubby man standing there, examining the top of the house and the telephone wires which stretched across the street. He looked dangerous. There was a young woman with him. She looked not at all dangerous. Sheila slid the chain onto the door quietly, then opened it two inches.

"Yes?"

"Oh, hello, you must be Mrs. Flint?"

"That's right."

"I was wondering if I could see your husband."

"I don't know. Can you?"

The man laughed a short impatient laugh.

"It's a business matter," he said.

"My husband's not here."

"Oh."

"He's gone off for a couple of days."

The man seemed almost heartbroken. Suddenly he looked more tired than dangerous. He looked as though he might collapse on her doorstep. She was about to offer them coffee when she remembered what Miles had drummed into her: never let in strangers, never, even if they look official—*especially* if they look official. She stood her ground.

"A couple of days, you say?"

"That's right. Good day."

And with that she closed the door slowly but firmly on Jim Stevens's hopes and prayers. Still, a couple of days. It was nothing. He could wait. What choice did he have?

"Told you so," said Janine. "I told you he'd left, suitcase and all."

"Clever little bugger, aren't you?" said Stevens, wondering how the hell he could afford to pay her next month. He had little enough money as it was. "Come on," he said, "you can buy me lunch."

"Around here?" she cried, flabbergasted. "It'd cost a week's rent for a bacon buttie. There's a café in Camden, though, dead cheap. I'll treat you to a salami sandwich."

"Wonderful."

"Come on then," she said, flitting down the steps. "It's called Sixes and Sevens."

PART THREE
Sixes and Sevens

CHAPTER 19

"Ah yes, Mr. Scott."

And with that the courier ticked his name off the list. Belfast airport was near empty, which was fine by Miles; it was also, to his surprise, very modern and very clean. He didn't know quite what he had been expecting, an old RAF-style hangar perhaps, ringed by steel. But this was not like arriving in a country at war. No soldiers paraded their weapons. The atmosphere was . . . well, ordinary. Perhaps he would have an uneventful few days after all. If only he could get away from Mrs. Nightingale.

"Coo-ee, Mr. Scott! Over here!"

And here she was, in the ample flesh, wading towards him as though through water, her hand waving like a distress signal.

"Coo-ee!"

She had been sitting next to him in the Trident, humming along to Handel's *Fireworks Music* and crunching barley sugars with real ferocity. To her questions, he had decided that he was a widower and a civil servant. Wrong answers both: she was a widow (her wedding ring had tricked him) and a civil servant too, executive officer, Inland Revenue. He wondered now why he had not played the old card of pleading homosexuality. Perhaps he still could. What he could not do was retrieve the past excruciating hour of tales about the tax collector's office. His head throbbed like a gashed thumb. When, oh, when was he supposed to slip away?

"Mr. Scott, have you asked him about the baggage?"

"Not yet, Mrs. Nightingale."

"No, silly, call me Millicent."

"Millicent."

"Well, go ahead and *ask.*"

The courier, however, saved him some small embarrassment by answering the unspoken question.

"We'll go and collect it now, shall we?"

"We'll go and collect it now, Mr. Scott," repeated Mrs. Nightingale, putting her arm through his. Miles wondered if the courier were in on the deception. Everything which had seemed so well planned in London now seemed tenuous and half baked. He might yet end up on a tour of Ireland. Seven days and nights with Mrs. Nightingale.

Outside, baggage collected, they boarded a minibus. The country around them was darkening, as though the wattage of the bulb were fading. On their way out of the airport Miles noted a checkpoint where every second car was being stopped and searched. Sleeping policemen bumped the minibus out onto a main road. There were no signs visibly welcoming them to Northern Ireland, but pasted onto a road sign was a Union Jack poster with the legend ULSTER SAYS NO printed in large black letters. Miles closed his eyes, hoping to feign sleep. Mrs. Nightingale, a little later, placed her hand on his.

The hotel was unpromising. His room was a single (giving Mrs. Nightingale a whole range of options), the bar was dowdy and full of nonresidents, and the view from his window was of a flat rooftop where the matted carcass of a cat lay as though it had died of boredom. It might have been London. In fact it was much quieter than London, for not even the wailing of a police siren could be heard.

There was a knock at his door. Not Mrs. Nightingale, for he doubted very much whether she would have bothered to knock.

"Come in."

It was the courier.

"Mr. Scott, sir. You'll be leaving us first thing in the morning, so get an early night if you can. Someone will be here with a car for you. They'll come to the door, so make sure you're alone, eh?" The courier gave an exaggerated wink. He was the sort of despairingly jolly fellow so beloved of holiday-package groups. He did not look like a member of the services.

"Do me a favour, will you?"

"Yes, Mr. Scott?"

"Try and keep Mrs. Nightingale out of my hair."

The courier smiled and nodded.

"Understood," he said, and was gone.

Miles settled back on the creaking bed and flipped through a magazine which, having noticed that every traveller was carrying some sort of reading matter, he had bought at Heathrow. It was filled with book reviews. Not a word on coleoptera, though. He supposed that he could try the bar again but was afraid of what he might find there. He recalled Mrs. Nightingale's clammy hand on his, and he shuddered.

There was no telephone in the bedroom, but there was a battered pay phone at the end of the hall. He would call Sheila. He slipped out of the room in his stocking soles and padded through the deserted corridor. He had only the one tenpence piece, but that would be sufficient to reassure himself that Sheila was all right. . . . Did he mean all right, or did he mean chaste? He wasn't sure. He dialled his home number, but there was no reply. Well, she could be anywhere, he supposed. He dialled his own number, the one for his study telephone. Still no answer. Finally he decided to call Billy Monmouth, just, so he assured himself, to hear a friendly voice. This time the call was answered. Miles pushed home the coin. It stayed in but nothing connected.

"Blast this thing." He slapped the front of the apparatus. "Damn and blast it." The telephone went dead. He had lost his only coin.

"Mr. Scott!"

"Mrs. Nightingale."

"Millicent, Mr. Scott. You must call me Millicent. Who were you phoning?"

"Trying to reach my son."

"You didn't tell me you had a son, Mr. Scott!"

"Oh?"

"Let's go down to the bar and you can tell me all about him."

She was already tugging at his arm.

"I don't have any shoes on, Millicent."

She looked down at his feet, then laughed.

"In that case," she said, "we'll just go along to your room and you can put your shoes on. I've been dying to see your room anyway. Come on."

In the small, smoky lounge bar the hotel guests were being treated to jokes and songs by a local, who, unshaven, his cap askew on his sweat-beaded head, seemed irrepressible. Miles noticed, however, that the man's eyes remained as sharp as a fox's. He was working hard and methodically to win the free drinks which were his right, and he wasn't about to let any of the pale-faced guests escape. He swayed before them like a snake before its prey, seeming to entertain when in fact it was already digesting its victims.

Everybody laughed, of course, but it was a laughter coloured by fear. They could all see that this was a potentially dangerous man, and they would gaze at the barman when they could, pleading with their eyes: make him stop.

Miles sipped his lager. Ordinarily, he would have drunk Guinness, but he did not wish to appear patronising.

"Go on, Declan, tell them the one about . . ."

Yes, Declan needed his prompters, needed the whispered reminders from the wings.

"Remember, Declan, that time when you . . ."

In truth, several of the party could not make out one word of Declan's stories, and their smiles were the most enthusiastic of all. Mrs. Nightingale was one of these. Her laugh was a garish parody of fun. Well, at least she's quiet, thought Miles, thankful for the smallest of mercies.

It was not quite dawn when, a light sleeper at the best of times, Miles heard a key turn in the lock, his door open, and saw two shadowy figures enter the room. By then he was already out of bed, keen to appear efficient. "Packed and ready to go, gentlemen," he whispered. The men seemed satisfied. Miles was already dressed and had only to slip on his shoes. One of the men lifted his case, then headed out of the door, checking to left and right as he did. The other man motioned for Miles to go ahead of him and relocked the door behind them. Within ninety seconds they were out into the chill darkness. A Ford Granada was revving up beside the pavement. Miles was ushered into the back of the car beside the first man, who held his suitcase on his lap. The second man, getting into the passenger seat, motioned for the driver to move off. Nobody had said a word, except for Miles's smug little whispered announcement. He regretted having said anything now: silence should have been maintained. Then, in sudden panic, he thought of another potential and horrific error: how did he know who these men were? They could be anyone at all. He had not asked, had seen no identification, had not heard their accents. But the city streets outside told him to be calm. Morning was approaching, bringing with it a waking serenity. He would wait and see, that was all. He would sit back and say nothing and trust to the fates.

After all, it was time for a definite change in his luck.

"Mr. Scott?"

"If you say so," said Miles.

"Well, that's what your lot told us."

"Then I suppose it's true."

"I'm Chesterton." The man thrust forward his hand, his eyes still glued to the papers he held. Miles shook the hand.

"Any relation?" he asked, smiling.

"To whom, Mr. Scott?"

"Never mind, nothing really."

Chesterton looked up at Miles suspiciously, then, seating himself at his desk, continued to read the papers. Miles examined the room. It was much like the room in which he had been interrogated by the Scottish policeman. A table, three chairs, wastepaper basket, one barred window.

"Is this a police station?" he asked.

"Sort of." Chesterton looked up again. "The normal differences between Army and police tend to blur a bit over here. It's a lesson you'd be wise to learn, Mr. Scott. Everything here is just like reality, just like London, but distorted slightly, out of kilter. Something can look very safe, very ordinary, and then blow up in your face. A taxi driver turns into a gunman, a discotheque into a booby trap. Are you with me?"

"Yes, I see."

"But that's just it, you *won't* see. You'll have to learn to use your sixth sense. You're our guest here, Mr. Scott, and we don't like our guests to get themselves killed. It's bad for our reputation." He spoke like the maître d' of some expensive hotel.

Miles nodded slowly. He was thinking of London, of how shopwindows could blow out into your face, of how people hesitated before passing a parked car. He wanted to say, We've got bombs in London, too, mate, but thought the remark might be taken the wrong way. Besides, having made his point, Chesterton seemed happy. He folded the papers and tucked them into a drawer of the desk. Miles heard something rattle as the drawer was pulled open. A gun, he thought, lying ready for any confrontation with distorted reality. Billy Monmouth, a few years ago, had spoken with him about the troubles.

"Who wants them to stop?" he had said. "It's the best training ground Britain's got. NATO's learned a lot from our experiences, medicine's learned how to treat skin burns more efficiently, the Pilgrim cousins have tested their own men in the field. It's just one vast laboratory of human endeavour. Everybody over there treats it like a game."

Miles did not believe that. Reading the newspaper reports, it didn't seem much like a game. Billy's, as always, was the comic-book version of events. He had never been to Belfast and would never go.

"I know what you're thinking," said Chesterton.

"Oh?"

"Yes, you're thinking about breakfast, and rightly so. Come on."

Breakfast. It had not occurred to Miles to feel hungry. Meekly, he followed Chesterton out of the room.

Initially, Chesterton's moustache and bulk had caused Miles to place him in his late thirties, but now, studying him at leisure in the relaxed atmosphere of the canteen, he was obliged to subtract five or six years from that estimate. There was something in Chesterton's face which should have deserted him in Northern Ireland but had decided to remain: a trace of youthful innocence.

It was well hidden, of course, but it was there. Was he Army or Special Branch? It was hard to tell. From what Miles had seen thus far, it was true that any distinctions blurred. Even rank seemed to merge with rank, so that, in the queue for breakfast, Chesterton had spoken with real friendliness to a much younger and inferior-looking man. Miles envied them their camaraderie. Here, he felt, real friendships could be forged. What was that old proverb about adversity?

"All right, is it?" Chesterton jabbed his fork in the direction of Miles's plate. "The food, I mean."

"Oh, yes, it's fine, just what I needed."

Miles cut and lifted a section of bacon, and watched a nodule of fat drip back into the pale yolk of the egg.

"The operation is due to take place tonight," said Chesterton, mopping his plate with a thin slice of white bread, "if there are no hitches. We don't expect that there will be any, not at this stage of things."

"I see."

"You know the setup, of course?"

"Well . . . I have London's side of it."

Chesterton laughed.

"Very good, Mr. Scott. Very well put. Yes, there's often a rather wide gap between their—I suppose I should say *your* side of things and ours."

"Well, while I'm here, please try to think of me as being on *your* side, making it *our* side."

"Lined up against the mandarins of Whitehall, eh?"

"Something like that."

"Have you heard of the initials NKIL, Mr. Scott?"

Miles pondered, tricked at first into thinking it some new terrorist organisation. Then he remembered.

"Not known in London," he said.

"That's right. If it's not known in London, then it might as well not have happened. Intelligence here was being run down prior to this new bombing campaign. But now, well, we can hardly keep track of all the undercover squads, the nameless individuals who tiptoe in here, then tiptoe out again, heading south. Some of them we never hear from again. I don't know whether they return directly to their bases on the mainland or are caught by the enemy and turned or executed."

"Have the . . . enemy turned many people in your experience?"

"Top secret," whispered Chesterton with a wink. "I'm not allowed to know. There have been rumours. Rogue personnel bombing their own units. If you really want to know, ask Whitehall."

"Whitehall isn't quite as close-knit as that, I'm afraid."

"Isn't it? You could have fooled me. Are you going to eat that egg?"

Miles shook his head, and Chesterton pulled the plate towards him.

"Waste not, want not," he said.

"Would you mind explaining things to me," said Miles, "about this evening's operation?"

"Of course. Though there will be a formal briefing later this afternoon." Chesterton looked up from Miles's plate. "You can stay here, you know, you don't have to go. No one would be any the wiser back home, and it would save us from having to look after you."

"All the same," said Miles.

"Well, it's entirely up to you, Mr. Scott. We'll be heading south. I don't suppose I should say 'we' really, since I'll not be going along."

"Oh?"

"No, but there will be a Mobile Support Unit with you. They're from the RUC. Probably four of them. And one or two others."

"From E4A?"

Chesterton, impressed by Miles's ready knowledge, raised his eyebrows. E4A was a shadowy outpost of Special Branch, formed with the specific brief of deep surveillance of Irish terrorists. Miles knew very little about the group, except that it had a reputation for thoroughness in everything it did, with the possible exception of keeping within the law. On that particular point, E4A was known to be less than circumspect, and for that reason, as well as for others, it was not often mentioned within the firm. Chesterton shrugged his shoulders.

"From Special Branch certainly," he said. "As you see, Mr. Scott, your presence is hardly necessary on this little jaunt."

"Nevertheless," said Miles, "here I am."

"Yes," said Chesterton, pushing back Miles's plate, "here you are. Here you are indeed."

The room was full of smoke when Miles arrived, so he assumed that he was late.

"Ah, Mr. Scott. Welcome." This from the only man in the room not smoking with fierce determination. They were all dressed in civvies. It appeared that no one in the building wore a uniform of any kind.

"And you are?" asked Miles casually, taking the proffered hand.

The man laughed, glancing at his smiling colleagues.

"I'm nobody, Mr. Scott. I don't exist. Nevertheless, here I am."

Yes, thought Miles, here you are indeed.

"May I introduce you to the rest of the team for our little evening drive?" The man nodded towards a stocky character, his shirt open to reveal a sprouting chest, the hair as dark as a thicket. "This is One. One, meet Mr. Scott."

"Mr. Scott." They shook hands. One? Had Miles heard correctly? Maybe it was something Chinese, Wan or Wun. The man did not look Chinese.

"And this," pointing now toward a much thinner man with a pale, cruel face, "is Two."

"Pleased to meet you."

"Likewise," said Miles. He had not misheard.

He was, in turn, introduced to Misters Three, Four, and Five.

"I suppose," said his host finally, "you can call me Six."

They were all Irish, and this, after the crisp English of Chesterton, made Miles a little more nervous. He was drifting further and further from the safety of the raft, moving deeper into the dark waters around him. He was as isolated as he had ever been in his life.

"Let's proceed," said Six, while Miles tried to work out the identities of his colleagues. Two, Three, Four, and Five might well be RUC men. They had the look about them of policemen not entirely used to this life of intrigue and double-dealing. They looked as if they were enjoying the novelty of it all. One was a different proposition again. Special Branch maybe. A brute of a man. Six was brutish, too, but more intelligent, and as he went on with the briefing Miles began to see the Army training stamped all over him. Not quite SAS, but then what? Something shadowier still. Something unpleasant.

With the eyes of an executioner.

"A simple arrest procedure should be sufficient on this one, but we'll be armed for safety's sake. As you know, Circe has been keeping an eye for several months on a small electronics factory south of Belfast. How far south I'm not going to say. We now have proof positive that this factory is an IRA front, set up specifically to buy in electronic timers and other such devices from the Continent. These devices then go to make up fairly specialised little bombs, such as those being used on the mainland at this very moment."

Seated on his hard plastic chair, Miles noticed from the corner of his eye that the others looked at him from time to time, curious perhaps. Still they smiled and puffed away at their chain-lit cigarettes.

"We shall," continued Six, "arrest and bring into custody the ringleaders, two men who will be, so intelligence informs us, alone in the factory this evening. They will not be armed"—he looked up—"we hope. I've got some photographs of them here with full physical descriptions on the back." He handed out glossy black and white blowups of two young and handsome men, taken without their knowledge. One was leaving his car, while the other was standing by a petrol pump, examining his wallet. The photographs were impressively sharp and focused, the work of a real expert.

"These were taken this morning," said Six.

Miles stopped being impressed and felt a sense of awe in its place.

"On this sheet of paper is a breakdown of what each man is wearing today."

Studying the details, down to shoe colour and jewellery, Miles was again impressed. He was not dealing with a "half-cocked bunch of Paddies and Paddy-watchers," as Billy had termed the operation in Northern Ireland. This was a classy show, and these men were just about the most professional thugs he had ever encountered.

"We've just time for a cuppa and maybe something to eat," said Six, his voice more relaxed, "and then we'll be off. Any questions?"

There were none.

"Mr. Scott, I'd be obliged if you would check that you have nothing on or about your person which could identify you, no wallet, spectacle case, letters or envelopes, or name tags on your underpants."

Miles nodded as the others chuckled.

"Then," continued Six, "you'll be just as naked as us, should anything go wrong. From now on I think we'd better call you Seven. Is that all right with you?"

Miles nodded again.

As naked as us. But they were not naked, and he most definitely was.

Although trained in the use of firearms, Miles loathed the things. They were noisy and unnecessary most of the time. But Miles wanted a gun now, just to even things up. In the canteen he noted that the others were packing fairly heavyweight pistols. So he asked Six.

"Oh," said Six, stirring three sugars into his mug of tea, "I shouldn't think that would be necessary. I'm told that you're only here as a spectator, not as a participant. If you were to be given a weapon, you would automatically become a participant, and we wouldn't want anything to happen to you, would we?"

Hadn't Chesterton said the same thing?

"Don't worry," continued Six, "I'll put it on the record that you requested the use of a firearm and that your request was denied. Just sit back now and enjoy the ride, that's my advice. And let's just double-check that there's nothing on you that would give the game away."

"I can see why they call you covert security," mumbled Miles, turning out his pockets like any small-time crook.

"We have to be careful," said Six, running his eyes down Miles. Was there contempt in his look, hatred of this nuisance factor which had been embedded into an otherwise straightforward job? Well, to hell with him, thought Miles. I'm going to see this through whether I'm in the way or not. "There was a time," said Six, as much for the others as for Miles, "when we could be sure of these things going as smoothly as a greased runner. The enemy were just cartoon cutouts toting half-baked bombs, getting themselves blown up more than anybody else. There wasn't any problem."

"The Paddy Factor," interrupted Miles, wishing to appear knowledgeable and immediately regretting it. Six looked towards the others, who were not smiling any longer.

"One of your smart London phrases," hissed Six, the door to his prejudices open at last. "You lot sit at your desks all day smirking at newspaper reports of another soldier killed, another part-timer crippled, and you can laugh as loudly as you like because it's all happening a million miles away from your bowler hats and tea trolleys, but here, well, we see things through different eyes."

Go on, thought Miles, spew it all up.

"Over here everything changes. There's no Paddy Factor because there are no Paddies anymore. Everyone's grown up now. They don't learn their trade in the haylofts and the barns. They've all been to college, to university. They've got brains, they're open-eyed, they know the score. If you go along on this trip expecting to meet Paddies, then let me assure you that you're in for a bit of a surprise."

Behind the speech Miles could hear a cry of frustration against Whitehall's cumulative neglect of the "troubles." Finally, almost in a whisper, his breath coming fast and hot from his lungs, Six said, "Just to put you in the picture, that's all," and fell silent as he gulped at his tea. The silence was more unnerving still, and Miles felt as though he had been cajoled onto a roller coaster, only to find himself wanting to get off as the machine reached the top of its climb.

Too late to get off now, he thought, his hands clutching at the table rim. Far too late.

The car flew over the rise in the road and headed downhill even faster. Miles felt his stomach surge and craned his neck to catch a glimpse of the speedometer. Seventy. The country was a darkening blur outside his window, and he began to feel a claustrophobia which had not assailed him since his youth. The day had become a sort of recurring nightmare. Here he was again, sandwiched in the back of a car. In the front sat Six and his equally deadly ally, One. And somewhere behind, the remaining two members of the team were following in a transit van marked MURPHY'S MEAT & POULTRY.

The car had the body of a Cortina, but what lurked beneath the bonnet was something else entirely. From the moment the engine had been brought to life, Miles had been aware of an extraordinary power, 2.6 litres or more of it. The thing accelerated like a test rocket, sending its passengers back in their seats. The roller-coaster effect was complete.

There was little conversation during the drive. For one thing, the engine was too noisy, the whole interior of the car seeming to vibrate, and for another, no one seemed in the mood for speaking. Miles could feel his back cloying with sweat, his hair prickling. Yes, this was a foreign country, everything out of kilter, just as Chesterton had said. So, as though he really were on a roller coaster, Miles gritted his teeth and sat back, determination replacing the fear in his stomach, his eyes narrowed so that he would have to take in only very little of what was happening and what was about to happen.

Although he could not be said to be an expert on the scale and geography of Northern Ireland, it did seem to him that they had travelled a good long way south. Of course, there might have been several twistings and turnings toward east and west. They could be anywhere. All the same, their destination was supposed to be due south of Belfast, and now that he thought about it, "south of Belfast" had come with ominous vagueness from Six's mouth. How far south exactly? He had heard of border raids, but only rumours. Of course mistakes had been made by patrols in the past. But this was different, wasn't it?

"Nearly there," roared Six. He rolled down his window and waved with his hand, signalling this information to the van. One of the slices of bread sandwiching Miles slipped the pistol out of his jacket and gave it a quick check.

"Browning," he explained, weighing the gun in his palm and smiling.

Why did they all smile? Miles remembered that monkeys smiled when afraid, but there was no fear in these men. They were about to enjoy themselves. They had been built with this operation in mind, and now they were about to be made very happy indeed. Yes, these were knowing smiles, and Miles, despite his every effort, could not make himself smile back.

It was as cold as a tomb, a deep freeze, a mortuary: as cold as all the images of stasis and lifelessness which were conjured in Miles Flint's head. It was dark, too, but his fevered mind hadn't got round to cataloguing similes for darkness yet. The six men walked slightly ahead of him, though they glanced back often to make sure that he was still with them and had not glided off into the night.

The factory was a small, self-contained unit within a cluster of about a dozen, the site itself seeming new, doubtless part of some regeneration programme for the economy. There was a light on in the small office. Six had explained the layout to them in enormous detail. A front door led directly into the office. There was a larger warehouse entrance, but it would be locked at night. Entrance to the factory could be gained only through the office. If they made a run for it, they would run into the factory, a small hangar of a place, equipped with two fire exits. Three would cover one of these exits, Four the other. They branched off now, at the entrance to the site, and made their way around to the back of the buildings. Only one of the factory units was lit.

"That's our baby," said Six, breathing good deep breaths. He looked ready to swim the Channel. Then he drew out his pistol, some huge, anonymous, nonregulation model. It glinted metal-blue in the faint light from the office window. He didn't look like a swimmer anymore. He looked ready to club some seals.

"Let's go, gentlemen," he whispered.

They did not rush the door, not until they were one step away from it. Six knocked once and opened the door with split-second force. One was right behind him, gun trained, and the two RUC men stepped in afterward, leaving Miles to walk through the door last, last and unarmed, as though he were in charge. Three men stood behind a desk, gawping at him. Their hands were above their heads, and on the table lay some plans. To Miles they looked like the blueprints of some piece of circuitry.

"We'd better have those," snarled Six, and one of the rather timid-looking RUC men lifted the plans and began to roll them up.

"Who the hell are you?" shouted one of the men behind the desk. Miles recognised him as the more handsome of the two men in the photographs. He was wearing the clothes in his description, but his tie hung loosely around his neck. He looked every inch the harassed businessman, with orders to be despatched and deadlines to meet.

"Never mind that," said Six in an even more Irish accent than he had used with Miles and the others. He pointed toward the third man with his finger, his gun hand steadily trained upon the handsome businessman. "Who the hell are you?"

This third man was somewhat older than the others. He looked ready to expire at any moment. Innocence was written on his face in pale, trembling letters.

"I'm Macdonald," he managed to say at last. "Dicky Macdonald. I ordered some circuit boards. I just . . . I mean, this hasn't got anything to do with me, whatever it is. Jesus, I've a wife and kids. Have the lads not been paying their protection money, is that it? I've not—"

"Mr. Macdonald," said Six, "will you please go outside. Two, look after Mr. Macdonald. Get him into his car and get him away from here."

Two nodded, relieved to be going back outside. The office, despite the cold which was coming in through the open door, was stuffy with fumes. A portable gas fire burned away furiously in one corner.

"Cosy," said Six, his voice almost a whisper. "I mean, the whole setup's cosy."

"Look, pal, what's this all about?" This came from the other man, his voice quieter than that of his partner, but his eyes infinitely wilder.

"This is about bomb making, this is about the murder of innocents and of Her Majesty's forces, this is about the two of you."

"You're right out of order," said the handsome one.

"You're over the damned border!" shouted the other one, confirming Miles's worst fears. His eyes were burning, but those of Six burned right back at him. "The bloody English Army! I don't believe it. You're way out of your territory. You better get the hell out of here. This is an international incident!"

"Listen to it, would you?" said One, speaking for the first time, and in a voice as cold as his gun. "A terrorist calling *this* an outrage."

"They never learn, do they?" the handsome one said to the wild-eyed. "They think they can do whatever they like."

Miles knew for the first time that he was about to witness an execution. Reason demanded it. They could not cross the border and take these men back: there would be too many questions at the trial, accusations, witnesses (Macdonald for one), and the shit would hit the fan all around the world. Nobody had any intention of letting that happen. This was an assassination run, and he was right here in the middle of it. He wanted to speak, but his jaw muscles would not move. He felt paralysed, like the prey of some insidious and poisonous insect.

"Seven?" said Six, and it took Miles fully a second to realise that he was being addressed.

"Yes?"

"Come here, would you?"

"Are you in charge here?" said Wild-eyed. Then, to Six, "Is he in charge?"

It was only when One laughed, a low, heartless chuckle, that Miles knew for certain that he was in trouble, though really he supposed that he had had some inkling all along. They were about to incriminate him in the act. They were going to make him fire the shots.

But I'm a watchman, he wanted to shout. That's all, I just watch, I don't *do*. Someone else always does the doing, not me, never me.

Instead of which he shuffled forward, his legs full of sand and water, noticing several things as he moved: the girlie calendar on the wall, the fact that one window and one door of the office led inward, right into the factory itself, the sheen of animal fear on the faces of everyone, and the facts of his isolation and his unfitness to be here at all. Throughout his adult life he had trained himself to blend in, to be anonymous and invisible, and now these men were destroying his life's work. They were turning him into the main attraction.

And then the pistol was pointing at him.

While the look on Six's face said everything there was to say about domination and betrayal.

"Will you go and stand with these gentlemen, please?"

"What the hell is this?" Miles tried to sound amused, realising deep within himself that this was no joke.

"Will you go and stand with these gentlemen, please?"

"Do what you're told, prick!" This came from One, who was laughing again, clearly a man upon whom no trick had ever been played. He had the look of a machine, preprogrammed for this moment.

Miles's head was spinning.

"There's been some terrible—" But the words seemed far too vague and inadequate.

"Some terrible mistake?" mimicked Six. "No, there's been no mistake. The orders were unambiguous. Orders always are. These two," waving his gun at the terrorists, "and you."

"Whose orders?" Miles was trying to think fast, while half his mind tried to control his suddenly aching bladder.

"There's no mistake, Mr. Scott, honestly." Six was speaking very gently.

"My name's not Scott. It's Miles Flint. You can check that."

Again, very quietly, "There's been no mistake."

Three of them in front of the desk. Three behind.

"Get it over with," said Handsome.

"Patience, Collins," said Six. "It's not every day we get to execute some-one."

One was about to laugh again, his stomach distending and his head arching back, and Miles was opening his arms to make another attempt at explanation, when the wild-eyed man heaved the desk with sudden fierceness onto its side, sending Six and One off balance. The handsome man opened the door into the factory, while his counterpart made a spectacularly clumsy dive through the window. After an almost fatal second's hesitation, Miles followed them, and the first shot flew an inch above his head.

In the darkness of the factory there was nothing to do but survive for the moment. Every second he stayed alive now was a bonus. He slipped behind some machinery, ran through a maze of what appeared to be lathes, then crouched. He breathed hard, summoning up all the adrenalin he could, and shook his head to clear it of dizziness and any lingering indecision. That pause back there had nearly cost him his life. For the moment he could think of no way out, but he was not dead: that was a start.

He heard One, Six, and the spare RUC man come into the darkness, quite close to him but not too close. There were two fire exits, but both were covered from outside. The shot would have alerted the two men keeping watch. He was as trapped as a baited badger.

A shot rang out suddenly from the other end of the building, and Miles heard One screech, "They've got guns!"

Good for them.

"Find a light switch," hissed Six. "Must be around here."

"Or maybe back in the office," whispered One. "We want to kill the lights in there anyway. We're sitting targets while they're on."

"Right, Five, slip back into the office."

"Why me?" Five sounded in some distress. Miles judged that if he were going to move further away, then this confusion was offering him his best cover. The problem, of course, was that in moving further away from the assassins he was moving closer to the enemy, who might mistake him for their foe. A badger had never been so baited.

His eyes becoming accustomed to the gloom, he moved silently forward, bent double, watching the floor so that he did not bang his feet against anything metallic. Noise would travel far in here.

Rather than travelling in a straight line towards the opposite wall, he moved around the edge of the interior, staying well out of any stray bullet's way. Perhaps there was another means of exit, but he thought not: the planning had been immaculate, well, almost immaculate. His pounding heart was proof of a slipup. Six would be hoping that the slipup was temporary. So would One. Miles did not fancy having to tackle either of them on the issue.

And then, coming around one corner, he found the mouth of a pistol staring him in the face.

"I think I'm on your side," he whispered. The handsome one put his finger to his lips and motioned for him to follow.

Wild-eyed was crouching behind a bench. He ignored Miles.

"They've got both fire exits covered," Miles told Handsome, "and they're trying to turn on the lights in here." He felt a shiver in his abdomen: he was betraying his country, and it felt good. He remembered fights he had been in, drunken half brawls at university. He had to relearn that old aggression, and fast.

"Then we'd better get out before that happens," said Handsome, "otherwise they'll pick us off with no trouble at all."

"Give it a few more seconds," said Wild-eyed, "give the bastards outside time to relax again. If they heard the shots, they'll be as jumpy as a bitch in heat."

Looking behind him, Miles saw the faint outline of one fire exit. There was a bar halfway up the door which had to be pushed, and the door would open easily. It was a godsend, really, for the quickness with which it could be opened would, with a little luck, surprise those waiting outside.

Wild-eyed looked at Miles.

"There's no time for questions now," he spat, "but there'll be plenty for you to answer afterward. You come with us, or you stay behind. Suit yourself. I couldn't give a monkey's."

And with that he leapt to his feet and threw himself at the door, beginning to fire off shots as he went.

"Keep low when you run," called Handsome, running after his friend, and Miles, still crouching, followed like a circus monkey out into the cool fresh air.

Where no RUC men awaited him. A shot came from their left, and Wild-eyed and Handsome returned the fire, still running. The RUC men were covering the wrong exits. They had gone to the adjoining unit!

There is a God, Miles screamed to himself as he ran through the long grass, there is a sweet Jesus Christ and he loves me, he loves me, he loves me!

But another shot, whinnying past him from the factory, brought Wild-eyed down onto his face.

Leave him, thought Miles, watching Handsome run on, never glancing back. Then he stopped thinking altogether and concentrated on running for his life.

They crossed a landscaped border of soil and small trees and then a road. And after that a field, the soil heavy underfoot, trying to suck his weary feet down. Hide here, it said, hide under me. But Miles kept on running. There was an explosion behind him: the factory. Flames lit the sky.

Over the fence, trousers snagged and torn, then a pasture, and finally a clump of trees with a glade, a lovely spot for a picnic. He had gone past the collapsed figure of his fellow runner before he noticed him. He brought his legs to a juddering halt and fell to his knees. His lungs felt like the stoked boiler of a steam train, and his mouth was full of a sticky saliva which, when he attempted to spit it out, clung to his lips and his tongue, so that in the end he had to wipe it away with his sleeve. He rubbed his hands over the wet grass and licked the palms, feeling the moisture refresh him.

And seemed to pass out for a time, lying on his back, while the trees and the sky whirled above him, restless, never stopping, like some automated children's kaleidoscope. . . .

CHAPTER 20

The gun was pointing at his pineal eye, and perhaps this was what had brought him awake, his back chilled with damp, his lungs still fiery and raw. Above the gun, Miles could just about focus on the milky face of Collins. That was what they had called him, Collins.

"There are some questions need answering."

Miles nodded slowly, aware of the barrel of the gun, its explosive potential. Fire away, he almost said, but swallowed instead.

"Why did they want you dead?"

"I don't know," said Miles, his mouth thick.

"Who are you anyway?"

"My name is Miles Flint. I live and work in London. I work for Military Intelligence." Collins seemed unimpressed. "I am a surveillance officer," Miles continued slowly, aware that his answers meant a great deal. "I was supposed to be witnessing the arrest of two suspected terrorists. That's all."

Collins smiled wryly. His hair stuck to his forehead like great leeches at feeding time. There was a considerable intelligence behind the large, deep eyes, but also an amount of fear. Miles knew that his life was still in danger. He very much did not want to die, not yet, not without knowing why.

"You thought you were going to see us arrested, eh?"

"That's right."

Collins laughed quietly.

"There aren't any arrests these days, not here. This is no-man's-land. Shoot to kill. They'd crossed the border. It's easier to kill than to take us alive. Don't you know that?"

"I know it now. What was that explosion?"

"Just a little something I left for your friends. Which brings us back to you. You could be a plant. You could be anything or anyone. This whole thing could be a setup. So why don't you persuade me otherwise, eh?"

The gun was as steady as the trees around them. Miles swallowed, feeling hunger and thirst and a whole welter of emotions within him.

"I'll need to take off my trousers," he said.

"What?"

"I'll need to take off my trousers," he repeated, "because back there I was so scared that I wet myself."

They were running again, together, through the fine drizzle blowing across the fields. It had grown light, and so they moved with caution, though the only sounds around them were those of the waking birds. Miles felt more tired than he had ever been, and yet he moved easily enough, as though in a dream. He did not even feel the constant chafing of his damp trousers against his legs.

Collins moved ahead of him, the pistol out of sight beneath his shirt. He had discarded his tie altogether, burying it in loam, and he moved now like some wild species, quite at home in both terrain and situation. I'm on the run with a terrorist, thought Miles. In a strange land, not knowing quite what I should be doing. He replayed the events of the previous hours, trying to answer his own questions. Had there been a mistake? No, there had been no mistake. The notion of Six making that sort of error was unthinkable. The truth was that someone somewhere, someone in authority, wanted him dead and buried as privately as possible. He had been sent into this nightmare without a weapon and without any means of identification. He carried only his money and a handkerchief.

He was the invisible man now all right, because that was the way they had wanted him to die.

From behind, Miles thought he caught the faint drone of a motor vehicle. He called to Collins, who crouched. Miles fell onto his knees in the long grass and shuffled towards him. Collins had drawn his gun.

"What is it?" he whispered.

"Some kind of vehicle," said Miles, bending lower as the sound moved more obviously towards them, travelling slowly.

Both men watched through the filmy rain as the van juddered past, both driver and passenger staring out of the side windows. Miles gazed at the words MURPHY'S MEAT & POULTRY written on the side of the van.

"That's them," he said. "There was that van and a Cortina."

Collins levelled the pistol and followed the slow progress of the van. He did not shoot, and Miles started breathing again when the vehicle had disappeared from view and the pistol was lowered again and replaced inside the shirt.

"We'd better wait here a few minutes," said Collins. He lay back and studied Miles. "You're genuine enough," he said at last. "I knew it when I watched you sleeping back there. I thought to myself, No plant would ever be able to sleep at a time like that."

"Your friend . . ." Miles began, trying to apologise or explain.

"We all know the risks," said Collins. "He knew them better than some." He pulled at a piece of grass and began to chew on it.

"Do I just call you Collins?" asked Miles eventually.

"My name's Will, but yes, you just call me Collins."

Miles wondered at that; Will, short for William presumably. It did not seem a likely name for a Catholic, not from what little Miles knew of the Boyne and King William of Orange.

"I'll tell you what we're going to do," said Collins, spitting out the grass. "We're going to make for a farm I know, where we'll be relatively safe. We'll stay there for a while until these bastards have to call off the search. Then"—he patted his shirt—"I'll decide what to do about you. Meantime you can tell me about yourself as we go. Maybe that'll help me to make up my mind."

"That sounds reasonable," Miles said, wondering whether or not he had meant it to sound ironic. Irony would not be in his best interests here. He had to keep everything straightforward, since this world into which he had plunged seemed to him about as straightforward as Hampton Court maze. He had already decided one thing: if he could get his hands on Collins's gun, then he would take the risk. The thought made him tingle, as though he had been bitten by a radioactive spider. Despite himself, Miles Flint broke into a huge, early morning smile.

The farmhouse was an old two-storey building, galloping towards dilapidation. The door was not locked, and inside Collins motioned Miles to sit down and remain silent, while he went upstairs as quietly as was possible. The stairs were a perfect burglar alarm, creaking ponderously with every footstep. The upstairs landing, too, joined in the fun, identifying for Miles the progress Collins was making.

The room in which Miles sat was part kitchen, part lounge. He sat at a heavy wooden table, upon which lay a loaf of uncut bread and a huge pat of butter. There was a wood-burning stove in one corner, with a teapot of truly Brobdingnagian proportions sitting on it. Sheila had always wanted a wood-burning stove. All Miles wanted was a cup of hot, sweet tea and a slice or two of buttered bread.

He knew that he could make a run for it, could take off across the gritty farmyard in his second escape of the day, but Collins was counting on his tiredness, hunger, thirst, and the fact that this place provided shelter from those who might still be searching for him.

Collins was a shrewd man. Miles bided his time, making himself comfortable on the long wooden bench.

A few minutes later, with accompanying squeals of tortured wood, Collins reappeared from upstairs. He stared at Miles, then smiled; Yes, you've stayed put, just as I knew you would. He went to the stove, opened it, and dropped a fire lighter into it. This he lit with a match, then crammed small, neat peat briquettes into the iron interior. A blaze started almost immediately, and Collins closed the door with a satisfied chuckle. He warmed his limbs, motioning for Miles to join him, then filled the old kettle with water and set it on the heat.

"No time at all," he said quietly, while Miles rubbed his hands and felt the life still in them, the tingle he had felt in that damp field.

"Nobody'll bother us for a while," said Collins. He cut thick slices of bread and spread butter over them. Miles, busy with the kettle, accepted one and bit into it. The kettle had boiled, and above the sink was an old tin tea caddy. He washed out the huge teapot, then opened the caddy. Inside, wrapped in clear polythene, was a small handgun. Miles looked quickly to Collins, who was busily slicing more bread, then pulled the gun out and slipped it into his pocket. Its weight there felt comforting. Silently, he replaced the caddy and tried another tin box. This contained loose tea and a rusted scoop. Collins still had not looked at him. Miles filled the teapot with hot water, threw in a handful of leaves, and touched his trouser pocket to check that he had not been hallucinating.

"Here we go," he said, pouring the tea out into tin mugs. He was trying to forget about the gun, for he knew that Collins would spot any change in his attitude or even his tone of voice. He did not have a gun, he did not have a gun, he was still at the absolute mercy of Collins.

But he *did* have a gun. The question now was, would he use it?

"Have you decided yet?" asked Collins, wolfing down the last of the bread. They had eaten the entire loaf and were on to a second pot of tea.

"Decided what?"

"Decided why your friends should want you dead."

"I've got a few ideas, too many ideas in fact." Miles sipped at his tea. "A colleague of mine tried to warn me before I came out here, I think, but he was vague. He wouldn't say much."

"Some friend," said Collins.

"I didn't say friend. I said colleague."

"What's the difference?"

Miles shrugged.

"Anyway," he said, "what about you?"

"What about me?"

"Well, I take it you *are* a terrorist, an enemy of the British state?"

"I'm not a Sunday school teacher," said Collins, smiling, "but I'm no terrorist. I'm a freedom fighter."

"That's just the same thing viewed from a different angle."

"Robin Hood was a freedom fighter. Would you call him a terrorist?"

"Robin Hood may not have been such a hero after all. Historical research tells us—"

Collins hooted.

"Would you listen to him?" he said, raising his eyes to the ceiling as though consulting some friend up there. " 'Historical bloody research.'

Aye, Mr. Flint or Scott or whatever, history's a funny thing though, isn't it? I mean, look at what history's done to Ireland, and look at how successive British Parliaments since God knows when have twisted the real situation here into a pack of lies for their own use. *That's* all the history I need to know, and a right biased bastard it is. Shall I give you a history lesson, Mr. Flint? No, perhaps not. Instead, you can tell me, what do you know about the situation here, about the roots of the trouble?"

Miles shrugged his shoulders, feeling suddenly tired.

"Not much," he said, "I confess that."

"Just what you read in your newspapers and see on TV, am I right?"

"That's about it."

"But you see, it goes back a lot further than that, a whole lot further. It goes back nearly five hundred years. Ireland was Catholic, you see, just when it shouldn't have been. That was its only mistake. And the people wouldn't change their religion, so Protestants had to be brought in instead, and they were given the land which had belonged by right to the Catholics."

"Yes, plantation, they called it, didn't they?"

"Plantation is right. The English turned our princes into slum landlords, and that's been the way of it ever since." Collins stretched. "Ach, what's the point?" He pointed to a door at the foot of the stairs. "There's a spare room through there. We'll get some sleep, then see what's to be done."

"Where are we exactly?"

"County Monaghan," said Collins. "That's all you need to know. Better for you if you *don't* know. OK?"

Patting his shirt again, he rose from the table. Miles resisted the temptation to pat his pocket in reply.

There was a small bed with a horsehair mattress, and a large armchair in the room, and no space for anything else. The place smelt damp, musty with disuse. But Collins found a two-bar electric fire and plugged it in, sparks flying as the layer of dust which lay upon it ignited. Soon, however, it had heated the room. Collins chose to sleep in the chair, so that he could keep an eye on his "prisoner," as he put it. He pulled one of several thick quilts from the bed and wrapped it around himself, then manoeuvred his way out of his clothes, which he threw in front of the fire, telling Miles to do likewise. The bed was chilled, but Miles soon warmed up. He would have given everything for a hot bath and a shave, followed by a change of clothes, but contented himself for the moment. He had slipped the gun under his pillow before throwing the trousers over toward Collins, who had patted the pockets conspicuously.

What if it were discovered that the gun was missing from its caddy? Well, he had nothing to lose in any case. He felt woozy and welcomed sleep, but Collins seemed to have wound himself up by talking of Ireland,

and he continued his monologue, snatches of which Miles heard, becoming distorted and echoic as he fell toward darkness and release.

When he awoke, the sun was shining. His watch said ten, which meant that he had slept for only three hours, yet he felt utterly refreshed and wide awake. He felt for the gun and stroked it, then looked across to where Collins had pulled the quilt right up over his head and was breathing with the deep regularity of sleep. Miles slipped out of bed, leaving the gun under the pillow, and picked up his clothes from in front of the fire, which was still burning. His clothes were dry, except for a patch of damp here and there. The faint odours of sweat and dried urine were not inviting, but he dressed anyway, leaving off his shoes. Collins's breathing was becoming rather too deep, and he might wake himself with a snore soon. Quickly, Miles returned to the bed and slid the gun into his pocket, wrapped still in its polythene packet.

What now? He could disarm Collins, or he could make his escape. He had heard no sounds from the kitchen or from upstairs. The farm seemed utterly deserted: no hens clucking in the yard, no dog, no tractors or Land Rovers, no clanking of machinery at all. This was the *Marie Celeste* of agriculture: the bread and butter lying out, the kitchen still warm from the previous evening, the door unlocked. It all seemed to him—for the first time—very strange, and he wondered why he had not mentioned this to Collins, who now snorted once, turned beneath the quilt, and began to breathe more regularly again.

Miles, stepping over the pile of clothes, the outstretched legs, the shoes, managed to pull open the door without a sound, watching the figure in the chair as he did so. He entered the short hallway and tiptoed into the kitchen, closing that door behind him. So far so good.

Then he caught sight of the girl at the kitchen table and felt his chest tighten into a clenched fist. But the girl stared at him as though it were the most natural thing in the world for a stocking-soled stranger to appear before her. She was eating bread and jam, and, sure enough, Miles could smell the unmistakable aroma of newly baked bread, half a loaf of which sat on the table alongside a new wedge of butter. The girl turned her sleepy gaze back towards the table. She was nine or ten, her eyes and hair dark, her face thin and sharp. Miles could think of nothing to say, so he decided to ignore her. He started to walk towards the kitchen door, deciding at that moment, shoes or no, to leave, but he kept his eyes on the girl in case she should set up a hue and cry.

Finally he decided to make a sign to her that she should remain quiet, and that was what he was doing when the door pushed itself open and Will Collins came in from the yard, clean clothes on his back and black wellington boots on his feet.

"No need for that, Mr. Flint," he said casually. "Marie's dumb, can't utter a sound. She won't give you any trouble."

"Who the hell is that in the room?" gasped Miles.

"Oh, that's Champ. He lives here. Has he fallen asleep by any chance? I take it that's why you're out here. And about to leave us by the look of it. Well, go ahead."

Collins made a sweeping gesture with his arm, holding the door ajar for Miles.

"Go on," he said. "Though I should warn you that your friends are still in the neighbourhood. They won't be for long. I've just telephoned the local Gardai with an anonymous tip-off that they're here and have broken the immigration laws in the process. They'll be chased off in a hurry, I should think, but if you want to take your chance just now, be my guest."

Collins was smiling like a schoolboy: he'd gained the upper hand again and was delighted with himself. Miles walked back to the table and sat down across from the girl. He smiled at her, and she smiled back.

"Suit yourself," Collins said, closing the door with a slam which eventually brought the man called Champ staggering into the room.

"He's made off, Will!" he shouted, before seeing Miles seated quite peaceably at the table. "Oh, Jesus, mister, what a fright you near gave me."

Laughing, Collins went to the stove to pour out more tea.

In the rich, primitive warmth of the kitchen they smoked cigarettes and played gin rummy. Miles took long puffs of those cigarettes which he won, though he had not smoked for years. As an undergraduate, he had affected a liking for Gauloises so as to appear bohemian. Now he smoked to blend in with Collins and Champ. It was an old and trusted psychological ploy— become like your captors. It made their minds easier to read and also made it more difficult for them to justify murdering you. So he smoked, not heavily or with any conspicuous show, just enough. And, playing cards, he made sure that he lost as often as he won, even if it meant cheating against himself.

More often than not they used candles instead of the low-wattage electric lighting. This made the room more intimate still, so that everyone felt very comfortable in the presence of everyone else. Just the desired effect. Miles was practising on Champ now, trying to ingratiate himself. Champ was a simple man, but not simple-minded. He had told Miles that working the land gave a man time to think, lots of time, and offered also the opportunity for a kind of communion with natural justice, so that the man-made farce called "justice" came to seem utterly ridiculous.

The farm, however, was no longer a working concern. Most of the fields had been sold to a property developer in Dublin, who would let it moulder until the time was right for building or selling. Miles reckoned that Champ was fifty, though he might be a bit younger or a bit older. The land did that: it made the young old before their time, and the old seem eternally young.

During the days Collins wandered through the fields and around the farm, keeping himself to himself. He had agreed to allow Miles an amount of freedom, and so Miles, too, walked the farm, inspecting the carcasses of rusting cars and antiquated machinery, watching the wooden planks of the cowshed crumble to dust beneath his palm, rotten with woodworm. Everything here had run down in accordance with the rules laid down by nature itself. Soon the rusting scrap would be covered by earth and grass, wild seedlings of oats and barley, bright flowers.

In the warmth of the kitchen, kitted out in some of Champ's old work clothes, Miles thought of London. What would Sheila be thinking? He wondered, too, about the traitor, the smiling Arab, the whole game. He had swallowed a great draught of fear, and it had destroyed a tiny, important part of him. There remained a maddening need to know the truth, even if the reward for knowing that truth was received point blank and without mercy.

But he would never discover the truth unless he could escape from the farm. He needed Collins's help, needed to persuade him to arrange passage to London, and that, finally, meant telling him everything.

CHAPTER 21

"We're going to Drogheda."

"Who's Drogheda?"

"It's not a who, it's a where. Champ's gone to pick up a car for us. Can you drive?"

"Yes."

Miles wondered, Is this it, a drive into the country, down a lane, into some woodland, and then the gun at the base of the neck? Dying, somewhere in Ireland, a lowly statistic which might never even come to light.

"About Champ . . ." Miles began, curious and trying to calm himself.

"What about him?"

"Is he your . . . father?"

Collins roared with laughter.

"Of course not. Jesus, I wonder if I should take that as an insult?"

"I shouldn't if I were you. He's a very clever man, and a very sane one. What about Marie?"

"Oh, Marie's his daughter right enough."

"And his wife?" They were in the yard immediately outside the kitchen door. Collins seemed to be scanning the horizon for some kind of prey.

"She ran out on him when the farm started to collapse. She's always been a survivor."

Miles nodded slowly. Collins was still shaking his head and grinning.

"Me the son of Champ," he said. "Jesus, I'm not even a Catholic."

There was smoke in the distance. But the chaff had already been burnt, hadn't it? Collins had seen it, too, puffing into the air, growing ever nearer as though carried on the wind, though there was no wind.

"Collins—"

"It's Champ!" Collins was already reaching into his waistband, producing the handgun which Miles had not seen since the night of their escape. Looking up the winding farm road, Miles saw Champ's car veer sharply and take the last hundred yards or so of track as though heading towards a finishing line. The car, dust enveloping it, slid to a halt in front of them. Dust, thought Miles, that's what it is, not smoke.

"What's the hurry, Champ?" shouted Collins, his eyes still fixed on the track.

"Being followed!" Champ bellowed back at him, lurching out of the car. "Get in!"

Miles had no choice. Collins pushed him into the driver's seat, then ran around to the passenger side, hauling himself in. There was blood on the steering wheel.

"Champ's hurt," said Miles.

"Never mind Champ. He's indestructible. Get us out of here."

"Same way we came?"

"No, round the side of the barn. There's an old track there through the fields."

"That's never wide enough—"

The barrel of the gun stuck its cold, probing tongue into Miles's neck.

"Drive," said Collins.

Taking the car in its circuit around the farmhouse, Miles had time to glimpse the other car heading down the main track towards the farm. Oh, he'd recognise that car in his dreams, in his waking nightmares, and he had no doubt that Six and One would be in front, the one driving, the other angling his gun out of the window.

He drove.

Champ had gone into the farmhouse. It struck Miles that he would be reaching into the old tea caddy, searching for his own weapon, the weapon with which to protect Marie and himself. Oh, God . . .

"Just drive!"

He had pulled the car out of one rutted ditch, foot hard down on the accelerator, and now pushed it through the tortured track, no more than a walkway, while the fields complained all around him and the motor whined its plea for a third gear change.

"It's them!" he shouted.

"Well, I didn't think it was Christian Aid," Collins called back as the first hollow bang told them both that bullets were angling towards them.

The fields, once pockets of green, now seemed huge and barren. Miles knew that one slip would plunge the car into another, larger ditch. He had to keep his hands steady, steady despite the smear of blood on the steering wheel, despite the sweat pouring down his face.

Collins slid into the back seat and smashed the window with the butt of his gun. Another whine, as of a blacksmith's hammer, came and went, and Miles was still alive. There was the terrible sound of sudden thunder as Collins tried his luck. As his ears cleared, Miles risked a glance in the rearview mirror. The car behind had slowed.

"They don't like that!" Collins shouted.

Then Miles found the ditch.

The car plunged in, its back wheels leaving the ground and remaining suspended. Collins was screaming at him.

"I need your weight on the boot," Miles said, feeling a sudden calm, the tranquillity of the doomed. The other car stopped abruptly, as Collins scrambled out of the back window frame and landed on the large boot, still firing off bullets like a man possessed. Miles was no racing driver, no stock-car expert. This was instinct, nothing more. He put the car into reverse, waited until Collins had hammered the back wheels onto the dry clay soil, and let the engine go with everything it had. The unrestrained clamour of machinery filled the air, and the car jolted back, climbing onto the road again, sending Collins tumbling into the back seat, where he whooped and sent a shot through the roof of the car.

Nothing to lose, thought Miles. In fact it's inspired. He kept his foot down hard on the accelerator, yelling to Collins to watch out, and sent the car screaming back into the Cortina, where it crumpled the bonnet. Collins, ready, sent four or five shots into the intact windscreen from a range of three feet, while Miles found first gear and prayed that their own car had not been damaged in the collision.

They flew, while the wrecked Cortina let off steam, no bodies apparent in its interior. The windscreen was still intact.

Reinforced glass. Very. He'd seen it before. The thing was a veritable tank.

None of which worried Collins, who gave several more victory whoops as he climbed back into the passenger seat.

"We showed them," he said. "We showed the bastards where to get off."

But Miles doubted that.

"What exactly," said Miles, "did you mean back there?"

The fields had opened into a lane, and the lane had opened into a two-lane highway. Miles, getting to know the car's whims, had relaxed a little but still felt queasy.

"When?" Collins was reloading, picking bullets out of his pockets and pushing them into the ammunition clip. Cordite was all around.

"When you said you're not a Catholic."

"Neither I am."

"Then why do you fight on their side?"

"Jesus, you can ask that? When you just saw what the other side looks like?"

The car coughed, reminding Miles that it was old and rusty, as unused to any of this as he was. It was the kind of car you would steal only if contemplating a one-way trip.

"I've heard," said Miles, "that even the Eire government isn't in favour of the IRA or their methods."

"You're not seeing, are you? You're still blind. Those men back there have been hunting us for days, they're madmen. And they're the supposed security force. Now do you see? Your government's put this country into the hands of the insane, and then gone and torn up the rules to boot."

"It doesn't explain how you come to be in the IRA."

"Turn left here." Collins slipped the gun back into his pocket and rested his feet on the dashboard. "When I was a teenager there was a big recruitment drive for the UDA and UVF. They were coming out of the woodwork like rot. I joined. Once you joined, though, it was hard to get out. I'd killed a man before I was twenty, Mr. Flint. I was a good soldier." He turned to gauge Miles's reaction. His teeth were bared, and the words came out like slashes from a bright blade. "I took my orders and I did what I was told to. For thirteen bloody years, working for men like those ones we just left."

"So what happened?"

"You wouldn't believe it. You'd laugh."

"Try me."

"I don't see why I should."

"Because of what happened back there? Because you need to?"

"Maybe."

"So what happened?"

"What happened?" mimicked Collins. "I found myself crying for Bobby Sands, that's what happened."

They needed petrol and decided to eat at a transport café behind the pumps. Miles's senses were sharp now, and he examined the lunchtime customers for gun-toting executioners, while Will Collins wolfed down fried potato farl and eggs.

"I've got something to tell you too, Will," he said.

"Oh?"

"But I'm not sure yet where to begin. Meantime, what about your story?"

Collins patted his shirt, signifying this time that he had eaten well. He lifted the mug of tea to his lips, still chewing, and studied Miles over the discoloured ceramic rim.

"Where was I?"

"Crying over Bobby Sands."

"Oh yes." Collins turned his gaze to the greasy windows and the asphalt gathering of elderly trucks and cars beyond. "Well, I'd seen some things, maybe too much for my age, but I'd seen nothing like that hunger strike. So I decided to see how it would feel to go hungry. I locked myself in my room for a couple of days, survived on nothing but sips of water and my own company. I near went crazy, but it set me to thinking that to starve yourself slowly to death you'd have to be clinging to something worth dying for. Do you see? Dying with a gun was one thing, quick, a hero's way to go, but a lonely starvation, well, that needed something *more.*" He paused to light two cigarettes, handing one to Miles. "There were two of them died that year on hunger strike, and each death made me feel worse. It was as if *I* was the one starving them."

"So you switched allegiances?"

"It wasn't as easy as that, so don't think it was. I had to leave my family and friends behind, knowing I could never go home, knowing they'd be after my blood. And there was no telling what the other side would do to me anyway. I mean, would they believe me, or would they just shoot me dead? I was walking blindfold into it."

Miles thought that he could see now why Will Collins had been so gentle with him, so willing to believe: his existence, too, depended upon belief.

"But they did believe you?"

"I'm not sure. I work hard and well for the cause, but there's still a suspicion there, always the thought that if I can turn once I can turn again."

Collins was staring out of the window again, towards where their car sat.

"At any rate," said Miles, "you're still alive."

"Alive and kicking, no thanks to your friends. You know what I can't understand? Why plan such a big operation to net a very small fish?"

Why indeed. Miles had been thinking the very same thing.

"And there's something else bothering me."

"What's that?"

Collins nodded towards the window.

"What does it say on that van just behind our car?"

Miles looked. He had to screw up his eyes to find a focus, but the writing was clear enough: MURPHY'S MEAT & POULTRY.

"Christ, they've found us," he hissed, turning back to Will Collins, but Collins was out of his seat and heading jauntily towards the toilets, leaving Miles on his own. He panicked: follow Collins or head out of the door? He chose the door, and stood beside it for several seconds, staring out at the van. There were two faces behind its windscreen, but he did not recognise them, and they seemed not to recognise him. At least, their eyes glanced towards him and away again, intent on the car, the car with Champ's blood on it.

"Let's go."

It was Collins, moving past him and out of the door.

"Just follow me and try to look casual."

They were crossing the asphalt, passing right in front of the van and behind the crumpled boot of their car. Miles thought that Collins was about to stop there, but he merely paused while Miles caught up, then put his arm around his shoulders.

"—and then he says to me, "Mickey," he says—" Collins began loudly, going on to tell some garbled anecdote, all the while gently propelling Miles towards the far corner of the car park. He stopped beside a Land Rover. "Here we are now." And then, to Miles's astonishment, he produced a key from his pocket and opened the driver's door. "Get in," he whispered, walking around to the passenger side. Miles got in.

"How the hell did you—"

"An old boy having a pee back there. I just tapped him on the head and took his keys. Before that he'd been telling me about what a fine Jeep he had. Thank Christ there was only this one parked here. Our lucky day, Miles, is it not? Thanks be to sweet mother Mary."

Miles was grinning like a monkey as he turned the ignition and drove sedately back past the butcher's van and out of the lot. Collins rested his feet on the dashboard again.

"Just follow the signs for Drogheda," he said. "Now, what was it you were going to tell me?"

"You mean apart from telling you you're a genius?"

"Well, that'll do for a start. Would it have been anything to do with our friends who seem so keen to see us again?"

"In a way, yes."

"No subtlety, these people. That's their problem."

"But they were right, weren't they? I mean, you were supplying parts for bombs?"

"Oh yes, but they could have cut our supplies at source. They must have known where the stuff was coming from. And they'd known about the factory for nearly a year to my knowledge."

"What have you been doing recently?"

The question smacked too much of interrogation, and Collins gave him a hard look.

"Sorry," said Miles. "I shouldn't have asked."

"Let's see . . ." Collins checked his watch. "It's half past three. Well, I suppose I can tell you now, since it was due to go off at quarter past."

"What was?"

"Our biggest job yet, a nice big bomb due to explode at three-fifteen in Kew Gardens, just as the Home Secretary was planting a tree for some new trust or whatever."

"Jesus Christ," muttered Miles, and then it hit him: *that was why they had needed a gardener!* Harvest had borne its bitter fruit all right, but the final clue had eluded them. They needed to plant the bomb. They needed a park keeper. "I was part of that surveillance."

"What?"

"Watching the cell in London, the cell responsible. We were called off a week ago. A woman and three men, one of the men a park keeper."

"Somebody slipped up then," said Collins.

"More death." Miles wiped at his forehead, then stared at his hand, seeing the dull stain of Champ's blood still upon it. His back hurt and he felt a little dizzy. In fact he was tingling all over. The road was rising and falling, and his stomach heaved like a sea squall. "So much needless death," he said. "Why?"

"I don't know, Mr. Flint," answered Collins. "As time goes on I find it harder to explain. To myself as well as to others." His voice had become very quiet. "To myself especially. I've seen it from both sides. And do you want to know something? They're both the same."

Miles nodded. He knew that now too.

"Can we stop for a breather?" he asked, already slowing the Land Rover, signalling left, ready to explode into the fresh air.

"They could be onto us at any moment," warned Collins.

"Yes, I know, but we have to talk. There's nothing else for it."

Somehow, it was easier after that. They sat on a five-barred gate at the side of the road, facing in towards the fields, the Land Rover behind them on the verge, and the traffic roaring past beyond it.

Miles knew where to begin now, right at the beginning, smiling Cheshire cats and all. His initial fears, the disappearance of Phillips and the warning of Sinclair, and Billy's warning too. But he was surprised by the immediate interest of Collins, by the way he frowned, his face a mask of concentration.

And when he had finished, Collins jumped down from the gate into the field and began to walk away from him. He seemed, to Miles, to walk the length of the field, a good hundred yards. It was the furthest they had been apart since they had met. What was more, the car key had been left in the ignition. He could make his escape! He would not be caught; he could be away before Collins, running full pelt, was halfway back up the field.

But he didn't; he sat there and watched Collins walking back towards him. His eyes were bright, and there was a wry smile on his lips, as if to say, I knew you would not go.

He heaved himself back onto the gate, which rattled ominously but held firm.

"So that's it," he said quietly.

"It's as much as I know," said Miles, while another lorry clattered past, pouring out rich, choking fumes.

"Maybe," said Collins, "you know more than you think."

"What do you mean?"

"Well, since we're in a mood for stories, how would you like to hear another one?"

Miles nodded, watching while Collins lit another two cigarettes, then jumped down from the gate again, leaning against it while he watched the traffic.

"It makes me nervous, all this traffic. Everything moving so fast, while I'm standing still. We're targets."

He stared intently at the traffic, using up the burning tobacco as though it were oxygen and he a drowning man.

"I did a job once, rather a strange one, when I was very young. An assassination, you could call it, no questions asked. I'd been told that this man was a spy, something like that, and that he was dangerous to us. My job was to get to know him, then eliminate him. But then I found out that it wasn't quite as straightforward as I'd thought."

How straightforward is the murder of a stranger? Miles wanted to ask.

"Go on," he said instead.

"Oh, the man was a spy all right, just like you, Mr. Flint. But he wasn't any danger to us. No, there was payment involved. A hundred rifles, as I recall. I'd been used as a hired assassin. There was nothing political in it, nothing to do with the cause, just plain payment of some guns in exchange for my services. I couldn't do anything about it, of course. That would have been dangerous. So I played it by the book, their book, and I looked for a way to burn the pages. But I found a martyr instead." He rested for a moment, stubbing out the cigarette and lighting another. "The weapon I used, and the rifles, were delivered by an Israeli gentleman."

Miles felt his fingers go limp, the cigarette threatening to fall to the ground.

"Coincidence?" he said.

"Maybe. But you say that this Israeli who died in London was a gunrunner?"

"A suspected gunrunner, yes."

Collins nodded.

"A couple of years ago," he said, "an old friend, still active in the north, sent me a message. It was brave of him. If he'd been caught, Christ knows what would have happened. He told me that there was a man asking questions about me. A funny guy, my friend said, spoke like an Englishman but carried an American passport."

"Did he have a name?" asked Miles, thinking of Richard Mowbray, his heart beating wildly.

"Yes, Gray. Andy Gray. I remember because it's the name of a foot-baller, too."

"Andy Gray," Miles repeated, thinking hard. But he was thinking through great wads of cotton, his head like a dispensary. The name meant something to him. Andy Gray, yes, a footballer. Andrew Gray. An ana-gram of Mowbray? No, not even close.

Then he remembered: Billy Monmouth's friend.

I've been in France. A company-funded shopping trip.

Billy hadn't mentioned that he was American, though. What was it Richard Mowbray suspected? That there might be CIA moles within the firm. Billy Monmouth and his American friend. The "company" being slang for the CIA itself. Well, well, well. Was it all coming together at last? Or was it exploding into too many fragments, like Kew Gardens this last half hour?

"Does the name mean anything to you?"

"I'm not sure," said Miles, "not yet." Here perhaps was the trump card which would save his life: Collins was curious, and Miles held all the answers.

"What about the assassination?" he asked now. "Did you learn the victim's name?"

"Yes," replied Collins, staring into a distance of his own, "and I'll never forget it. His name was Philip Hayton."

"Philip Hayton?"

"Did you know him?"

"I know of him, yes." And Billy had brought him into the conversation only a few weeks before. There was no coincidence.

"Did he have a family? A wife and kids?"

"No, I'm sure he didn't," said Miles generously, unsure of the facts.

Collins nodded. He seemed almost soporific now, while Miles's thoughts were moving faster and faster, trying to identify the terrain through which they travelled. Billy. Andrew Gray. The Israeli. And now Philip Hayton. Where was the connection?

There had to be one. There *had* to be.

"What happened to this Gray?"

Collins shrugged, as though trying to heave a great weight from his back.

"He asked around, flashed around quite a bit of money, according to my friend, but what could anyone tell him? I was a traitor as far as they were concerned in Belfast, and no one wants to advertise their traitors, do they? Not unless they're dead. I'd have thought *you'd* know about that."

"I'm not a traitor."

"Then why the hell are they after you?"

"It's not me they're after, it's *us*. I couldn't see it until now, but the Israeli is the connection. He's the lowest common denominator. What's more, I know where we can find out more about this man Gray."

"Where?"

"From a friend of mine."

Collins gave him a steady look, his next question a formality.

"I don't suppose this friend lives in London by any chance?"

"Yes, he does."

Collins shook his head.

"No way," he said. "There's no way on God's earth that I'm going to let you go to London."

"Then come with me."

"It would be suicide."

"And if you stay here? Do you think they'll stop coming at you?"

"There's a chance."

"Sure there's a chance. A chance that you'll be blindfolded and shot in some field, dropped into the sea like so much dead meat." Collins shivered, and Miles knew that he had hit another nerve. Of course: Hayton had been dumped at sea. It had been called a sailing accident, hadn't it? A sailing accident with a great big bullet hole in the victim's skull. The firm had covered that one up nicely, but why?

"A chance," Miles continued, licking his parched lips, "that you'll die without ever knowing why. At least if we go to London we might find out what it's all about."

He jumped off the gate, hoping it wasn't too dramatic a gesture, and began to walk down the field, just as Collins had done. Will Collins was not a stupid man, and Miles was sure that, finally, he would agree to go. There was just the one problem now.

Would they reach Billy Monmouth alive?

Collins was lighting another cigarette from the butt of the old, and Miles, approaching, was about to say something about chain smokers dying before they were forty. But he thought better of it when he saw the pistol in Collins's hand.

"No," Collins said, "no, we're not going to England, Mr. Flint. We're going to Drogheda where I can be rid of you once and for all."

CHAPTER 22

"It's on the coast then, this Drogheda?"

Collins nodded. He had been silent throughout the rest of the drive and had given Miles a cold look whenever he attempted to start up a conversation. So, Drogheda was on the coast. The coast meant boats, and boats meant quick and invisible trips across the Irish Sea. Perhaps things were working themselves into a pattern much more to his advantage than anything he could have planned.

"Drogheda," said Collins at last, as they turned into the town. Miles imagined himself as Perseus, entering the stony land of the Gorgons, but it was no use. The last thing he felt was heroic.

"It was near here I killed Hayton. We went out to sea, and I shot him."

"Very neat," said Miles.

"Not really. Have you ever killed anyone, Mr. Flint? Neatness doesn't enter into it. There's blood everywhere. It finds you and sticks to you. I kept finding flecks of it on me for days afterward."

"And no questions were ever asked about Hayton's disappearance?"

Collins shrugged.

"I don't know. I don't think so. I went back to Belfast and tried to forget all about it."

"Until you found out you'd been tricked."

"You know, I'll be glad to be rid of you, Flint. You sound like a conscience, but your eyes are full of tricks."

Miles tried to smile. "I'm parched," he said. "Can we get something to drink soon?"

Collins pondered this. Yes, they had not had anything to drink for a long while, and there had been much talking since then. Miles watched as Collins was forced by the workings of his own mind into a remembrance of their joint confessions.

"Yes," he conceded finally, "let's find a pub."

While Miles finished his whisky, Collins made a telephone call, watching him intently from the wall-mounted pay phone. Miles smoked, feeling a taste in his lungs as though he had smoked twenty a day since childhood. He studied the bar, wondering what the chances were of a sudden, dashed escape. Will Collins's stare told him that they were nil; his mind had been read. Collins was no fool. He knew that the nearer a man walked towards execution the stronger became the life force, the desire to struggle and kick.

The bar's conveniences lay somewhere outside at the back of the building. A straggle of men wandered in and out of a great oak door which bore the legend CAR PARK AND GENTS. The Land Rover was not parked out there, however. It lay some hundreds of yards away outside a fish and chip shop which had been opening for the evening as they arrived. Collins had eaten a bag of chips, but Miles had not felt hungry. The whisky, however, was beginning to bite at his empty stomach, the fumes as heavy as smoke within him. He examined his empty glass philosophically, motioned to Collins that he was having another, and approached the bar. Collins indicated that he did not want another drink. His half pint of stout sat on top of the telephone, a few sips missing from the top. He had not

spoken into the receiver for some time, and this was his second call. Perhaps there was no judge and jury to be found at this time of the evening.

"Another Jameson's, please," said Miles, and the barman, nodding, sullen, went off towards the row of gleaming optics, while the few regulars,
looking comfortable in their regular seats, stared into space, resolutely
ignoring the Englishman and his English accent. An old and well-worn
Rolling Stones record was playing on the jukebox, the sound so muted that
it might as well not have been playing at all. Miles sneezed three times and
blew his nose, wishing of a sudden that he could announce his Scottish-
ness. I'm not English, he would tell them, I'm not to blame. To which they
would, he knew, have replied that the worst of the Protestant incomers
had been Scots. So he kept quiet, paying for the drink with the money
given to him by Collins. He had not had the chance to change any of his
own money, and he wondered, in a mad second, whether he could claim
expenses from the firm for this part of his assignment.

"Mr. Scott!"

Turning sharply, he found Millicent Nightingale beaming at him, her
handbag clutched to her prodigious bosom. Behind her, three more members of the tour party were glancing around them, having just entered the
bar.

"Mrs. Nightingale!"

"Millicent, silly. Call me Millicent."

"Millicent, how good to see you again." Looking across to where Collins stood, the receiver limp at his ear, eyes wild, Miles knew that the
moment had come to a crisis. "Did you get my note?"

"Your note, Mr. Scott?"

"Yes, saying that I'd had to dash south on urgent business. Don't say
they didn't give it to you at the hotel?"

"But, Mr. Scott, the guide told us that you'd been taken ill."

"Really? How strange."

"Anyway, you're here now. Are you going to join us for the rest of the
trip?"

"Why, yes, Millicent, I might just do that."

Collins had slammed down the receiver and was approaching. Miles
decided to take the initiative. The whisky had given him a poise which he
hoped would outlast the situation.

"Millicent, this is Mr. Collins. Will, I'd like you to meet a friend of
mine, Millicent Nightingale."

"Pleased to meet you, Mrs. Nightingale." Collins made a pretence of
checking his watch. "Eh, we'd better be going, hadn't we?"

"Nonsense," screeched Mrs. Nightingale, "not now that I've caught up
with you at last, Mr. Scott. We must have one drink at least. The trip has
been *so* exciting. There's lots to tell you. We're going to the cathedral

tomorrow to see the head of the Blessed Oliver Plunkett. And besides, how can you leave when you haven't even started your drink?"

Miles, smiling broadly, jiggled his glass of whisky in Will Collins's face as proof of this final remark. Drinks were being bought by the other members of the party, and Miles professed the need of another Jameson's. It was then, seeing the look of complete and utter panic on Collins's face, that Miles felt sure for the very first time that he would return home safely. It was a nice feeling, and he drank it in. Collins's eyes might be as cold as the contents of an ice bucket, but nothing could scare Miles anymore, not even the obvious patting of a jacket pocket. He felt sure that everything was preordained, and therefore it made no sense to dither. He would get home safely; that was the main thing. How he went about it was, really, of little consequence and worth little preparation. He knocked back the whisky in one satisfied gulp.

"Just nipping out to the little boys' room. Won't be a moment." He smiled at Mrs. Nightingale, then at Collins, and headed toward the oak door.

Before he was halfway outside Will Collins was behind him.

"People will start to talk," Miles whispered, beginning to chuckle. He continued to chuckle on the short walk across the gravel-strewn yard.

"What the hell was all that back there?" hissed Collins. "And none of your tricks this time."

"That," said Miles, his mouth slack, "was the divine, the enchanting Mrs. Millicent Nightingale, executive officer in Her Majesty's Inland Revenue, holidaying in this fair country. I met her in Belfast. I'd come across here, you see, in the guise of a holiday maker. Quite the most ridiculous and obvious cover imaginable. My name was Walter Scott. You know, the novelist, *Waverley* and all that."

"You've had too much to drink," said Collins.

They had reached the toilet, a ramshackle affair with an ancient, soured urinal and a dark, festering object in one corner which might once have been a washbasin. Miles relieved himself noisily, smelling his whisky breath in the chilled air. Collins stood in the doorway, arms folded.

"Not having any joy contacting your friends?" Miles asked, zipping himself in the half-light.

"Not yet. But they know I'm in town."

"It's a start."

Miles was in the doorway now. He stared at Collins, his eyes a little glassy.

"I know what you're thinking," he said. "You're thinking that it would be nice to shoot me here and now. Then you could relax. But your bosses wouldn't be very happy about that, because they would have wanted to interrogate me first, and they might think it a bit suspicious that you killed me before they'd had the opportunity. They would trust you less than ever, especially after your friend died at the factory and you managed to escape. Besides, what would Mrs. Nightingale say?"

Collins smiled.

"No," he said, "if I was going to kill you, I'd do it out at sea."

"Very good," said Miles, wagging a finger. "A boating accident, as with poor old Philip Hayton. Yes, very professional. Well, shall we go back in?"

He made a sweeping gesture with his arm, and for just long enough Collins was fooled into moving off ahead of him. Miles brought out his own gun and pressed it into Collins's back, pressed it hard so that there could be no mistaking it for a piece of wood or a bluffed finger.

"One move and you're no longer of this earth." It was hissed, snakelike, into the suddenly frozen ear. The breath which had seemed so full of drunken gaiety was filled now with nothing but sober, real threat. Miles grabbed the gun from Collins's pocket and stuffed it into his own. Then he stepped back one pace.

"Turn around slowly," he said, breathing deeply. The sudden implant of adrenalin was threatening to make him really drunk, and he gulped air as though it were water, diluting the alcohol.

Collins's face was a mask. Was there hate there, or surprise, or a touch of relief that the weight had been shifted from him? His arms dangled now as though the life had left them. He was acting like a puppet, trying, thought Miles, quickly to do to me what I've just done to him.

"Well," he said, "maybe you'd have taken me out to sea, Collins, but I've no such finesse. I'll shoot you here and now if you so much as sneeze, so I hope you haven't caught my cold."

"What now?" said Collins. Miles shrugged.

"I'll have to think about that," he lied. "I've got time to think now. A rare luxury on this trip." He took the car keys from his pocket and held them up in front of him. "You'll be doing a bit of the driving from now on. It gives me a sore back."

He dropped the keys at Collins's feet and stepped back.

"Pick them up very slowly indeed." Collins did so. "Now, I would imagine that you know some fishermen in this part of the world?" Collins furrowed his brow, uncomprehending. "We're going to do a little fishing," said Miles. "I wonder what kind of fish we'll find."

As they moved across the car park and out onto the road, Miles could hear Mrs. Nightingale's voice as it cooed to him from the oaken door:

"Mr. Scott? Mr. Scott? Mr. Scott?"

PART FOUR
Homing

CHAPTER 23

The office telephone rang, and since Billy Monmouth was alone, he was forced to answer it for himself.

"Monmouth here."

The receiver clicked and went dead. Billy replaced it with a sigh but left his hand hovering above the desk. The ringing recommenced, and he pounced.

"Monmouth."

"Billy, it's Andrew Gray. Any word on your friend Miles?"

Billy sighed again.

"I was about to ask you the same thing," he said. "No, there's been nothing at this end."

"He's probably alive then?"

"Or probably dead. Who can tell?"

"I bet our mutual friend is shitting himself all the colours of the rainbow."

"I doubt that, Andrew. Our 'friend,' as you put it, is not one to make himself conspicuous. But let's hope *something* happens soon. What about Sizewell?"

"Leave him to me, Billy."

"That's what frightens me, Andrew." And with that he dropped the receiver back into its cradle, which chimed once and once only.

Sheila phoned again from the office, but Colonel Denniston had no news, and Billy had no news. Had her husband disappeared then? she had asked, but both had been cagey in their replies.

"Well, we don't know where he is," said Denniston, "but he may well have gone off on his own for a few days. He completed his work in Belfast before he vanished. You must realise, Mrs. Flint, that Miles has been under rather a strain of late, hasn't he? Too much pressure and all that."

"What are you saying?"

"Merely that he may have felt the need for a break."

"Without telling you? Without telling his own wife?"

"A *complete* break, Mrs. Flint. I have to say that he had been acting a little strangely."

"How strangely?"

"That's not for me to say." Denniston sounded suddenly and irrevocably bored. "Look, I'm sure there's no cause for concern, but we've let the chaps in Belfast know to keep an eye open for him. If there's been no contact or sighting in the next day or so, we'll reconsider the situation, reevaluate it."

"You talk as though he were a row of figures."

"I'm sorry, I didn't quite catch that, Mrs. Flint."

"Nothing, Colonel. Thank you so much. Goodbye."

Colonel Denniston was not stupid. He knew that something was wrong in Ireland. But there were other, more important things on his mind. Another head was due to roll, probably from the very top of the heap. He read again the newspaper report in front of him, its subdued headline— KEW TERRORIST ATTACK KILLS ONE, INJURES SEVEN—serving only to highlight the horror. Londoners were agog. At times like these, he had noticed in the past, a sense of wartime stubbornness overtook the capital. People went about their business, jaws set defiantly against the enemy, and everyone talked to everyone else in bus queues, showing once more that humanity bloomed in adversity.

Heads would roll, for it was already evident that one of those responsible for the bomb was the gardener who had been involved in the Harvest surveillance, and the surveillance, if sustained, must surely have put a halt to this atrocity. Goodbye to the old boy then, and, most probably, hello, Mr. Partridge. Partridge was no friend to Colonel Denniston. There would be hard times ahead, arguments over accountability, the need for a new broom, a clean sweep. All the old clichés of business. It was bound to come out sooner or later that the firm had known about the gardener. Special Branch would blabber, in order to cover their own backs. And who had ordered the surveillance to cease? Mr. Partridge. Perhaps that, if nothing else, would save the watchmen from his wrath. But, of course, they would be in the firing line for everybody else's sticks and stones. Everything would hit them and would stick to them.

Nothing, of course, would stick to Partridge. He was the Teflon man.

Harry Sizewell wanted to make statements from his hospital bed, but the doctors weren't having any of it. The best he could manage was to relay messages to the press outside via his agent, and then watch the television in his room as Giles repeated it all to the waiting cameras at the hospital gates. Not very telegenic, old Giles, too nervous, trying to answer any queries truthfully rather than handing out the stock responses. And those journalists knew it. They asked more and more barbed questions, honing them each time, and Giles looked into the camera as though he were a Peeping Tom at somebody's keyhole. Blast the man. But bless him, too. He had been at Harry's bedside constantly, probably having nowhere else to go. The whole situation was tailor-made for the creating of political capital and public sympathy, but Giles just wasn't up to it. Why not? The man had been involved in politics for years, after all. Ah, but always as an invisible man, always one step behind Harry. He was not meant for limelight and the immediacy of media pressure. Poor man. He was making a balls of the whole thing.

The door of Harry Sizewell's airy room opened silently, and the attractive nurse came in.

"All right, Mr. Sizewell? Got everything you want?"

"Oh, just about, nurse, just about." And he laughed with hearty false humour. *'Yes, he's sitting up and making jokes with the staff,' said one pretty nurse earlier today. He's not the kind of man to let something like this stop him or defeat his principles.*

"Good. Just ring if you need me." And with that she was off, vanishing as briskly and as efficiently as Jimmy Dexter had when the bomb went off. It had been like a vacuum inside Harry Sizewell's head, everything being sucked in toward the centre, more implosion than explosion, and there had been a smattering of warm rain, light, dust, heat. A moment's silence, and then the first scream, male, but piercing, and the recognition of carnage, a shattering of the whole scheme of things.

The Home Secretary was elsewhere, probably in a more private room than this private room, or a more private hospital even. But then his injuries were greater than Sizewell's, if the media were to be believed. Burns, it was said. A team was being flown in from Belfast, best burns specialists in Europe. Well, one could see why. And Jimmy Dexter sprinkled over the turf like so much fertiliser, nourishing the very tree that they had gone there to plant. So there would be a vacant post for someone, and surely he would be the obvious choice from the media point of view.

"And now today's other news . . ."

He pressed the gadget and the television burned out to darkness. Yes, there had been a bout of immediate nausea, followed by a frightening darkness. Dear Lord God, I'm going to die, he had thought, though the notion had seemed quite absurd. In any event, he had wakened to searing white echoes, and then had been given gas, slipping away again, wanting to kick and to shout and, above all, to stay awake. I may never wake up again, you bastards.

MURDERING BASTARDS, the headline had screamed.

Well, of course they were. To pick such an open place, such a public spot. But such a sweet target: how could they have refused the opportunity? There had been security, of course, there always was, but how secure could one be? It was a fact of life that politicians were targets. It was part of the hard-won image. As soon as one gained one's seat there were policemen on one's doorstep, opening car doors, one step ahead and one step behind during every trip. It gave one a sense of power, and Sizewell had always enjoyed it. It was a mark of attention, a badge of his importance in the state.

All the same, intelligence should have caught wind of this one. He knew that he would have to have a few words with his old friend Partridge. But first there was another statement to compose. *I would like to be seen as a symbol perhaps of this country's determination never to give in to . . .*

He thought again of the phone calls and the threats, of the snooping newspaperman. This would settle his hash. Let him try and dig up dirt on me now, thought Sizewell, no one would dare publish it. He lay back contentedly, fingering his singed eyebrows delicately. Partridge would know what to do, he was sure of that.

Partridge was on the hunt, hunting out his superior, who had gone underground. Partridge knew that when the old boy needed to think, or to escape, the railway stations were often not enough for him, and he would find a half-decent platform on the Underground and sit there, watching the ebb and flow of the day's travellers, until he had made peace with himself. On a day such as this, though, he might just be of a mind to push his way right to the front of the platform, waiting until the scream of lights from the tunnel gave him the momentary courage to leap onto the rushing tracks.

Bond Street, Oxford Circus, Tottenham Court Road, Holborn, Russell Square, King's Cross, Euston, Warren Street, and Goodge Street took him the best part of the morning, and by the end of it he had only a sense of utter hopelessness and a raging headache to show for his odyssey. The old boy could be anywhere. What was the use? He came up into blinding light, the Ascension-clear light of early winter. The air was as brittle as glass, and the paving stones were like permafrost beneath his feet. He bought the noon edition of the *Standard* and read of Harry Sizewell's continuing recovery. Well, that was something anyway. God, what a mess this whole thing had been. What an utter shambles.

He knew of a small sandwich bar near the museum where he might have lunch before heading back (in a taxi perhaps: he could not face the Underground). There were reports to be drafted, questions to be avoided (not evaded: he knew the difference), files to be unfiled and refiled, and the Harvest team to be summoned from their individual locations. All except Miles Flint. Where on God's earth was he? Partridge had read the cryptic note from the Mobile Support Unit: the arrest had been going to plan, but then there had been a skirmish, shots had been fired, and one of the suspects had escaped, taking agent Scott with him. What the hell did it all mean? Had Flint been kidnapped? Partridge had spent a great deal of the taxpayers' money on telephone calls while he tried to find out. He had been bounced like a rubber ball from one extension to another, from one barracks to another, and always the person to whom he most wanted to speak was not available, was "still in the field," could not be contacted. What did they mean, "still in the field"? The operation should have ended days ago. It looked as though Circe had blown up in his face. And, as ever, Miles Flint was the fuse.

The receiver burning in his hand, Partridge had finally given up. For some reason a poem by Yeats came to him. He had never been one for poetry, but a few lines, rote-learned for school examinations, stayed with him: "Things fall apart; the centre cannot hold." Well, he was damned if he was going to fall apart, though everyone and everything around him might. No, he would be the centre, he *would* hold, he must.

He found the old boy in the sandwich bar, examining his shoes and his reputation, perhaps thinking both to be in need of repair. Partridge sat down at the scarred, formica-topped table.

"Sir?"

"Partridge, what are you doing here?" The voice was tired out, like froth in the bottom of a cup. "Harvest went all wrong, didn't it? We pulled them out too early."

"That happens, sir."

"It shouldn't. We should have hung on. London in the middle of a bombing campaign, and we pull out of a terrorist surveillance."

"We may have a larger problem than that, sir."

"No sign of Flint yet?"

"None, sir."

"What do you think?"

"It could be anything, but the probability is that he's been taken by the IRA, maybe even turned by them."

"He knows too much, you know. We can't let them get anything out of him."

"I'm aware of that, sir. There are men in the field just now. They'll find him."

"Then give them the order. Nobody must come out alive."

"That's a bit—"

"Nobody!" The Director seemed close to tears, but they were tears of anger. Things were moving away from him too fast, and he felt a sudden impotence.

"Yes, sir," said Partridge, realising for the first time just how close he was to the top job. The old boy would be lucky to last another week. Seven days only, at most. He had been summoned to Downing Street three times in the last five days. He was running out of answers.

"Bloody Miles Flint," he said now, "where is he? What's his game, eh? Just what's his game?"

CHAPTER 24

There were splendour beetles everywhere, which made for a fairly depressing homecoming. Look at them all, besuited and betied, the suits French, the ties silky soft but unobtrusive. Obtrusively unobtrusive. City shoes of polished leather clacking the length of the expensive streets, the streets of gold. There was nothing splendid in this show. Latin, *splendere,* to shine. But the splendour beetles buffed up to the nines, *Buprestidae,* their larvae fed on decomposing matter. There was always this furtive decay beneath the casual and splendent display. What secrets did they hide from the world, these busy businessmen, their shoes sounding like the rubbing together of insect legs? Everyone had their secrets, their little cupboards of treasure, private diaries locked away in bureaux, the pile of salacious magazines in the bottom of the wardrobe, the unquenchable taste for the illicit.

Miles heard the sounds of guilt as he walked with Collins, and he thought, Is this what I've been paid all these years to protect? He had been put in charge of everything, from the whitest lie to the guiltiest of traitors, all in the cause of the sanctity of secrecy itself. Was that it then? Yes, that was it. That was all. He had been a schoolboy, collecting things for the teacher, no reasons needed, no excuses. He flagged down a taxi and motioned for the sullen Collins to get in. He was fairly certain that Collins wouldn't attempt to escape, not now that he was in the enemy heartland. Miles had noted the newspaper headlines. The hunt was on for the Kew bombers. Besides, Miles had offered him a very generous incentive to stick around.

The new Miles had not been surprised when their return to England had turned out to be so uncomplicated. He felt that he could accomplish anything. The spider's bite still tingled in his blood. He ducked into the taxi after Collins, and felt warm and safe and snug.

Snug as a bug in a rug.

"St. John's Wood," he said to the driver, then sat back to watch, as Collins was doing, the parade of all those who had been fitted out for the annual ugly bugs' ball.

He couldn't be sure which, to the taxi driver, would seem the more suspicious—perfect silence during the drive, or Collins's accentuated brogue. He decided finally to play it as it came. The driver, in any case, seemed preoccupied. He was in the midst of an argument with the world at large and other drivers in particular, and he carried on the argument vociferously from his cab window.

"Why St. John's Wood?" asked Collins, trying, Miles noted, not to make his voice sound too Irish.

"That's where I live," said Miles, quite loudly.

The driver looked in his mirror, interested for a split second, then turned back to harangue a pedestrian who had dared to step onto a zebra crossing.

"But won't they be watching your house?"

Miles shrugged and smiled.

The traffic was crawling like flies through a pot of glue. Time was of the essence now that Miles had sneaked back. He had to finish this off while the element of surprise was his.

"Do you know London at all?" he asked Collins, whose eyes were transfixed by the passing parade.

"Never been here in my life."

"It's hell," said Miles.

"Yes, I can believe that," murmured Collins, his hands planted firmly on his knees.

St. John's Wood, however, was reassuringly the same, though the renovating and building work continued all around. Miles held the last of his money in his hand, ready to pay the driver, his wallet empty now, no credit cards, no chequebook, nothing. His identity lay somewhere inside the house in Marlborough Place, but he could no longer be sure that he wanted it.

He realised that it was, in its way, a blessing that he had been ordered to leave his identity behind him, for the firm had given him plenty of cash to make up for the lack of plastic money. The owner of the fishing boat had taken a fair whack, but that had been worth every penny. Then the rail fares had been expensive, but he had never enjoyed travelling by bus. In their carriage he had read in the newspapers of the aftermath of the Kew bombing. It seemed that two people were still in hospital. Collins read, too, and his eyes registered a mixture of disgust and accusation that Miles found reassuring. He had changed sides once before; perhaps he would do so again. He knew what Collins wanted. He wanted what everyone, be they terrorist or spy, wanted eventually—he wanted out, plain and simple. But it was never plain and simple. It was not like quitting at roulette when you had won or lost. There were forces in this game, the old invisible rules, which chained you to the table. No croupier ever said *"Rien ne va plus,"* no wheel was ever still. But Miles was about to try to beat the table. He was going to break the whole system. And Collins, soulful, questioning eyes or not, was going to help him.

As the taxi turned out of Wellington Road and into Marlborough Place, Miles saw the figure. A woman, standing opposite his house, and quite obviously watching it.

"Just keep driving," he said. The driver nodded. Passing her, Miles risked a glance. She was a brazen one, though, wasn't she? They didn't train them well enough these days. Well, let her wait there. He wasn't going to announce his arrival.

"I thought this was where you lived," whispered Collins.

"It is," said Miles. "But I thought you might like to see where the Beatles made *Abbey Road*. It's just up here. It would be a shame for you to come to London and not see that famous zebra crossing after all, wouldn't it?"

Collins shook his head slowly. He had left a nightmare and entered a farce.

He hit him again, and this time the fanged alien stayed down, but as he walked towards the exit another one came at him, hitting him hard in the back, and just as he crossed the threshold out of the room his energy pack registered zero and he crumpled to the floor. A small angelic figure left his prone body and, to the music of the "Funeral March," ascended to the top of the screen.

"Damn!"

He had scored twenty-seven thousand, not even enough to put him on the top ten high scores. Jim Stevens turned from the machine and looked around the noisy arcade, seeking out another game to play. Nobody seemed at all curious about a middle-aged man in an amusement arcade full of children, which was just as well, since he was in no mood for looks and stares.

The Sizewell investigation had turned sour on him, and he had a raging toothache at the front of his mouth. He was also a little hung over from the previous night, a night spent wining and dining Janine. She had not fallen for his charm, but he *had* fallen to her gracefully executed karate chop to the neck. He had forgotten two important points: one, that she was a feminist, and two, that she attended self-defence classes in what free time she had. There was certainly nothing repressed or downtrodden about the blow she had given him. It still hurt when he turned his head to right or left. So, with everything conspiring against him, he had come down to the arcade to blitz a few aliens and shoot hell out of King Kong, Commando, The Frog, and Dizzy Miss Lizzie. All to the accompaniment of bleeps and squeals and the tight, businesslike sound of heavy rock music from the arcade's sound system.

"Give me another quid's worth of change," he said to the beautiful, bored girl in the booth, whose languid features had first attracted him to this place. Forget it, he had enough woman trouble as it was. When the bars opened again he would sink himself in whisky and beer and damn the consequences. Everything was going wrong. Business as usual. Sizewell would be impenetrable now that he had the media behind him. He almost had a halo over his cursed head. In addition to which, the spy, Flint, had never come home, which left Jim Stevens with nothing but a pocketful of change and a screaming desire to blast hell out of the Zorgon Battle Fleet once and for all.

Sheila parked the Volkswagen with her usual care, reminding herself that the passenger-side taillight needed a new bulb. Taillight, taillight, taillight. She picked up her briefcase and a large hardback book from the back seat. The book was about literary Paris in the 1920s. What she remembered about Paris personally were the appalling toilets in some of the buildings, and the outrageously priced café au lait of Montparnasse. She had not caught even a whisper of existentialism there, though she had found plenty of evidence of a dog-eat-dog philosophy.

Taillight, taillight.

The door opened fluidly and closed behind her with a slight echo, as if she needed reminding that she was alone in the house. The silence embraced her like a frozen coat, a chill smother of mothballs. She would cook up some mushrooms in wine and tomatoes, and eat them hot with rice or pasta. Rice probably. There was no pasta in the house.

In the kitchen she noticed that one of the chairs had been pulled from the small table. It hadn't been that way this morning. She always pushed it in after she finished breakfast. Always. She felt her stomach constrict and her face begin to tingle. Oh, God, she thought, oh, God. There were sharp knives hanging on hooks above the cooker. She lifted one down and clutched it to her breast, looking around her for other signs of ingress. Hearing a cough from the living room, she took a deep breath and started out of the kitchen.

When the living-room door flew open, the man started up from his seat, ready to do battle with almost anything except the wild-eyed harridan who, teeth bared, held a glittering carving knife before her in striking position.

"Jesus, missus, there's no . . . I can explain . . ."

She was only a yard away from him, and she looked huge, fear pumping her up to twice her normal size.

"No need to explain," she hissed.

"No, I can explain, really I can. Your husband . . ."

She was moving towards him, needing only the excuse of a wrong movement to send the knife plunging down. Two feet from him, then a foot, her breath as loud as any wild animal's . . .

"Sheila?"

Miles came clattering down the stairs.

"Sheila?

He was dressed in the blue towelling robe which she had bought last Christmas. His hair was wet and stringy, his eyes trying to pierce the blurred air. His glasses had been left behind in the bathroom.

"Oh, Miles."

They embraced, pulling each other inward hard.

"Oh, Miles, where have you been? I've been so worried."

"No need," he whispered, stroking her soft hair, feeling her weight against him, and then, in embarrassment, remembering the presence of Collins, he pulled away from her, but slowly, tenderly.

"How did you get in?" she asked. "You left your keys behind."

"My friend here is a dab hand with a locked door. This is Mr. Collins by the way. Will, this is my wife, Sheila." Miles examined the knife, which was still trapped in Sheila's fist, as incongruous now as some cheap joke-shop toy. "It looks," he said, "as though you've already been introduced."

Sheila smiled towards Collins, her face as red as a funeral wreath. Collins shrugged and smiled back, a little humiliated at his own show of cowardice. It surprised him that he could feel humiliation without any concomitant anger. Something was changing inside him, but what?

They ate the mushrooms, which Sheila had cooked to her special recipe. During the meal Miles and Collins glanced at one another, smiling conspiratorially. Both were thinking how strange this food seemed after the huge Irish breakfasts, the solid and comforting amounts of fatty meat, the potatoes and veg. While they ate, Sheila asked her questions, and Miles tried to parry them, feigning tiredness and artlessness. He had introduced Will Collins as a friend of long standing, but Collins was no actor and Sheila, sensing that here was the weak point in her husband's armour, had begun, gently but skillfully, to interrogate Collins. At last, some scraps of rice still untouched on her plate, Sheila put down her fork.

"You're lying through your teeth, both of you. It's quite transparent. Miles, I thought we had some kind of an agreement. Truth in marriage and all that. Is our agreement at an end?"

Miles chose to stare at Collins.

"Not here, Sheila, not now. Later."

"Why don't you trust me, for Christ's sake? Why does there always have to be this screen between us?"

"Of course I trust you, Sheila. Don't make a scene."

"Am I making a scene, Mr. Collins?"

"No, Mrs. Flint, you are not." Miles looked at Collins in silent horror, while Sheila turned to her husband in victory. "Your husband," Collins continued, "likes to think that he's armour-plated. That much I do know. But"—he paused to sip some wine—"I never set eyes on him until last week. I don't know why he's lying to you, frankly I don't *care,* but I don't see what point there is to it. He . . . *we* need all the friends we can get. You've got to see that, Flint. Else we could both be corpses by the morning."

Sheila put her hand to her mouth, her eyes dancing with shock.

"For God's sake, Collins," spat Miles.

"It's true though, isn't it?" asked Sheila quietly. "Isn't it? Tell me."

"Over coffee then," said Miles, placing his napkin on his plate. "The dinner table is no place for a horror story."

So they cleared the table, mouthing pat phrases and stock responses, and Miles poured out the last of the wine into their glasses and found a bottle of Bowmore whisky.

"Take this through, will you?"

"All right."

"And some glasses."

"Will these do?"

"Yes, fine."

"Coffee ready?"

"Just about. Do you take sugar, Mr. Collins?"

"Three, please."

"And two for me, dear."

"But you don't take sugar, Miles."

"I've changed."

It was all very civilised, but it was fake, too, and they all knew it.

"Will you help me?" Miles asked.

Collins sat in the corner, realising that he could be nothing more than an onlooker here. He smoked a cigarette, but Miles had refused the offer of one.

"Not unless you tell me what's going on." Sheila had folded her arms, such an obvious gesture of defiance that Miles was forced to smile.

"I need your trust," he said, "and I need you not to ask questions."

"Then I simply won't help you, Miles. I want to know what it's all about."

"So do we," muttered Collins to himself. He stubbed out his cigarette and drew another from the packet. Miles signalled that he would like one too. Collins had already started to place both cigarettes in his mouth to light them, when he realised what he was doing. They both laughed, and he first offered Miles the packet, then threw across the lighter. Miles lit and drew on the cigarette as though it would be his last.

"Sheila," he said, "I'm a spy."

"Of course," she said calmly.

"You had an inkling?"

She laughed at this.

"More than an inkling, darling. You didn't marry a wooden doll, you know, you married *me*. And I wasn't born yesterday."

Miles sat back, not daring to look towards Collins, who might be smiling a little too happily. Had it always been like this? Had he always been slower and more naive than those around him, standing outside the door listening while Sheila heard his every breath?

"Yes," he said, playing for time, "of course."

"That reminds me, actually," said Sheila.

"What?"

"A man's been pestering me. Said his name was James Stevens and that he wanted to see you on business. I know who he is though."

"Who?"

"He's a journalist on one of the Fleet Street—or should I say Wapping?—dailies. Investigative reporting is his forte, I believe."

"What the hell does he want?"

"I rather thought you'd know that. Or perhaps Mr. Collins does?"

"Not me, missus. I don't even *like* reporters."

"I wonder what he's after?" Miles said quietly.

"Oh, we'll find out, no doubt, now that you're back. Anyway, forget all that for the moment. What is it that you want me to do?"

It seemed to Miles that he did little else these days but take deep breaths and steel himself for action. He took one now, just for luck, and felt himself grow in confidence again. He went to the window and looked out to where a blackbird had balanced itself precariously on the pliant branch of a tree. The woman, standing across the road, turned and walked away toward Abbey Road. He had decided, after all, to give them a fighting chance. Let her call in. They wouldn't have time to react. Miles drew the curtains closed.

Janine had been mad as hell's own fires with Jim Stevens for his absolute lack of subtlety. The irony was that she rather liked him—not just admiration for his journalist's skills, but an actual like of the occasionally boorish personality which lay behind those skills. Yes, it was his plain and honest stupidity that had angered her, the way he had suddenly come to the conclusion that because *he* had had a bellyful of drink *she* would suddenly be putty in his arms, leading to a warm bed, and a late breakfast the following day. He had thought wrong, and she hoped that his neck and head hurt as much as she suspected they would. He had deserved everything he got, except perhaps her offer of money for a taxi when it transpired that he had spent every last penny on alcohol.

She was, however, seriously thinking of resigning her thankless commission. She had only come here today to show faith, so to speak, to work out her final days for him so that he could not turn around and accuse her of slacking. But she was glad that she had come, and felt sure that Jim would be interested to hear what she had to tell him. All she had to do now was find a telephone which still worked. In St. John's Wood, she didn't think that would be a problem.

CHAPTER 25

Billy Monmouth leafed through a book on Brueghel, purchased on his way home for no good reason except the sudden and desperate need to spend money. He skipped the commentary and concentrated on the paintings themselves, solid representations of peasant life and the natural cycle, followed by those few but powerful images of death and hell and the whole works. Billy clutched his whisky glass as though it were some kind of crutch, while the book, resting on his thighs and knees, seemed as heavy as sin.

From the seldom-used stereo came the sounds of the Rolling Stones. They were another of his secret vices, though he played their albums seldom and selectively. They were to him predictions of chaos as potent as any Cassandra's. Hell, Billy knew, was not some far distant region. It was a millimetre away, and all one had to do was scratch at the surface with one's fingernail to reveal it.

He thought of Sheila's insistent phone call. She had to see him, it was as simple as that. He supposed that she would need comforting now that Miles was gone, but he did not relish the task. And so he would allow her to see him like this, bemired in self-pity, allowing himself to be led into the Dance of Death to the music of a 1960s guitar wail. He just didn't care anymore.

There was a knock at the door. Why didn't she use her key? The knock came again. Ah yes, she had sent back the key, hadn't she? Well, he supposed he could just about manage to lift himself from his chair. He heaved the book onto the floor and heard the stereo switching itself off, the record finishing with a nice sense of timing. Should he choose something else? No, let silence be their coda.

As he opened the door he felt it push against him, causing him to stagger back, so that he was already—physically as well as mentally—completely off balance when Miles Flint strode into the room. He seemed taller than Billy remembered, and behind him came a taller man still, a mercenary-looking character with thick black hair and the beginnings of a beard, who seemed to have been conjured out of his own thoughts.

"Miles . . ."

"You'd better sit down, Billy. You look a little weak. Been having a drink? Perhaps we might join you. Mr. Collins, see Mr. Monmouth here to his seat."

It was Miles all right, but it was like no Miles Billy had ever encountered, not even the one who had slapped him on the face at the Vorticist exhibition. Miles's eyes roamed the room, checking this aspect and that, avoiding Billy. There was something sharper and quicker about him, as though he had been working on half power before. He seemed larger, too, muscular, his eyes keen and ready for anything. Billy might have taken this for posturing but knew instinctively, despite the haze of alcohol around him, that this was something real, something dangerous. He wanted to be very sober for this, whatever this might be, but instead found himself feeling woozier still. He needed cold water for his face and coffee for his bloodstream.

"Miles . . ."

Miles nodded, seeming to read his thoughts.

"Wait," he ordered his accomplice, who remained silent and impassive as a golem. "Take Mr. Monmouth to the bathroom and allow him to wash himself. I'll make some coffee, Billy. Oh, and Mr. Collins?"

"Yes, Mr. Flint?"

"Don't let him out of your sight."

"I surely won't."

Sweet mother, thought Billy, being led away, this man is Irish. Who the hell is he?

Miles watched the wretched Billy being led away, his face ashen as though the extermination trucks were parked around the corner of the lounge. So far so good. Miles felt rather pleased with himself, and noticed that Collins was entering into the spirit of the thing, too. They had scared the utter living shit out of an utter living shit. Now they could examine at their leisure Billy's hollow shell.

He drank the first scalding cup of coffee without his lips once leaving its rim. Miles stood over him with the steaming jug, pouring more out when requested. The second cup Billy drank more slowly, almost gingerly, taking deep breaths between mouthfuls. Collins, standing behind him, mimed the sticking of fingers down his throat to Miles, indicating that Billy had made himself sick in the bathroom. The weak strands of Billy's hair were still beaded with water, a few drops falling occasionally onto his pale, heavy face, where they sought the safe shadows of his throat.

"OK?" asked Miles.

"A bit better, yes."

Miles motioned for Collins to sit in the other armchair and then made himself comfortable on the sofa.

"I have a lot of questions, Billy, and I *know* that you know the answers. Before beginning, I should point out that Mr. Collins here is a member of the Provisional Irish Republican Army, and I've given him a promise that if I'm not satisfied with your answers I'll hand you over to him. You'd like that, wouldn't you, Mr. Collins?"

The nod was slow, the eyes fixed on those of the trembling Billy. Miles decided to himself that he would have made a damned good interrogator. No, perhaps not: he was enjoying it too much.

"Miles, what is this all about?"

Miles pulled a small cassette recorder from his pocket and switched it on, placing it on the low coffee table.

"That's not the kind of answer I need, Billy, that's not a good start." Billy looked down into his lap in a show of obeisance. "Do you remember," continued Miles, "on one of our lunch dates, not so very long ago, how you introduced me to a . . . how did you put it? . . . an 'old friend' of yours, someone you saw only at dinner parties?"

"Yes," replied Billy, holding his coffee cup in both hands, quite sober now. "It was Andrew Gray."

"Oh, yes," said Miles, nodding, "yes, that was the name, Andrew Gray. Do you happen to know, Billy, why Mr. Gray should have gone to Ireland looking for Mr. Collins here?"

If such a thing were possible, Billy actually grew paler. He looked over to Collins.

"Time for explanations, Billy. Time to get it all off your chest."

"Miles, this is madness. Do you know the danger you're in?"

Miles shrugged. Billy rested for a moment, seemed to make up his mind, then leaned forward in his chair.

"You know me, Miles, I've always liked to know what's going on in the world and in the firm particularly. I like to think of myself as the eyes and ears of the place. Well, that goes for past events as well as present. You know that your sidekick here murdered Philip Hayton?"

"In exchange for some guns, yes."

"And that the middleman on the job was—"

"The Israeli assassinated by Latchkey, yes."

Billy nodded.

"Then you know a great deal," he said.

"But you, Billy, you knew it all the time. And you knew that something was up, that someone was trying to get me out of the way."

"I tried to warn you when you were leaving for—"

"Some warning," spat Miles. He rose to his feet and walked around to the back of the sofa, where heavy net curtains hid them all from the darkened city.

"Some warning," he repeated evenly. "You let me walk right into it every step of the way, without knowing what I was getting into. You and your friend Gray. He's CIA, yes?"

Billy nodded.

"Something like that."

"And you're his eyes and ears, Billy, his puppet, nothing more than a puppet. Yes?"

Billy touched the side of his face but said nothing.

"Yes," Miles answered for him, "or maybe a performing monkey would be a better description. At first I suspected you of being behind the whole thing, but it didn't fit. You wouldn't have gone near Sheila if you had been." He turned toward Billy and rested his hands on the back of the sofa. "She had nothing to do with this, did she?"

Billy thought about his answer for a long time. He had detected a hint of pleading in Miles's voice. If he were to lie and say yes, she was involved, then he could reverse the roles, could . . . But he was past all caring. The game had become too complex, and he couldn't be bothered anymore to read the new rule book. So he shook his head.

Miles nodded, thankful and satisfied. Collins just sat there. This was a revelation to him, like some grand, unfolding soap opera. But, he had to keep reminding himself, this was for real. He couldn't allow himself to forget that.

"So," Miles continued, "you were a magnet for gossip, bits and pieces of information, and Gray used you as an informer."

"It was mutual," said Billy, growing more confident. "He gave me information too. He knew quite a lot, about the other side, about his own people, and"—he paused—"about us. He knew, for example, about the Hayton business, not all of it, but enough. Between us we put together a pretty fair picture of the whole thing. Philip Hayton had been . . . involved."

"Meaning?"

"The love that dare not speak its name."

"He means homosexuality," Miles said to Collins, who had furrowed his brow.

"Yes," said Billy. "Well, nothing new in that, is there, Miles? Not in our profession. But the man with whom Hayton was involved was trying to break it off. Perhaps he had been scared by the whole 'Fourth Man' business. Hayton didn't want to lose him, was threatening public exposure, moral blackmail, all that sort of thing, I suppose. I'm a bit hazy on this part of the story. There was a kind of triangle, you see, and Hayton was going to cause trouble for all. So he was eliminated. It looked like a terrorist killing"—he looked to Collins—"and so was hushed up, but it had been arranged from within the firm, quite clandestinely, utilising the firm's own channels and techniques."

"All a very long time ago now," said Miles as Billy sipped at his coffee, made a face, put it aside, and rose to fetch a bottle from the cabinet. They all sipped the whisky for a moment or two, savouring the break in tension. Miles checked the tape in the cassette recorder.

"It's not as good as the Irish stuff, is it, Mr. Flint?" said Collins.

"You're right, Mr. Collins," said Miles.

"So," began Billy, not sure quite whether he were joking, "you've gone over to the other side, eh, Miles?"

"Perhaps," answered Miles. Then, "Do go on with your story, Billy."

"That was it so far as the Hayton thing went. No one was any the wiser.

He was seen as a victim of the troubles, nothing more. But Gray got hold of something, I'm not sure what. Hayton's lover, having used the firm as cover for the operation, had aroused some interest. The Israeli, I would guess, worked for everyone: CIA, Mossad, us. I think Gray got his information from him."

"And?"

"And"—Billy paused again, rather overplaying his hand—"the trail led back to our own Mr. Partridge."

"Partridge?"

"None other. He'd been Philip Hayton's lover all those years ago, had tried to break it off, and had, well, finally taken stronger action."

"My God," whispered Miles. It was beginning to fit into place. "You mentioned a third man?"

"Quite a lowly political huckster then, as now. Harold Sizewell."

"Who was almost blown up at Kew?"

"Quite. He's my local MP actually. I've a place in his constituency, Chillglade."

"Well, well." Miles had the feeling that he was burrowing quickly into some warm and rotten piece of wood.

"But all this was, as you say, Miles, a long time ago."

"So what happened?"

"Several things. A concatenation of circumstances, you might say. For one thing, Partridge has worked his way up to a position where he is next in line to run the show."

"He's worked hard and fair to get there, hasn't he?"

"Oh, yes, I'm not disputing that. But skeletons do have a way of appearing from the cupboard just when one doesn't want them to. So our friend decided to tie up the only loose ends in his past."

"Which necessitated putting out of action those people who could be dangerous to him: Mr. Collins here, the Israeli, and Sizewell."

"As to Sizewell I can't be sure. Gray seems to think that the bombing was coincidental. No, Sizewell wasn't the threat. He would have as much to lose as Partridge should anything have emerged from the cupboard. But as for the others, yes."

"Where do I fit into all this, Billy?"

"You were an accident, Miles. Partridge had arranged it so that the tail on Latchkey should lose him. Gray reckons it worked something like this." Billy was on the edge of his chair now, becoming something like his old brash self again. "Partridge had found out that Latchkey's target was to be the Israeli—"

"How?"

"Well, the closer you come to the top of the chain of command, the more intelligence comes your way. Perhaps it was a trade-off with one of our allies or our enemies."

"Go on."

"All Partridge had to do, having gleaned this information, was to ensure that the surveillance, which had already begun by this time, botched the job. *Voilà,* one of the thorns in his past disappears, and no one's any the wiser. It was beautifully simple really. He must have thought it divine intervention when the opportunity arose. But then you entered the picture, just when you weren't supposed to. You went along on the surveillance, *you* ended up being the one to lose Latchkey, and you became suspicious. In Partridge's mind, you became another problem."

Miles shook his head.

"He was way off the mark, Billy. Yes, I was suspicious, but I hadn't a clue what was going on, and I certainly wasn't getting any closer to solving it."

"*I* know that, Miles, but Partridge thought that you were. That was what was so important."

"Sounds to me," said Collins slowly, "as though you were set up, Mr. Flint. Set up by this bastard here and the Gray character."

Miles nodded.

"That's the way it looks to me too. What do you say, Billy?"

"Well, Miles . . ." Billy had already lost what confidence he had gained during the telling of his tale. "It was Gray, you have to understand that."

"You were trying to flush Partridge out, using me as bait?"

Billy looked into his lap again but saw little comfort there.

"Something like that," he mumbled.

"But why was Gray so interested in the first place?"

"Oh, good reasons. For one thing, and even you must see this, Miles, it is in nobody's interest for someone like Partridge to step into the old boy's shoes. The Americans have been nervous of our setup here since the 1970s. They've kept tabs on us. And for another . . ."

"Well?"

"It doesn't matter."

"Billy, it looks to me as though Mr. Collins is itching to do you some violence."

"A lot of violence," corrected Collins.

Billy sat back in his chair, staring at the ceiling.

"Then go ahead and do it."

It was Miles's turn to lean forward in his seat.

"You were going to tell me about Gray, I think. Well, you're not the only one who can put two and three together and come up with a conspiracy. What about this: Sizewell is on a committee investigating cooperation and the lack of it amongst the security services, as well as other highly secret and confidential proposals. The Americans would like to know what's being said and would simply love to have someone in there putting forward their own views. Sizewell was the obvious candidate because of the Hayton killing. They'd had him tucked away in their files since then in the hope that they could use him in just such a way at a later date, and that date is now. So your friend Gray was attempting to put the frighteners on a member of the British Parliament, to blackmail him, and the only way to stop blackmail like that, as we both know, is to root out the evidence. So Sizewell got in touch with his old friend, and Partridge was given another reason for eliminating the past. They must have thought the world was falling down on top of them." Miles looked over to Collins, who had started to sweat a little, though the central heating was temperate at most. "You're a wanted man, Will. You're the last one left alive who can jeopardise this whole stinking thing."

"Except that now you have it all on tape," said Collins.

"Suppositions, theories. *You're* the only witness, the only physical obstacle left."

"Which is why this CIA bastard was looking for me, to protect me?"

"Yes. Where is Gray, by the way, Billy?"

Billy shrugged.

"France maybe. He's heavily involved over there just now. Antiterrorism."

"A real troubleshooter, eh? It's a pity. I'm sure we'd have liked to meet him, wouldn't we, Will?"

"Yes, Mr. Flint, we would."

"So Partridge had set it up so that Latchkey could escape. Simple enough to do, I expect. An anonymous warning that he was being followed. But one of our men had to be in on it." Miles thought of splendour beetles and Sobranie cigarettes. "Phillips?"

"Of course."

"Yes, he of the lateral promotion." But hadn't Phillips been in Mowbray's camp? "What about Mowbray? His little setup was surely more of a threat to Partridge than I was?"

"Not at all."

"Not with Phillips in his camp, keeping Partridge informed of all Richard's doings?" Miles was thinking back to that night at the Doric. But hadn't Felicity first approached him while Phillips was parking the car? That would mean that her first sally had been . . . coincidence.

"What about Cynegetics? Where does it enter the scheme of things?"

"Well," said Billy, "shadowy as it is, we do know that Partridge set up the group and staffed it with agents loyal to him, so that he could monitor anyone within the firm who might be trying to dig up the dirt on him."

"But he never guessed that it was you who was doing the burrowing?"

"There were too many others for him to keep busy with. Andrew Gray saw to that."

"Others like me, you mean?"

"Yes. But now I have a question to put to you." Billy was rubbing at his face tiredly.

"What?"

"Just what happened to you in Ireland?"

Collins manufactured some rough and ready sandwiches, and they ate them, washing each one down with mouthfuls of tea. During which time Miles, as he thought only fair, told Billy his own story.

"Incredible," was Billy's response. "Partridge didn't overestimate you. If anything, he underestimated you. We all did, Miles."

"What's this fellow Partridge's first name anyway?" Collins asked through a paste of cheese and tomato.

"Nobody knows," said Billy, still in awe of the Irishman.

"Somebody must know," said Collins, "even if only his mammy."

"Let's come back to Gray," said Miles. He was obsessed now and was not about to be led away from his obsession. He had turned the tape over, and now he switched the cassette recorder on again.

"Gray," he repeated, "was using me as bait, was he?"

"Not especially," answered Billy lethargically. "But you did help discomfort Partridge, which was all to the good. Gray wanted to create the maximum panic, so that Sizewell would give in. It wasn't just you. I think he kept dropping hints and clues to Mauberley, too, knowing that Richard, no matter how stupid, was bound to come up with something eventually. Then there was a newspaper reporter called Stevens. Andrew did his anonymous phone call routine on him, sending him clues, so that Stevens would go after Sizewell. He's probably still after him."

"Stevens, you said?"

"Yes."

Miles looked at Collins.

"That's the man Sheila said had been pestering her about me."

"Well, well, well," said Billy, "he must be a better reporter than we'd thought if he's tracked *you* down."

"But all this," persisted Miles, "the reporter, me, the whole thing, was designed merely to pile on the pressure?"

"That's about it."

"Using human lives as bits and pieces in a game?"

"Isn't that what we do for a living, Miles?"

A fair answer, thought Miles, but it didn't help to make any sense of it all. But, he supposed, if he were in a game, or even a game *within* a game, there must be a way out. All he had to do was keep on playing.

"I'll tell you this, Billy, it's got to end, and it's not going to end with me as the corpse and you lot as the grieving colleagues."

"It was never planned that you'd—"

"Wasn't it?"

"Christ, Miles, how long have we known one another? If I'd thought that Partridge was planning anything so drastic, I'd have stopped you from going to Ireland, and I mean that."

Miles stared at him hard, and Billy had to fight to keep his gaze matched to that of this new Miles.

"I wonder," said Miles, not in reproach or disbelief but with real curiosity. "You know, Billy, you've been sitting back throughout, letting anyone and everyone become involved except yourself, afraid of committing yourself, of being on the losing side. We've been walking around with third-party insurance, and you've been fully covered. I could admire that to some extent. I could, but I don't."

"What's done is done, Miles. There's no escaping it."

"True."

"Listen, confession's over on my part, no more to tell. Except to say that you must be mad, running around with the man behind the Kew bombing. He'll be public enemy number one any day now. But I suppose none of this is my concern. Do you mind if I put a record on, something relaxing?"

"No, go ahead."

Billy went to the stereo, slipped the record back into its sleeve, and began to search through his collection.

"You've got a lot of records," said Miles, coming up behind him.

"Oh, yes, well, I like to think that my tastes are eclectic." He brought out a classical album, thought better of it, and looked for something else.

"Can't you find anything suitable?" said Miles.

"Well, it *is* rather a strange occasion."

"Do you mind if I take a look?"

"Not at all. What are your tastes, dear boy?"

"Oh, eclectic, I suppose, like yours." Miles crouched down, while Billy, having decided upon a Dave Brubeck album, stood in front of the stereo. "I usually just start at the beginning," said Miles, "and work my way through. Take this section, for instance. I'd start here on the left with Pink Floyd, Liszt, Janis Ian, Michael Nyman, Tchaikovsky"—Miles fingered each record in turn—"and so on, right up to . . . let me see, yes, Miles Davis." Billy had moved back from the stereo without switching it on. "Look, Billy, it's a funny thing, but if you take the initials of these records there's a message spelt out. It says, "Flint on to you." Isn't that a coincidence?"

"Sheila told you about our little code?"

"Of course," said Miles, rearranging the records. "Oh, *you're* the clever one, Billy. And I've been your dupe for far too long. Time for a change, my dear old friend and comrade. Time for everything to change. But you needn't bother with this little code. We're not taking you anywhere."

"What are you going to do?"

"Well, firstly I'm going to have this tape copied, and the copies sent to

Richard Mowbray and to this journalist Stevens. That should ensure that, even if I don't survive, something is done to pull this whole cheap façade to bits. Then I am going to *demand* your silence."

"You'll have it."

"I know I will. You're going to arrange for me to 'come in.' Get in touch with the old boy and insist that Partridge and he fetch me themselves. Tell them that something went badly wrong in Ireland but that I'm sure it was all a mistake and now I want to be met by people I trust."

"Partridge won't fall for it."

"That's what I'm hoping for. But then he won't know about Mr. Collins here, will he? As long as I have Mr. Collins with me, I hold the trump card. I can expose Partridge."

"That brings me to another question, Miles. Our friend here"—Billy pointed a brittle finger at Collins—"how did you ever enlist his cooperation?"

Miles smiled, then produced a gun from his pocket.

"Cooperation is a dead principle, Billy. You of all people should know that. The new religion is coercion. From the Latin, meaning to shut in. I feel as though I've been shut in for far too long. It's time to close some doors on Partridge. And I know just the place to do it."

"Where?"

"My home territory," said Miles, smiling a smile that would have chilled a good glassful of gin. "I've been playing away from home for far too many matches, and I've only just realised it."

It was as dark outside as the half-moons under Jim Stevens's eyes when he finally switched on his answering machine and heard Janine's excited voice.

A few minutes later he was wrestling with his jacket again, trying to pull it on with one hand while he tied his tie with the other. He staggered against a wall, swore to himself, and opened the door back into the wide and humourless world. He was relieved to have an excuse to get out of the flat. He loathed its emptiness and the fact that he maltreated it. But now he had a mission, and had evidence, too, that Janine had forgiven him, though she had said nothing on the telephone. Well, all that could come later. The spy was back in town, and Jim Stevens was ready to confront him.

Though he had forgotten for the moment just why he wanted to speak with him in the first place.

He rode the tube for two stops, began to feel dizzy and sick, and came up into the chilled night. A black cab was there, as though he had hailed it, and he stepped inside, pulling open the window so that he could breathe whatever was out there. It had been a very long forty-eight hours.

The streets were empty and the traffic lights were with him. Soon enough the taxi came to a halt.

"Marlborough Place, guvnor. That'll be eight quid and tenpence."

Muttering to himself, he paid off the cabbie and felt a sudden tiredness descend upon him as he climbed out.

"Jim." It was Janine, standing before him in her private-eye raincoat and headscarf.

"You look the part," he said. Then remembered. "Look, Janine, I'm sorry about—well, about everything. I mean it."

"This is not the time for self-pity, mister. Where have you been? No, never mind. I can guess from your look. Come on, let's go get your spy."

He watched her cross the road, wondering what he was doing here so late at night when he could be zapping aliens at one of the all-nighter arcades down by Piccadilly. But the way she moved . . . There was nothing to do but follow, even though it took the final drops of his energy to climb the half dozen steps to Miles Flint's front door. By the time he pushed at the doorbell he was dizzy again and breathing hard. Janine gave him a peck on the cheek.

"Forgiven," she said with the briskness of a priest.

Flint's wife opened the door. She looked drawn, as though they had disturbed her in the midst of a crisis. She looked dazed, too, with the sluggish motions of a shell-shocked survivor. She didn't seem to recognise Stevens and spent the first few seconds concentrating her attention on Janine.

Stevens himself felt about as unhealthy as a human being could come without actually being on a slab.

She recognised him at last.

"Not you again," she said.

"I know he's here," puffed Stevens. "He's back. Can I speak to him now?"

"He's gone off again."

"But I saw him this evening," said Janine.

"Yes, but now he's gone." Sheila Flint opened the door wide. "Take a look if you like. He told me never to let strangers in, but I don't suppose it matters now."

The look on Jim Stevens's weathered face would have melted the heart of the meanest crone. Janine thought he was about to cry and put a hand on his shoulder to comfort him.

"Where's he gone?" he asked.

"Edinburgh, I think," said Sheila Flint, her face wrinkling slightly as she remembered something. Then, slowly and quietly, she closed the door again.

"This is a nightmare," said Stevens. There was no other explanation for it. Soon now he would wake up and everything would be as it had been five years ago, when he was on the crest of his career. Edinburgh? People *came* from Edinburgh, they didn't *go* there. Why in God's name had Flint gone to Edinburgh?

"We can follow him," Janine was saying. "You can pay for the fares out of the money you've saved by not paying me any money this past week."

"How did he get away? I thought you were watching?"

"Well, I had to find a phone, didn't I? There was this pub, and I thought I could call from there, but then the barman offered to buy me a drink. He was Scottish, and the place was quiet. I suppose he wanted the company. Anyway, I had a drink and then I telephoned . . . Jim? Jim?"

Slowly, with great calculation and perhaps even a touch of heroism, Jim Stevens had begun to bang his head against the solid mahogany door.

CHAPTER 26

"I'd be a lot more use to you if you'd give me a gun."

Miles blew his nose, breathed in the sharp, brand-new air, and examined the Sir Walter Scott monument. He was seated on a damp bench in Edinburgh's Princes Street Gardens, with Collins, cold and looking it, standing in front of him.

"How do you know that you can trust Monmouth? He's been screwing you around all this time, what's to stop him now?"

The monument, darkened by time to a suitably Gothic shade of black, pleased Miles more than he could say. He remembered climbing to the top once, back in his student days, and feeling claustrophobia while he climbed the narrow, winding stairwell, then fear when, at the top, he found that there was only a narrow circuit to traverse, the wind blowing fiercely and too many people trying to move up and down the stairs. It had seemed the perfect image of Scott's novels.

"I suppose this is why they called you Walter Scott, eh?" said Collins now, changing the subject in an effort to elicit any kind of response from Miles.

A bitter wind was blowing the length of the gardens, and Miles was the only person mad enough to be sitting down in such unpleasant conditions. Those who walked past, swinging heavy shopping bags, mistook him for a tourist and smiled sympathetically, as if to say, Fancy coming to Edinburgh at this time of year.

Collins didn't look like a tourist. He looked like a beggar. He wrapped his coat a little more tightly around him and decided that, if Flint would not answer him, then he would not speak. He had been to Edinburgh once before, many years ago, on a fund-raising venture. He knew that fifty minutes would take him to Glasgow, and that from there it was a simple if lengthy journey by train and boat to Larne. Waverley Station was a short walk away: why didn't he just make a run for it? Would Flint be crazy enough to shoot him in so public a place? One look at that contemplative face gave him his answer: of course he would. Flint had changed into the kind of man Collins was used to dealing with, and he wasn't sure that he liked the change. He had felt some sympathy for the old, scared, confused Miles Flint. This new character would not appreciate such sentiment. But then what did it matter? He couldn't run back to Ireland anyway, not like this. Those men in the meat van would still be sniffing around, and what could he tell his commanding officer about his own kidnapping by a member of MI5? If he had blown great big holes in Flint and that snake Monmouth, then yes, he could have returned. But he was not at all sure that he wanted to go back, for he knew that, once back, he would be forced to take sides again. He wanted to disappear, to become ordinary and invisible, to escape Miles Flint's smile . . .

Miles was thinking of Sheila. He had come to this spot with her several times, of course. Right now, following his instructions, she would be clearing out of the house and selling the Jag to the dealer in Highgate. He had emptied their bank account for the price of the train fares north and the hotel. No one would think of looking for him at the most expensive hotel in Edinburgh, would they?

He watched Collins shuffle backward and forward in front of him, becoming ever more impatient, becoming agitated. That suited his plan too. Everything would fall into place. He had given Collins his own room, showing his trust. But there was a connecting door. The hotel clerk had looked askance at the request, but Miles had gone on smiling. Trust me, his smile said, as I am trusting Will Collins, the enemy become ally.

Collins sat down on the damp bench. He needed Flint's trust, the trust which would give him one of the handguns. With a handgun he would feel warmer and so much more secure. He still couldn't believe Flint's tale of finding the pistol in Champ's tea caddy. What had the old fool been doing hiding it there in the first place? With a gun in my hand, he thought, I would shoot Miles Flint. He didn't want to, but he would, in the way that one would extinguish a smouldering fire. Miles had become too dangerous by half and did not realise that he could not win whatever game it was he thought himself playing. Collins would shoot him, but only enough to cripple him and make him safe again.

Then he would head south and seek out Monmouth, and he would shoot him dead. There was no question of that.

"Let's go up," said Miles.

"Up where?"

"Up the monument, of course. Come on." And he almost sprinted to the doorway, where the attendant took his money and mentioned that this was the last day the monument was open.

"Closing for the season," he said.

"Is there anyone else up there?" Collins asked.

"On a day like this? No, not a soul."

Good, thought Collins, then this is where it ends.

Miles climbed ahead of him, his hands touching the cold stone walls. He had given Billy precise details of which train Partridge and the old boy were to take, and what they were to do upon arrival. He was not giving them time to think or to plan. He wanted them dazed, fuggy, off balance. Especially Partridge, for whom this little circus had been arranged. They would travel north by the slowest of trains, one which stopped at countless small stations. They would feel like death when they arrived.

But could he trust Billy? The man had betrayed him, had betrayed everyone. He was an agent of chaos, and he would produce chaos whenever and wherever he could. Miles didn't care. No matter how much Billy gave away, Partridge would still come north. He might not come unprepared, but he would come.

And that was all Miles needed.

"Not far now," he said, feeling the blood pumping through him, taking rests at the various levels of the ascent. Still, he didn't feel like a museum beetle anymore. He was the hunter.

"Why is it," he called back to Collins, "that human colonies work towards chaos while insect colonies work towards harmony?"

"You and your bloody insects," came the reply up the steps.

Collins was gaining strength with every moment, filling himself with the power and the speed that would be needed to disable Flint, to take him out of the game. He had to exhaust him, had to keep him talking, using up vital stamina.

"We're dead men," he called into the half-light. "I can see it clear as day."

"The good guys never die," said Miles Flint, his breath short.

"Yes, they do, they do it all the bloody time. Give me a gun."

"You're going to have to trust me, Will, at least until tomorrow morning."

"Well, don't blame me if you die a terrorist instead of a martyr." Collins had reached the top step and walked out into a fierce squall. The walkway was tiny, and there was no safety mesh, nothing to stop anyone from plummeting to the well-tended ground below.

"Jesus," he whispered.

"Scared of heights?"

"Not until now." His face had lost all colour, and he began to feel a vein of sweat on his spine.

"But what a view, eh?" said Miles, pointing northward towards the Forth estuary. "I should never have left this place."

"There's probably some truth in that, sure enough."

"Are you all right?"

"I'm fine. It's just this wind; it could blow a man right off here to his death."

"Do you think that's why I brought you here?"

"Well, is it?"

"No, but I did think you might have a similar plan in store for me."

"Maybe I did."

"You've changed your mind?"

Collins pointed to Miles's coat.

"Your hand's not in that pocket because it's cold."

Miles nodded.

"Even so," said Collins, moving forward, "maybe it's worth the chance, eh? I mean, if someone was pushing you towards your grave, wouldn't you try just about anything to stop him?"

"You know what I'd do."

"Well, what are you going to do now?"

They were a foot apart, and as Miles began to draw his hand from his pocket, gun firmly in place, and Will Collins made to grab his shoulders, planning to break maybe both legs, they heard a noise on the stairwell, and both froze, listening as the steps grew nearer, two individual rhythms, two people approaching. Miles angled the pistol away from Collins and towards the doorway.

The face in the doorway froze, eyes fixed on the gun, then was framed by the two arms which came up, trying to stretch above the head in a show of surrender.

"Mr. Flint? Mr. Miles Flint?"

"And you are?"

"Jim Stevens, Mr. Flint. I'm a reporter."

"Well, Mr. Stevens, you'd better join us. And this is—?"

Stevens was followed onto the walkway by Janine. She had her hands in her pockets and seemed determined not to look afraid.

"My assistant," said Stevens.

Miles recognised the woman who had been watching his house.

"Put your hands down, Mr. Stevens. I'll put this away. It wasn't for your benefit, rest assured."

Miles slipped the gun back into his pocket, and Stevens lowered his arms.

"I want to ask you a few questions about—"

"No need," interrupted Miles. "I've sent a tape recording to your newspaper office. It should make everything clear."

"But I don't work there anymore."

"You don't what?" This from Janine, who had taken her hands from her pockets and now stood with them planted firmly on her hips.

"This is Mr. Collins, by the way," said Miles. "His is one of the voices on the tape." Collins smiled towards Janine, who smiled back at him, her eyes showing interest.

"By the way, how did you find us?" asked Miles, resting against the parapet.

"Oh, I've still got friends here. I worked here for years. A wise newspaperman gets to know the hotel clerks, the night porters. And then I thought, well, you're the boardinghouse type, quiet, anonymous, but you're playing some sort of game, so you'd go for the opposite, try to outmanoeuvre anyone who might be looking for you."

Collins gave Miles a contemptuous look. Miles knew what he was thinking: If this man can outwit us, others can too.

"Oh, and I'm not the only person looking for you."

"What?"

"And what's your first name, Mr. Collins?" Janine was asking.

"William."

"What do you mean," said Miles, "someone else is looking for me?"

"That's right," said Stevens, part of his attention lost to the dialogue going on between Janine and Collins.

"Yes?" prompted Miles.

"Well, according to the hotel clerk I spoke to, someone else has been asking questions, flashing around a bit of cash. Only they didn't have my sources."

"Any idea who?"

"No."

"It looks to me," said Collins, "as though that snake Monmouth's been blabbering."

"Who's Monmouth?" asked Stevens, nose twitching. Janine had started to point out local landmarks to Collins.

"The other man on the tape," said Miles.

"And this tape will answer all my questions?"

"Oh yes, definitely." Miles was examining the parapet. "Long way down, isn't it?"

"Very."

"I love your accent," Janine was telling Collins. "Irish accents make me all shivery."

"Yes, it is a bit chilly up here," Stevens called to her, and she stuck out her tongue at him. "Look, why don't we all go for a drink, eh? I know a pub near the station—"

"Sorry, we have work to do."

"Well, later maybe. Or tomorrow?"

"OK," said Miles. "Tomorrow afternoon."

"Fine." Stevens was smiling. He knew when someone was selling him Korean tartan. "Do you know the Sutherland Bar?"

"I used to drink there as a student."

"Well, that's fixed then. Janine, let's go. I want to phone London and get someone to send me this mysterious tape."

But Janine and Collins were busy in conversation, their voices muted. They seemed not to have heard Stevens, who, beginning to blush, turned back to Miles Flint and returned his grin. "Well," he said, "she can catch me up." He made toward the stairwell. "Oh, and Mr. Flint?"

"Yes?"

"I hope you have a permit for that gun."

CHAPTER 27

Waverley Station, lying under glass and metal, had changed much since his last visit. It had become fashionably and garishly open-plan, with a taped skirl of maltreated bagpipes and a bevy of high-profile station staff ready to answer the traveller's every question. The flooring reminded him of some dappled ice-rink surface, and video screens everywhere informed passengers that all trains were running upwards of five minutes late due to a local dispute.

By the look of things, the early morning commuter rush had just ended. Taxi drivers were catching up on the day's news headlines, their beefy arms resting against warm steering wheels. The station was lit, the day being dark, a real hyperborean landscape. The glare of the interior was igloo-like, while the ramps leading up to Waverley Bridge were like bolt holes to the surface of the world.

There was little hurry here, the people moving at a winter's pace, retaining their energy. There were no tourists to deal with, only some business travellers and people coming into the city for a day's shopping. Although a public place, it was openly private in its attitude. It would do nicely. He signalled to his companions.

"You know what to do?"

"Yes, Mr. Partridge," said Jeff Phillips.

Billy Monmouth had told Partridge all he needed to know. He had said that Flint was planning a nasty little surprise. He had said that Flint was not coming in alone but had Collins with him. These revelations had made the logistics nice and easy. It didn't matter so much about Flint himself. For the moment, Partridge really wanted only the Irishman, for he was the last piece of evidence. He felt the absurdity of it all. At first it had seemed so simple and so viable, but when one killed someone a whole chain of events came into being which grew and grew and would not stop growing, leaving everyone powerless and trapped within the chain. He couldn't break that chain now if he wanted to. He wasn't coming empty-handed to meet Flint. He had a good enough proposition to put to him, one which

Flint was certain to accept. They would play it like an honest game of cards between two players who know each other for incorrigible cheats.

He had questioned Billy Monmouth thoroughly. Did Flint have any other evidence? No transcripts? No signed statements? Billy had been very definite in his answers, and it seemed that Flint had slipped up here: he had thought Collins such a strong trump that he had dispensed with any alternatives or backups. That was foolish of him. Billy had said that he was a changed man, that the incident in Ireland had unhinged him. He was uncoordinated, rambling, half living in a fantasy world of shoot-outs and car chases. There would be none of that today.

Partridge felt himself prepared for any scheme Flint might throw at him. Slowly, with Phillips and the woman a few yards behind him, he made his way across the concourse toward platform 17.

He wished that he had taken the opportunity on the train to wash himself and maybe even shave. It had been an appalling journey, and the more frustrated he had become, the slower the train had moved, until it had seemed that everything was standing still and that he was moving forward by himself, was running, having broken free of his chains.

He walked to the end of platform 17, his hands by his side, intimating that he was not in possession of any kind of weapon. In fact he was carrying a small revolver in his jacket pocket. To combat the cold, however, he wore an overcoat, and the gun, buried beneath this coat, was for use only in the direst emergency. He didn't believe he would have any need of it.

There were no train spotters about. The end of the platform did not offer overhead shelter from the morning's needle-fine drizzle, and he turned up his coat collar. The trains which arrived at this platform were local services from Dundee and Fife, no further. He saw from the flickering video screen that a train was due in from Cowdenbeath. Now where on earth was that? He seemed to recall that a football team from there appeared somewhere in the Scottish league but couldn't be sure. Looking back up the length of the platform, he saw Phillips standing with the woman, who was held in towards him as though unwillingly. He motioned for Phillips to move further away. It would ruin everything if Flint were to see them both. Phillips moved away quickly, right out of Partridge's sight. He would reappear when the time was right.

There were no obstructions to Partridge's view. He would have fifty yards' warning of Flint's approach. It seemed extraordinary that he should have enlisted the aid of Collins under any circumstances. Partridge was still not sure that he fully believed it. Perhaps Monmouth was playing some sort of trick on him. Well, he would soon know one way or the other. They would be here at any moment.

From out of the Waverley tunnel came a slow, tired-sounding diesel engine, pulling three dingy carriages behind it. The Cowdenbeath train, he presumed. It pulled into platform 17 and drew to a halt. A crowd of people began to disembark. This, he thought, must be Flint's plan: he will arrive just at the height of the confusion, hoping to catch me off guard. Partridge craned his neck to search above the heads of the herd, who were now walking briskly along the platform away from him.

And so did not notice the last door of the train open and the two figures jump out, beside him in an instant.

Startled momentarily, he managed somehow to return Flint's smile and even held out his hand.

"Miles," he said, "good to see you. A nice trick that."

"We took a train out to Haymarket and another one straight back."

"Yes, damned ingenious, really." He turned to Collins. "And this is?"

"I'm sorry," said Miles, "I'd forgotten that any introduction would be necessary. This is Will Collins. Will, this is Mr. Partridge, the man for whom you murdered Philip Hayton."

Partridge managed a low chuckle.

"Well, yes, poor Philip. He was quite mad, you know. If he hadn't died, well, he could have done great harm to the firm."

The Irishman's hand was like a mechanism of steel and taut wires, not a human hand at all. The eyes were glassy, as though they too had been jogged into life by a motor of tiny coiled springs.

"Yes," Partridge said again, not knowing what to say.

"You don't seem surprised to see Mr. Collins," said Miles. "I presume that's because Billy told you about him."

"Oh, well, yes, Monmouth *did* mention him, I think."

"I told you you couldn't trust that—" Collins was silenced by a wave of Miles's hand. Miles turned to Partridge.

"Where's the Director, by the way?"

"Couldn't make it. Poor old chap's become a bit . . . well, emotional of late. No, he couldn't risk the trip."

"In other words, you've kept it all from him."

Partridge's face became a parody of concern.

"He's past it, Miles. He doesn't care anymore. Doesn't it make sense for someone to take over, someone who knows better than he does? Anyway, I thought it best to keep this strictly between ourselves. To save future embarrassment."

"There'll be plenty of embarrassment over those tapes."

"Tapes?" Partridge's face became quizzical. Caught you, thought Miles, caught you at last.

"Yes, you know, the tapes I made of Billy's confession and of Mr. Collins's version of events. Didn't Billy tell you?"

"Perhaps it slipped my mind."

"Well, they've been sent to the proper authorities, the PM, the press, that sort of thing."

Partridge's face had become the colour of sticky bread dough before the flour is sprinkled on. All it needed now was the kneading. He looked quickly along the platform but could not see Phillips. Phillips would not come forward until he was sure that Miles Flint had arrived, and how could he know that, since they had not been expecting him to arrive by train?

"Looking for someone?"

"Well, you never know who'll turn up at these do's, do you?"

"Still cracking jokes." This from Collins. "Aye, you're a tough one all right, but we'll see just how tough."

Miles rested a hand on the tensed arm of the younger man and left it there.

"I think," he said, "we should make a clean breast, don't you, Partridge?"

Partridge shrugged his shoulders, rubbing his numbed hands together. He dearly wanted to push them deep into the woollen haven of his pockets but felt that it was important to keep his body gestures open, unlike the heavily attacking stance of the Irishman.

"You know," Miles began, "I was never a threat to you, never."

"With respect, Miles, I have to disagree. The very fact of our meeting here today is proof of that."

"It wasn't until you sent me to Ireland, sent me to my own execution, that I began to piece things together, and then only with the help of Mr. Collins. I was never close to finding out your dirty little secret. It was Billy you should have been watching, Billy and his friend Andrew Gray."

"Gray?"

"An American operative. He was putting a sweat on your friend Sizewell."

After a moment's thought, Partridge shrugged his shoulders again and looked back along the platform.

"Well, what does it matter now? I've never been one for postmortems."

"Just so long as the executions went off all right. This all started so neatly, didn't it? A single death, all those years ago, hidden by time, as you thought. But it's been growing, Partridge. And you can't kill everyone."

"I don't want to kill *anyone.*" He pointed to Collins. "Except him. Give him to me, Miles, and that can be the end of it."

"What about the tapes?"

"They can be recovered. It's him I want."

Collins made a leap forward.

"You filthy bastard!"

Miles's hand tightened its grip on Collins's arm, and he looked at him the way a parent would look at an errant son.

"I'm going to have him, so help me," hissed Collins.

"This man is *our* enemy, Miles," said Partridge, "you must see that.

He's everything we've been fighting against for twenty-odd years. What's more, he murdered Peter Saville, or, rather, one of his devices did."

"Pete?"

"Blown to bits in Ganton Street."

"But they said in the papers that they couldn't establish identity. So how the hell can you know that it was Pete?"

Partridge faltered, looked down at his feet.

"Unless," said Miles, "your Cynegetics bullies, your little private army, was following him. Maybe putting the chill on him, eh? Frighten him off, was that it? Yes, I'll bet that was it. Your own little army. I'll bet that appealed to you, didn't it? Speaking of which, how did you inveigle Phillips's help?"

"Simplicity itself. He had a fairly shaky time getting into the service. I helped him. Old family ties, you understand. So he owed me something deeper than loyalty to the firm."

Miles nodded, trying to look calm though his nerves were like sparklers.

"And you were the man at the Doric Hotel, the man who paid that girl to keep me occupied?"

"Yes. Jeff telephoned me. I live close by, so it was no trouble. The firm had used Felicity before, so I thought she might be there. Actually"—Partridge's voice had taken on a confidence which it should not have possessed—"speaking of Phillips, there's something I've brought with me to trade off for our friend here." He nodded towards the far end of the platform, where Phillips was standing with his hand firmly attached to the arm of a woman in a green coat. Miles thought he recognised that coat . . .

Good God, it was Sheila's!

"Sheila," he whispered.

"Quite so," said Partridge, seeming to grow physically, while the colour flooded back into his cheeks, the drought of uncertainty at an end.

"You'll never—" started Collins.

"Oh, but I will, won't I, Miles? A fair swap, I think. I'm told that Sheila and you are getting along quite famously now."

Miles seemed to wilt. His grip on Collins's arm was already loosening, and Collins could feel, with the release of pressure, that he was being pushed away from his ally and towards his assassin.

"No," he hissed. "For Christ's sake, Miles!"

"Well, Miles?" Partridge's was the smug voice of every schoolboy smarter than Miles and every tutor who had rebuked him, and every moralistic preacher and politician. It was the voice, too, of a universal evil, a hypocrisy which had taken over the world, the sweet-smelling breath of chaos. It always won, it always won.

"It always will," he whispered from his tainted mouth, where bile and fear had suddenly become tangy beneath his tongue.

"Well, Miles?"

He couldn't see Sheila too clearly, she was muffled up against the chill, but that was definitely her coat. People were walking up the platform now, boarding the train which still waited there, ready to take them to their momentous destinations. Yes, that was the green coat which he had bought for her on a whim . . .

And which she had never liked.

A guard was standing nearby now, checking his watch. He, too, looked along the platform, saw that no one was hurrying for the train, then blew his whistle.

That coat, she had hated it. Hadn't she said something to him? What was it? Yes, hadn't she said that she was throwing it out for jumble? Jesus Christ, yes, and she *had* thrown it out, he had watched her doing it. She could never have worn it here today, unless . . . Unless . . .

"That's not Sheila!" he shouted above the new roar of the engine.

"What?"

"That's not my wife. I *know* it's not!"

"Son of a bitch," said Collins, reaching into his coat. Miles made no attempt to stop him; rather, as had been half formulated but never really discussed between them, he opened one of the train's slowly moving doors and heaved himself in.

Partridge found his mouth opening in a silent O as he saw the gun appear in the Irishman's hand, but then there was too much noise all around him and a hissing of pressure in his ears as he fumbled at his own coat, wherein was hidden, too deep, too late, his own pistol.

And then he screamed as the bullet leapt within him, burrowing its way like a beetle into the warm, dark interior. Collins, his teeth bared, turned to look at the train, but there was no sign of Miles Flint's head from any of the carriage doors. He hadn't even bothered to watch.

Past the guard, who was running in a stiff panic back down the platform, Collins could see the other man let go of the woman's arm and begin to walk towards him, before thinking better of it. But by that time Collins had made up his mind. He moved past Partridge, who was frozen against a dripping pillar, and homed in on the other one. He'd have as many of them as he could. Now that Flint had left him, what else could he do? The train had been the only means of escape. He was at the end of a blind alley, and the only way out of it was to move back into the heart of the station, back towards the terror of the crowd, the shouts of the guard. He passed the woman in the green coat. She had tripped and fallen, revealing short fair hair beneath her hat. Miles might have recognised her as Felicity, but Collins did not even glance down at her.

Phillips was climbing some stairs, loud metal stairs leading to a walk-way. He looked scared to death and tired out, his legs moving with fatal slowness. Collins knelt and took aim, while people dived to the floor or knelt behind their cases.

"Will, no!"

The shot went wild, about a metre high of the target, but it froze Phillips. Collins took aim again.

"Will!"

It was Janine, running towards him, having shaken herself free of Jim Stevens. Stevens was holding a camera by its strap. He had been taking photographs of the whole thing! Collins gritted his teeth and brought the pistol in an arc until he had Stevens for dead in the sight.

But Janine swerved into his path, blocking out the reporter.

"Get out of the way!" he yelled. But she had stopped and didn't seem able to move.

But Phillips was moving, damn him. He had found the top of the stairs and was above Collins now, careering along the walkway towards street level. Collins rose to his feet and followed, ignoring the cries from behind him. He took the steps two at a time, feeling able almost to fly, and heard the sirens below him, entering the concourse, filling the air with new panic. So quickly? Perhaps they had been alerted by that snake Monmouth. Well, he'd get him too, one of these days. So help him. But first this one.

On the street, though, there was no sign of Phillips, no sign at all. He hid his gun beneath the folds of his coat, Miles Flint's old coat, and looked up and down the street. A car swerved towards him and screeched to a halt at the kerbside. The passenger door was pushed open from within.

"Get in!"

He had his gun out again, the gun Miles Flint had given back to him that morning. His hands shook almost uncontrollably as he tried to aim it at this new stranger in his life.

"Who the hell are you?"

"My name is Gray, Mr. Collins, and right now I may conceivably be the only person in the world who wants you kept alive and well. Get in. I can always use a man like you."

The approaching howls of more police cars made up Will Collins's mind. There could never be any escape for him. Not now, not ever.

He stepped into the car.

Envoi

Miles Flint sat on the terrace and sipped a glass of the local wine. He looked out across two untended fields toward a forest where wild boar were said to live. It was early spring, and already the sun was doing what sun is supposed to do, warming him as he opened the newspaper. He had to drive into Castillon-la-Bataille for the English papers, which arrived three days late and at exorbitant prices, but he didn't mind in the least. The townspeople knew that he had bought the dilapidated farmhouse near Les Salles, and they thought him eccentric but friendly. In fact he fully intended to renovate the house and the two small fields which had now become his. Everything in good time. Meanwhile, he opened his newspaper with a keen and knowing smile on his face, eager for the latest part of James Stevens's exposé of spy shenanigans in England and Ulster, exclusive photos and all. It was fairly obvious that much of Stevens's material had been subjected to this and that D-notice, but there was still enough there to make a sizeable four-part "investigation" into corruption and the misuse of power. Harry Sizewell would be standing trial soon, and there were others, too, Miles knew, who would be nervous about every phone call and every knock at the door for a very long time to come.

He did not even know if he himself were safe. This part of the Dordogne was isolated enough, but one could never be wholly safe, not in his world. All one could do was enjoy the present, and he was certainly doing that. He sloshed more wine around his mouth, then swallowed luxuriously. Perhaps he could plant some vines in those fields . . .

"Miles?"

"I'm on the terrace."

Sheila, looking tanned and fit, came around from the side of the house. Her hands were cupped, and she was walking quietly, as though afraid of waking a child.

"What is it?" he asked, and she opened her hands to show him. "It's a little beetle," he said, impressed.

"Yes, I just found it in the vegetable garden. Any idea what kind it is?"

"I haven't the faintest." Sheila transferred the tiny, brightly coloured creature to his own open palm. "But I can find out. I'll just go to the study and check." And with that he was off, back into the farmhouse, weaving between unopened packing cases, beneath the gaping rafters of the first floor, until he reached his study, which was in fact the bathroom. He kept a few books there beside the toilet. Placing the beetle on the rim of the bath, he settled himself down and opened a page.

About the Author

Ian Rankin, ex-swineherd, taxman, viniculturist, was born in Fife, Scotland, in 1960 and now makes his home in North London with his wife. *Watchman* is his second novel for the Crime Club.